Eye of the Burning Man

Eye of the Burning Man

A Mick Callahan Novel

Harry Shannon

Five Star • Waterville, Maine

First Edition
First Printing: November 2005

Published in 2005 in conjunction with
Tekno Books and Ed Gorman.

Set in 11 pt. Plantin by Carleen Stearns.

Printed in the United States on permanent paper.

Library of Congress Cataloging-in-Publication Data

Shannon, Harry.
    Eye of the burning man : a Mick Callahan novel / by
Harry Shannon.—1st ed.
        p. cm.
    ISBN 1-59414-381-1 (hc : alk. paper)
    1. Drug addicts—Crimes against—Fiction. 2. Burning
Man (Festival)—Fiction. 3. Radio broadcasters—Fiction.
4. Psychologists—Fiction. 5. Abduction—Fiction.
6. Nevada—Fiction. I. Title.
PS3619.H355E96 2005
    813'.6—dc22   2005019075

Dedication

This one is for my daughter, Paige.

"The world is suffering—
The cause of suffering is desire."
—The Buddha (250 BCE)

Acknowledgments

Eye of the Burning Man is a work of fiction, and the resemblance of any character to an actual person, living or dead, is coincidental. Even the geography described has been aggressively altered for dramatic purposes. I wish I could say the same for most of the statistics regarding child pornography.

As always, I am grateful to my wife Wendy for her constant support, blunt criticism, and endlessly creative suggestions.

The Burning Man Festival serves, for many people, as both a significant counter-culture statement and a legitimate arts festival. No one should construe Mick's feelings about the festival as reflecting my disapproval.

Thanks also go to the following friends (in no particular order) for reasons they will understand: Joe Donnelly, Jennifer Davila, Joan Bellefontaine, Ed Gorman, John Helfers, Leyna Bernstein, Lynwood Spinks, John and Jill Boylan, Judd and Dory Kramer, Dr. Paul Manchester, and my gal pal and fellow author Gina Gallo. *Gracias* to my English teacher back in 1963, a man named Dennis Kelly.

Finally, I'm grateful to the many mystery fans and small booksellers who have supported Mick Callahan and helped to spread the word about his exploits. I can't thank you enough.

PROLOGUE

Panorama City, California, July 4th
A fat woman stepped out of the meager shade of a withering lemon tree. *"Madre de Dios, hace mucho calor hoy,"* she whispered; Mother of God, it is hot! She turned the hose on herself for a long moment. The cool water caused her huge breasts to bounce like beach balls in the blue-patterned dress. She shook like a lazy, wet dog and went back into her home to open another can of *cerveza*.

The sun had scorched the tattered roofs of the bleached-out, pastel barrio homes, causing tempers to flare and copious amounts of cold beer to vanish. There was no wind, and the 106-degree temperature squatted on the San Fernando Valley like a living thing. Filthy fans whirled like perpetual motion machines in splintering window frames. Even the ice cream carts were sweating.

Harvey Street is a few blocks east of Sepulveda Boulevard, and several north of Saticoy. That summer day, four brown boys in white, sleeveless undershirts ran back and forth through the lawn sprinklers, playing soccer with a flaccid volleyball. They were all under ten years old.

The smallest began to gasp. The largest stopped the game at once, ignoring the howling protests of the other kids, and ordered his tiny friend to sit. No one dared to challenge him. The leader's name was Manuel, but his friends called him *"Loco."*

9

Loco was a dark, wiry boy. He looked around, searching for something, anything to do. "The air is foul with smog. Take a moment and rest your lungs."

"We were winning," another boy said. "It is not fair to stop now."

"You would have lost anyway," Loco said. He pounded his chest like an ape, drawing laughter from the others. "I personally would have defeated you. Unlike you, I was only pretending to be tired."

The spell was broken. The boys sat quietly in the cool mist from the lawn sprinkler, waiting to be chased away, wondering what to do next. Loco fixed his eyes on a battered fence surrounding a lot overgrown with weeds, land that held the wreckage of a former crack house. His eyes narrowed. He rose.

"No, Loco," said Jose. He was pudgy and round and had a flat Indio nose. His family had recently arrived from Guatemala. "Don't even think about it, *ese. No vaya por alli!*"

"Why not go?"

"Malas cosas han pasado alli," Jose said. Because bad things have happened there.

Another boy said: "A monster lives in that house. I can hear noises at night from my bedroom window. *Mi mamá me dijo que si se entra en esa casa, no se sale nunca."* My mother says children who go in there never come out again.

"You mother is a fool," Loco said. "The North Hollywood Boys use that house to party."

"That alone should frighten you," Jose said.

"Todos ustedas son Corbardes!" Loco said. You are all cowards. He threw back his head. *"Soy el mero mero!"* I am a courageous man.

The others watched him stroll across the blistering blacktop, his wet sneakers making a sound like sloppy kisses. He approached the boarded-up lot. The old fence had been tagged more than a dozen times. Loco paused by the huge NHBZ sprayed in black paint. He could hear other boys following. He resisted the temptation to look back over his shoulder. A man must be careful of his reputation.

Loco kicked at a board, careful not to pierce his shoe with a rusty nail. He swallowed his fear and prepared to step through the space and into the fetid blackness.

"Espérame aqui si quieres," he called out, bravely. Wait for me here if you want to. He moved through the fence.

The smell hit him instantly, a stench like bad sandwich meat. Loco recoiled. Something dead was rotting away. His mind conjured bloodless human bodies in grotesque poses, stacked together like butchered pigs. He almost ran, like a foolish woman.

He told himself the gang arranged such things to strike terror into the neighborhood. It was probably just the carcass of an animal, something they had found dead in the middle of the road. He approached, and forced himself to look down. It was a decaying possum, stiff with rigor mortis, horrid teeth bared in a final act of defiance. Loco pinched his nostrils and moved past it, going farther into the gloom.

Broken, splintered boards lay scattered about, along with rags and cans of spray paint. His eyes became accustomed to the gloom. The NHBZ logo was everywhere. Empty whiskey, wine, and beer bottles lay in shattered piles. Some baseball bats were arranged in a neat row along the edge of the porch. The front door, smashed down long ago by a police assault, lay flat in the dusty living room. Loco felt something go *snap* beneath his feet. He looked down.

Although Loco had yet to do drugs, except for a bit of weed, he recognized the burnt glass tube as a crack pipe. Cocaine had destroyed his life. His father had gone to prison, and his mother had gone to rehab. Now he lived here, with his aunt. He spat in the dirt and wiped his hands on his jeans.

Loco went up the steps and into the house. Used condoms lay everywhere, along with small compact mirrors, cut straws, and tiny brown bottles which had once held mysterious powders. The NHBZ had been quiet for the last few weekends. It probably wasn't crystal meth. If they had been smoking or snorting crystal, there would have been violence and people would have gone to the emergency room.

CRAAAAACK. A board snapping. *Dios mio!* Was that someone coming through the back yard toward the house?

Loco tried to move quietly, but quickly, back to the front of the building. He tripped. His elbows came down onto a faded stack of *Penthouse* magazines. Dust flew up and into his nostrils and he fought back a sneeze. Something many-legged and hairy ran across his arm and down into the magazines. Loco stifled a shriek.

The tarantula was huge. He was fortunate not to have been bitten. He slipped back out onto the front porch, dashed for the fence. Behind him he heard several gang members stumble into the house from the back entrance. They were obviously drunk. Loco knew that he had nearly been caught. He blew out a long breath and then pushed a board aside, seeking the friendship of sunlight.

A face glared at him from the other side. Loco gasped.

It was Jose. "Loco, are you okay, *ese?*"

"*Estoy bien, menso!*" Loco hissed. I am fine, you idiot. "*Estuvo facil.*" It was easy. "Now get out of the way, some of them are right behind me."

Giggling, the four boys raced across the street and back into the tepid water. Loco washed his face and hands and tried to cleanse himself of the sweat and fear. He could still smell the stench of the dead animal that lay rotting near that cursed house.

"Te llamas Loco?"

The boy turned. He saw a tall, powerful gringo with a shaved head and a nose ring. He was considerably older, and he sat behind the wheel of an old Dodge Dart. He seemed tense.

"They call me Loco," the boy said proudly. "Why?"

"Escúchamé," the man said. He spoke badly, with a piss-poor accent. *"Tu mama me a mandado."* Listen to me. Your mother has sent me here to find you.

Loco narrowed his eyes. "I don't live with my mother," he said with a sneer. "My mother is away. That woman is my aunt. Go away, pervert."

He turned his back. The boys, emboldened by their number and their distance from the vehicle, began to jeer. They called the man *maricon,* faggot, and other names. He did not seem angered.

"Suit yourself," he said. He gunned the engine. "I was only doing her a favor."

"Do us a favor and fuck off," Jose said. The boys laughed again.

"Just so you know, Loco," the man said, *"tu gato a sido atropellado."* Your cat has been run over.

Loco stepped back, shaken. He regained confidence. Said: *"Como se parece mi gato?"* Okay stranger, you tell me what my cat looks like.

"Right now? A bloody black and white bag of shit," the stranger said. He shrugged with indifference. Then, in broken Spanish: *"Gato gordo. Negro, con manchas blancas."*

Loco loved his animals. He approached the car warily.

"Vámanos!" shouted another boy. Let's run away!

But Loco moved closer to the car. He leaned into it ur-

13

gently. In low tones, he said: "When did this happen?"

The muscular stranger grabbed the boy by the hair and yanked him into the car. A woman appeared in the back seat and tried to jam a rag over his mouth. Loco struggled. *"Ayúdame!"* he screamed. But the car was already away from the curb, gone with a squeal of brakes and a blast of black exhaust. The rag covered his nose. It smelled foul, thick with a chemical stench. The world spun away.

The gringo police came. They brought an older officer with Mexican blood. He acted very concerned. They put rows of yellow tape everywhere in the yard, and took a lot of pictures. They used this excuse to roust the North Hollywood Boys, although they already knew that this particular perpetrator was a white man. They saw every neighbor willing to talk to them, and then they went away again.

The aging detective of Mexican descent spoke to Loco's aunt, Blanca, even held her while she sobbed. He stayed the longest. One could see he was deeply troubled. He assured Blanca that he and his department would do all they could to find the boy.

As he and his partner walked back down the sidewalk, the Mexican-American detective lit a cigarette. He swore under his breath.

"What's the matter?"

"I'm getting too old for this shit."

"I know," said the partner. They got into the sedan. He started the car. "It sucks, doesn't it?"

"Damn right. One more kid who was born to end up on a milk carton."

The story made the evening news, but it wasn't unusual enough to dominate the headlines for long. Not with Iraq in flames and the economy in a slump.

ONE

Northridge, California, August

It was an ugly, sweltering summer. Maintenance had set the thermostat in the booth for seventy degrees, but it was humid as hell and I was soaked with sweat. The heat of the San Fernando Valley rivaled a nasty season in a faraway place like Nashville or Miami.

"Good evening. You're on the air live with Mick Callahan, so be sure to turn your radio down." I watched a drop of perspiration roll from the tip of my nose to splat on a lined yellow note pad, smearing the ink where, for the last two hours and forty-five minutes, I'd scribbled catch phrases, reminders, and first names. I looked up and through the tinted glass partition where my date was sitting.

Leyna was a tall and slender blonde, an intellectual who preferred dark colors and wore glasses. She tucked her legs up on the sofa. Leyna was reading a limited-edition hardback copy of *The Collected Works of Albert Camus*, an author I dislike, although I'd no burning desire to confess. She felt me staring, caught my eyes, and smiled warmly.

Who's the man? And it's about time.

The caller spoke. "Is this Mister Callahan?"

"Last time I looked, it was."

"Call me Kevin," the man said. A long expulsion of

15

breath followed his name. He had the frail, scratchy voice of a heavy smoker. "You're talking about love again tonight, right?"

"Right," I said. "What does that word mean to you? Who do you love?"

A pause. "Don't laugh at me, okay?"

"Nobody's laughing, pal."

"I love my dog."

Let's not go there. "Okay. And what's your dog's name?"

"Her name is Lassie."

No kidding.

The man coughed harshly. He was quite ill. I heard a dog barking in the background as if alarmed. "She loves me unconditionally. I've been real sick. Lassie, she's been right by me the whole time."

"What's wrong?"

"My lungs are shot."

"But you're smoking."

"Not that much," Kevin said. "I've cut way down."

"With damaged lungs?"

"It's hard to quit, you know?"

"With the dog there. With Lassie there."

"Yeah," Kevin said proudly. "She's always right by my side, no matter what. That's why I love her."

I sighed. "I'm going to make two observations here, Kevin. And you're probably going to get all pissed off when I do. Ready?"

Guarded. "Okay."

"One, if you really loved your pet, you would do everything you could to safeguard your health, so you'd be around to care for her. Smoking with a lung problem doesn't cut it."

"I know, but like I said, it's really hard to quit."

16

"Two, have you read up on the health repercussions of secondhand smoke?"

"The latest research is saying that's all bull."

"Maybe it is, although I doubt it. You're probably not just killing yourself, maybe leaving your loved one homeless, you may actually be killing the dog, too. She didn't ask for a pack-a-day habit, did she?"

Dial tone.

"Well, too close to the bone that time. Like I said before, love is not mere companionship, and it is not necessarily unconditional. It's a very complicated, interactive experience, best defined as an action. It is not a feeling, it is something you do. Anyway, let's all just take a deep breath here . . . sorry, Kevin." I winced. *That was one bad joke.*

I left a beat for the hoped-for audience chuckle. "Look, let me put it this way. I had a stepfather who used to beat me. He made me fight other kids for money. I have come to understand that he thought he was teaching me to be a man, but I certainly wouldn't call *that* love. Would you? Obviously that was a rhetorical question. Okay. We're going to go to a commercial. Back with you in a moment."

My fingers fed a CD to the board. A huge musical chord sounded, followed by several females chanting "Mick Callahan Live" like porn stars approaching orgasm. Three consecutive commercials would now play, one for an electronics store, one for an Arena Football team, and one for a crooked political candidate.

I winked at my date. We had been seeing each other for nearly two long, very frustrating months. Apparently Leyna Barton had also read, and often referenced, an ancient, dog-eared, first edition copy of *The Rules*. She came from Beverly Hills, and thus a higher caste, so we hadn't gotten into the damned ballpark, much less to first base. This date was going to be different. She had greeted me with a long kiss and whispered, "Tonight's your lucky night" into my hot-and-bothered ear. It was damned difficult to keep my mind on work.

Only ten minutes to go. The calls had been coming in regularly, but my message wasn't getting across. *Singing opera for the deaf?* I made a few more notes, decided to get back on the soapbox. The commercial for the corrupt politician ended.

"Oh sure," I said, before I could stop myself, "I'm going to run right out and vote for a candidate who is facing imminent indictment for perjury and obstruction of justice. This clown would sell his grandmother for more status. Oops, I shouldn't have said that. Just cost the station some money."

The phones lit up. I glanced down at the winking lights. "Those of you calling in please be patient. I'm going to run my mouth for a second. If you don't like it, you can always go back to listening to Howard Stern."

Leyna flashed me a seductive grin.

"Okay, love. Erich Fromm quantified it, Freud and Jung and Saint Augustine and Paul the Apostle tried to write about it, we have self-help books up the wazoo on the subject. But what do we really know? Not a hell of a lot, right? Most of us don't even give the matter much thought. Why is that?

"We live in a culture that wants us to eat fast-food for every meal, refuses to accept that delay of gratification is the cornerstone to all dignified living, and peddles us some kind of gooey excrement as erotic mythology with every popular song, television show, and feature film. Many of us think meaningless sex is love, or maybe helpless adoration. Some of us believe that love should be completely unconditional, like it is some kind of constitutional guarantee or government entitlement. It's not. 'I should just be loved for who I am' is one of the most selfish, not to mention downright foolish, things anyone ever said. What was it that idiot therapist Fritz Perls spouted back in the seventies? 'I'm not in this world to live up to your expectations, and you don't have to live up to mine, and if we meet somewhere along the way it's groovy.' *Excuse* me?"

I checked on Leyna, who seemed as entranced as I'd hoped. I modulated to a higher key.

"I'm no prude, ladies and gentlemen. Most of you know I blew myself out of the Navy and nearly killed myself and my career, all behind drugs and alcohol. This was back when a few of you had actually heard of me. But that kind of selfish, hippie idiocy has left us a complete social catastrophe to clean up. Okay, now I'm going to go on a rant."

I switched the microphone off and clicked on my telephone headset. Leyna was now watching with rapt attention. Like a dork, I got up and strolled around the booth, still talking. I could feel her eyes roaming my frame and it felt a bit silly, like a high school jock passing by the cheerleaders. *All I need is a few more hormones and some fresh pimples.*

"Don't worry, guys, I'm going to take a final caller or two, but let me get the rest of this off my chest. We have had more than thirty years of unbridled narcissism in this culture. For the uninitiated, Narcissus was the Greek boy in the myth who fell in love with his own image in a pool of water. That irritated the gods, so they froze him there to see nothing but his own reflection forever. Healthy narcissism is thinking you're a pretty good person, or that you look nice in that outfit. Unhealthy narcissism is to be so trapped within our own wants and needs that we are unable to connect and properly empathize with the feelings and needs of others. Otto Kernberg once called human evil just a kind of malignant narcissism.

"Living creatures are not objects, people. They are not *things*. And as much as we would like them to serve us unconditionally, they cannot. In fact, it is precisely the tension between us, the struggle to meet one another's needs without surrendering our own integrity, that produces adult love, real love that promotes growth and solves emotional problems, love that matures people and breaks down their infantile concepts and selfish impulses. I can recommend a great essay, although it reads about as easily as the Chinese phone book. It's by a Jewish philosopher named Martin Buber, and it is called 'I and Thou.' Go find it."

I sat down behind the console. "Okay. End of lecture. That diatribe probably pissed *somebody* off, so I'll take another caller now." I selected a button and pressed it.

"Good evening, you're on the air live with Mick Callahan."

"Hi Mick, I love your show," the woman said. "My name is Trudy."

"Thank you, Trudy. What's on your mind?"

"I was just thinking about how my marriage failed. And I was thinking about what you said just now."

"Yes?"

She chuckled ruefully. "The marriage ended with a lot of accusations, you know? You never gave me this or you never listened to me about that. Well, that and oral sex."

I cringed. "Excuse me?"

"Passing each other in the hall and saying, 'Screw you.' That's a joke."

I laughed. "Back to the divorce. The marriage degenerated into accusations, and a kind of stuck feeling? Just the

20

same issues over and over?"

"On both sides."

"Right."

"Funny thing is," she said, "my ex and I get along okay, now. It's like we are better friends than we were husband and wife."

"And what do you make of that?"

"Being married brought some things up in both of us that weren't there before," she said thoughtfully. "Something happened. And we both got really locked into what we weren't getting, instead of paying attention to what we could give."

"Brilliant," I gave her applause. "Thank you for saying that. Because that is one of the points I have been trying to make all week, and it feels great that somebody understands."

"Cool," she said, suddenly sounding very young.

"When old patterns surface," I said, "we revert to being frustrated children. We fall into habits created when we were the most egocentric we were ever intended to be." I looked down at her name on the note pad. "Thank you for calling, Trudy."

"Thank you, Mick," she said.

I killed the line and glanced at the clock. "It looks like we have time for one more caller. But now my phone is dead. Come on, somebody. I'll take the third caller right after this word from one of our sponsors."

I slipped in another CD, a musical spot advertising a chain of furniture stores. Leyna was watching with frank appreciation. *The lonely cowboy shoots . . . he scores! Yo, there is a God.* I kept one eye on the phone bank and began to pack up my things. *For an expert on the subject of love, I'm sure objectifying this enchanting young woman. Can we spell hypocrite?*

Line one flickered, then died. The second lit and continued to blink. "Hold on, please, I'll be right with you." I punched the line back to 'hold,' shoved the rest of my papers into a briefcase, located the computer mouse, and lined up the pre-recorded nighttime programming so it would start with one click. The commercial faded away. I dropped back into my chair just as my fingers killed the CD and flipped the mike back to 'live.'

"We're almost out of time tonight. I want to wish everyone a romantic evening." I grinned at Leyna and continued speaking. "From now until dawn, we're playing cool jazz and classic blues. I will be back with you again tomorrow evening from nine to midnight. But before I go, I promised I'd take one last caller."

I opened up the line. "Hello, you're on the air."

Traffic sounds, far away. Perhaps someone on a cell phone?

"Hello? Anyone there?"

A muffled chuckle followed the question. A man's voice. A chill jogged up my back. After a few seconds, the caller broke the connection with a gentle click. I shook my head and covered. "Just my luck, the last caller on a night devoted to the subject of love ends up doing horny breathing into the telephone."

I flipped off the lights and clicked the mouse. The computer started a choral station ID, which then led to hours of automatic jazz programming.

"Good night, everybody," I said. *Hey, girl . . . here's my best FM voice.* "This is Mick Callahan, signing off and thanking you for being with me this evening. I hope you'll join me again tomorrow night."

Just as the clock hit the hour, my cell phone rang. I put my briefcase on the console and flipped open the telephone.

"It's me."

I pictured a thin young man with a burn scar covering half his face. "What's up, Jerry? Are you in town?"

"No, I'm still in Nevada, just messing around online."

"I'm in a little bit of a rush tonight." A pause. "Are you okay?"

"Me? I guess so." Jerry was slurring his words slightly, like he'd been drinking again. "I just wanted to talk."

"No luck, huh?"

"No luck, Mick." Jerry's voice caught on a strip of barbed wire. "It's like she never existed."

I looked up. Leyna was growing impatient. "Look, Jerry, I have an important business meeting I have to get to." That lie hurt. *Don't be such a dick.* "Can I call you back tomorrow or something?"

"No, it's okay," Jerry sighed booze into the receiver. "I've just been staring at the monitor for hours. I can't find a trace of Mary, Mick, and I'm damned good at this. There's no driver's license, credit card, phone bill, store card, nothing. Maybe something bad has happened. I want to know if she's okay."

"She'll turn up."

"Maybe. I guess I just needed to whine to somebody. No big deal."

"I'll try to call you back in an hour or two." The second lie hurt worse than the first. "Take it easy."

"You too."

I closed the phone again and stepped out of the booth, briefcase swinging at my side. "A girlfriend?" Leyna purred, somewhat coolly. She had been filing her nails, and the file was poking up out of one fist like a miniature erection.

I shook my head. "A friend from Nevada, kid named Jerry. He's a hacker. He's been searching the Internet, looking for a girl who helped us out of a mess. She up and disappeared a few months ago. He really had a thing for her."

"That's romantic."

"I'm not sure he'd look at it that way. Good show?"

"Good show."

"Suitably impressed, madam?"

She nodded. "The lady is impressed. Do you want to stop for a coffee somewhere to unwind, or just take me home?"

I put my arms around her. "That depends."

Leyna giggled. "On what?"

I kissed her. She kissed back, pressing her lean body against mine. Finally, we broke away. "It depends on whether or not I'm staying with you in the three-ten area code tonight."

Leyna raised her hands to cup my face. She stroked my ear and whispered, "Eight-one-eight; you're invited."

I locked up rapidly; we walked down the plushy carpeted hallway, through the metal security door, and past the empty reception desk. I flipped the exterior lights over to motion detector mode, made sure the coffee maker was off, and opened the front door. We stepped outside, into a reasonably pleasant evening. The odd quirk about L.A. heat waves is that the parking lots and back yards end up cooler during the night than the buildings they surround.

I passed my hand in front of the motion detector and the parking area lit up. My dusty, old, blue Chevy was halfway down the row, standing alone. Her shiny black BMW convertible was beside it. I put my right arm around her waist and shifted the briefcase to my left hand. Leyna snuggled in close. Our hips bumped as we walked along, lost in lust.

"My car or yours?"

Leyna wrinkled her nose. "Mine, of course."

The bushes near her BMW stood tall, grew thick. One rustled a bit, just a flicker of movement. I caught it from the corner of my eye and hesitated, almost causing Leyna to stumble. The hairs on the back of my neck fluttered. I responded to something deep in my mind, the voice of my abusive stepfather: *Stay awake, damn you, boy! You got to keep your eyes peeled . . .*

I shifted my weight and rolled Leyna around to the left. Another rustling sound. My mouth went dry. The quicksilver ice of adrenaline pumped through me as I used peripheral vision to track the brush. I kept my face turned forward, towards the BMW.

I spoke in a normal tone. "Where is your apartment again, above or below Wilshire?"

Leyna looked puzzled. After all, I'd driven her home several times. "Below. Are you tired, or something?" We were almost to her car.

"Get down!"

The brush exploded. I shoved her onto a small patch of dirt near the asphalt. Leyna howled as she scraped her knee and elbow.

I was facing a strange apparition: one huge ape of a man dressed entirely in dark clothing. He wore a navy watch cap pulled down over his head, and his features were covered with a plastic Halloween mask that had been spray-painted black. One arm was stretched out towards me, as if pointing to something back at the radio station. A prominent tattoo on the forearm showed a black stick-figure in a circle of reddish fire.

"What the . . ."

But then, in that giant fist, Leyna saw the small gun. She screamed.

"Shut her up," the man whispered. "One more sound

and I splatter your brains all over the car."

I stood quietly, taking the measure of my opponent. *Watch his eyes, boy, the eyes always tell you what's coming.* I figured the man for six four. He probably weighed two-fifty, maybe thirty or more pounds more than me. *Maybe there's a way out of this. See what he's after.*

"I don't have much money. You can have what I've got."

"How much?" The whisper was theatrically exaggerated.

"I'd have to look," I said. "Maybe sixty bucks."

"And the Beemer?"

"Sure. And the car."

A black glove pointed to Leyna. "Maybe I'll take her, too."

"Not a chance." I shook my head but did not move my body. "Don't even think about it."

"Why not, motherfucker?"

"Do you want the sixty bucks, or not?" I asked, pleasantly. "No hassles that way."

"I'll take whatever I want. Including her."

He is going to kill you both, he's only playing around. "Relax. Don't worry. I can't identify you."

"Huh?"

"I'll just tell the cops we got jumped by some steroid junkie with shrunken balls who thought he was Zorro."

The eyes behind the mask widened slightly. The gun moved a fraction higher. The man tensed, debated pulling the trigger. I went in very low, swept my right arm up and away. The gun fired once, but I barely heard it.

I slammed into the man, drove him back into the Chevrolet, and head-butted the Halloween mask. He grunted. *Take this bastard down hard,* my stepfather whispered, *or you're dead.*

I bounced off a solid wall of gym-rat muscle. He clawed

desperately for purchase as the gun came back down. Leyna now had her purse open, her cell phone in hand. She was screaming for the police. Her voice seemed to come from another dimension.

To my horror the .22 started to shift towards Leyna, so I grabbed the thick wrist and let my body go slack. My weight forced his arm down towards the dirt. Another POP followed as I freed my left hand and grabbed at the crotch of the black jeans, clenched my fist fiercely, and twisted the testicles. The man bellowed and brought the gun down on my forehead. The world whistled the National Anthem.

My eyes filled with blood but I knew better than to release the gun hand, so I used my body weight again and dragged the man into an awkward position; he ended up bent in half, with his knees buckling. I forced the gun hand inward and began to pressure his fingers, trying to force the guy to shoot himself in the stomach. *Teach him not to fuck with you, kid.*

The man released the weapon and swung. He caught along the right side of my jaw. I fell backwards and forced the gun to spin away across the pavement towards Leyna. I kicked up at the attacker, but the bigger man dodged. I got up, spun around on one knee, and got back to my feet. *Now do it, just do it!* I was probably quite a sight by now, face contorted with anger and smeared with my own blood.

A cold, weirdly comfortable flower of rage blossomed. Without the gun, the man was just another mean-spirited bully, like all the ones I'd downed in a dozen pointless fights as a kid, or during the dark days of my drinking career. He was my stepfather, Danny Bell.

"Okay, asshole." I wiped the blood away. "Let's dance."

POP.

The two of us turned towards her, startled, and discovered that Leyna now had the little .22. She squeezed the trigger again and it went POP another time. That bullet shattered one of the white lights high up on the lamppost, plunging the area into darkness. She lowered the gun farther. It hit me that the first bullet had gone up into the sky. She was getting a feel for the weapon, trying to zero in. I looked back at the bad guy.

The man in black leaped impossibly high, rolled across the roof of the BMW, and raced back into the thick brush. He was gone so quickly, it was as if he had never existed.

"Leyna?"

She did not answer, just clung to the now-wavering pistol.

"It's over. He's gone."

Leyna dropped the gun and sank to her knees. I was still feeling half berserk from the confrontation. I walked in circles for a few moments, kicking at my car and swearing, tense, dizzy, and shaking from unused adrenaline. Finally I sat down next to her. I ripped a piece of my shirt away and held it against the scalp wound. "You okay?"

Leyna didn't answer.

I shrugged. "That's a dumb question, right? Me neither."

Moments passed. Heavy tires roared down the deserted alley and into the dusty parking lot, fierce headlights pinned us. LAPD in a good old black and white, bright colors whirling on top.

"Keep your hands where we can see them."

I pointed with a weary arm to the fallen pistol. "Only one gun here, guys. It's a little .22. He jumped us and then ran off into the trees."

"Did you call us, ma'am?" the other cop asked. He was approaching fast, one hand on a holstered Glock. Meanwhile his partner examined the darkened area and ran his flashlight beam through the flattened brush.

"Footprints here, Larry," the partner said.

"I got shell casings," the one called Larry said. He picked them up with a pencil and dropped them into a baggie. He resembled me a bit, similar in build with the same dark hair and eyes, but more Italian than Irish in appearance. He also had a long, straight nose that wasn't broken, unlike mine. He squatted down next to Leyna. "Someone tried to rob you? Then fired at you?"

"I shot at him with his own gun."

"What did he look like?"

I suddenly felt sick, but hurling in front of Leyna was not an option. I put my head between my knees. "He was a big son of a bitch, bigger than you and me. I'd make him six three or four, and going about two-fifty and change."

"What was he wearing?"

"Dressed in black, spray-painted some kind of a generic Halloween mask to cover his face. Tattoo on the forearm, a little stick-man in a ring of flames or something like that."

"Was he after money?"

"Maybe."

"The BMW?"

I raised my head, answered without thinking. "Maybe her."

Leyna gasped and shuddered. She pulled away from me. The cop looked at her, puzzled. He eyed my lacerated forehead. "You need me to call an ambulance for that?"

"No. Just a scalp wound. I don't have a concussion or anything. Don't sweat it." Another police car rolled up. The young cop waved them away and they drove off again. The San Fernando Valley gets pretty busy on a Saturday night.

The cop asked for some ID and we gave up our drivers'

licenses. He began writing in a notebook, then paused and chuckled. "I thought I recognized you. You're Mick Callahan, that radio guy. You were a Navy Seal, right?"

"Half-assed. I made it through BUDS and jump school." Damn, I get sick of that question. "I washed out while I was still on probation."

"I wore the trident," the cop said proudly. "Only did one hitch, though. I didn't much like getting shot at."

"Yeah, me neither."

"You used to be on television too, didn't you? You got fired for getting in a fist fight one time."

Jesus, you're not doing me any favors, here. "Yeah, but that was all a few years ago."

The cop shook my hand. "Officer Larry Donato," he said. He spoke in short, choppy, authoritarian sentences that belied the wide-eyed, pleasant expression on his face. "I used to watch your show when I was a kid."

When you were a kid, huh? "Gee. Thanks."

The cop tore some paper out of his book. "Hey, can I get your autograph?"

"As long as it's not on a ticket." I was hoping Leyna was impressed. I looked. She wasn't. I signed.

Donato took the paper, folded it, and stuck it in his shirt pocket. "Thanks a lot."

"You're welcome."

Larry chuckled. "Funny story, Mick. My cousin says she busted you once, but let you go. Nice girl, tough as nails. Works Hollywood, mostly in prostitution. Name of Darlene Hernandez. You remember her?"

"Yeah." I shrugged, genuinely embarrassed. "I did a lot of things when I was drinking. Getting arrested wasn't usually one of them. It stands out in my mind. Uh . . . tell her I said hello."

Leyna Barton blinked. Her jaw dropped open. I struggled to save the situation. "It was a long time ago, Leyna. I had some serious problems. I don't drink any more, you know that."

Larry Donato gave me his card. "I'm not kidding. I really was a fan. Take this and hold onto it. It has my cell number on the back."

"Why?"

"In case you need to reach me."

"What for?"

"A favor. Whatever. I'm a cop, remember? And I'm thinking you might need me."

Leyna Barton said, "Why is that?" She was pale and seemed one pubic hair from emitting a shriek.

Donato chuckled. "He pisses people off sometimes, Miss Barton. It's part of his act."

I sighed. "Oh, give me a break. Couldn't it have been a simple armed robbery?"

"Maybe."

"But?"

"Why a little .22, except maybe to keep the noise down? This parking lot is pretty out of the way. Me, I'd say the perp knows you. Otherwise, why was he right here waiting?"

I had one eye on Leyna Barton. I was losing ground rapidly. I felt like kicking Donato in the shin.

"Hey, it seems to me somebody was out to do you for personal reasons."

"Think so?" It was the partner. He had just tuned in. "Maybe they should come with us and see some mug shots."

"You see too much television, Bobby," Donato said. "Besides, they said he was wearing a mask, didn't they?"

"Oh. Right."

I was watching the death throes of my love life.

Leyna went grim. "You really think this might have been something personal, Officer Donato?"

"I'd say it's more than possible. This is the parking lot of a radio station, lady. Not a lot of cars around here, so we sure can't rule that out."

They filled out the rest of the paperwork in a hurry. "You guys don't need to come down to the station," Donato said. "It's not like I don't know where to find you, if I need you."

"Thanks." I tucked the business card into the pocket of my jeans. "And thanks for this, too."

"Don't mention it. Thanks for not laughing at me when I asked for your autograph."

"I never laugh at people with guns."

We were both numb and exhausted, but I followed Leyna home, over Benedict Canyon and down below Sunset. When we parked, I approached her car and tried to lighten the mood with a joke. She got out in silence. I walked her to her apartment building, but she stayed two feet ahead on the pavement, head down. She would not kiss me goodnight.

"You act like that was my fault," I protested. "What the hell did I do wrong?"

"I don't know." Leyna looked down again and far away, into some other reality. "You had an expression on your face, something I'd never seen before. You scared me."

"He was going to kill us."

"I know. And I thank you for fighting back." Leyna punched her code into the keypad. The gate buzzed open. She stepped through and let it close behind her. Her apartment was the first in the row. For a long moment, I thought she was going to go in without looking back. Finally she turned.

"I can't see you anymore," she said.

"What?"

"I'm sorry."

"You're kidding. Because I fought the guy?"

"No, Mick," Leyna said, as she entered her apartment. "It's not that. It's because you looked like you enjoyed it."

She closed her door. I waited until I heard the series of clicks from her deadbolts. I waited until her porch light went off. I waited until I finally got the message, and then went back out into the night alone.

This sucked. I drove the long way home, watched the city lights from the top of the canyon until my eyes grew weary.

At home, I tossed for an hour, consumed by guilt about having not called Jerry back and by some vivid sexual frustration. I finally slept heavily, dreamed feverishly, became lost in a pastiche of fantasy and memory . . .

Snapshots: A boy, fist-fighting other kids for money; a Seal jumping from a hovering black chopper; one lost weekend and an explosion of random, meaningless violence; a tall, hellish fire cackling up a wooden skeleton towards the unforgiving stars, until it finally burned a ragged hole in the fabric of the universe.

TWO

I came to face-down on a damp bed, feeling rode hard and put up wet. The knuckles of one hand were raw. I had a sharp pain in one rib and a sore lower back. My forehead was throbbing, and a small lump had formed above my right eye. I moaned into the pillow and rolled carefully over onto my left side. The day was already scorching.

I slipped my legs out from under the damp, twisted sheets and swung my feet to the wooden floor. I got down, rolled over, and pulled my knees up to my chest to stretch the lumbar muscles, then twisted the rib back into place and popped the lower back.

"You looked like you *enjoyed* it," I muttered. "What a bitch."

I sat up, crossed my legs, and did some meditation. I've never had enough patience for Zen, but have gradually become comfortable with a brisk form of visualization. I followed my breath, rode the dragon, and opened my eyes again.

The modest house wasn't much, but it was mine. I'd purchased the 1950s-style, three-bedroom, one-and-a-half bath, North Hollywood property only a few months before. The down payment had come from my first signing bonus in three years. I had a cozy, fenced front yard, a small pool, and a genuine sunken fireplace. I'd given it a Southwest décor, with pastel colors and Navajo designs, to remind me of the desert. It had finally started to feel like home.

I finished meditating, padded to the bathroom in my underwear, leaned over the sink, and checked for damage. The chipped mirror reflected a small scab between my short, black hair and broken nose. I popped two knuckles back into place, but with a wince and a hoarse groan, and ran some cold water over my scratched hands. I took a shower and searched for Murphy.

Murphy, named for Murphy's Law, was a torn-up, ancient, male alley cat that had moved in to my motel room while I was doing a brief radio stint near my home town of Dry Wells, Nevada. I hadn't wanted a pet, but couldn't leave the battered, old feline behind. Now Murphy, one ear missing and the other nearly chewed away, was lazily grooming on the back porch. I brought kibble and water. Murphy did a purring square-dance move between my legs and gulped his food.

After some strong coffee in a tall mug, a protein drink with creatine, and a bowl of oatmeal, I felt ready to face the day, one I'd intended to start in a different bed. I strolled into my small office—a madhouse of books, papers, and memorabilia—and booted up the computer.

"He stopped lovin' her today . . ." Some classic George Jones whined out through large, brand-new speakers. I'd been a virtual technophobe until that one long Memorial Day weekend in Nevada. Jerry had opened my eyes. I'd upgraded the computer promptly upon arrival in L.A., and now regularly used video-conferencing, as well as high-speed DSL for research. I pulled up the e-mail. Hal Solomon, my AA sponsor, wanted to reach me.

What the hell are you doing in Australia, old man? Hal was a retired investment banker, media mogul, and sometime venture capitalist. He now traveled incessantly, as if the grim reaper had his name on a warrant. I checked the time and called via the Internet. He was online, as expected. After a pair of false starts, we connected. Hal's silver hair and patrician features formed on the oversized monitor.

"Good morning, Callahan," Hal said. "You look like hammered owl excrement."

"I love it when you try to use my pithy little Western phrases. Only you would change shit to excrement."

"Call me a fecal alchemist. Seriously, you look like you relapsed and thoroughly insulted half of Los Angeles."

"You got the latter part correct. He was big enough to be half of Los Angeles."

"Who?"

"I don't have a clue. He jumped us as we left the radio station last night. The guy had me by a couple of inches and maybe thirty pounds."

"That's big," Hal said. He winced and bent forward for a moment. "Oh."

"Are you okay, Hal?"

"Certainly," Hal said. "A bit of stomach trouble."

"That's been happening a lot lately."

"It's probably just from the change in diet. How is Miss Barton doing?"

"She was fine when I took her home. A little rattled, obviously. Oh, and she arbitrarily decided to dump my sorry Irish ass."

"I see," Hal said. His face flickered, returned to normal. "I suppose all this would explain the sad, cruelly battered countenance I see before me now. Really, no idea who it was?"

"Just a big bastard with a strange tattoo. I guarantee you his nuts will be swollen for days."

Hal snickered. "You and your temper."

"That's what she said."

"Who?"

"Leyna Barton. And that's why she decided to end our semi-transcendental relationship, just as it had begun to blossom."

"Son, you lost me."

I leaned forward, head on cupped palms, and stared down at the keyboard. "You know how it is. I've told you about my childhood. I guess I lost it and went a little berserk. It upset her."

"Oh."

"I was starting to think I'd left the anger behind, but it came back fast."

Hal blinked. "Did you tell Leyna about Nevada?"

"No." I sat back in the tan executive chair. It rolled away from the desk. "I guess I wanted to keep that part of my life for later. She's a rich city girl, you know? And here I'd be describing that ugly mess with the Palmer family, Donny Boy, a mess of dead people. Jesus, it was a melodrama. I guess I was afraid that would turn her off."

"At the risk of sounding predictably sage, you know you can't run away from who you are."

"I'd like to."

"Get in line."

"Leyna has class, you know? A college education, and not from the crummy schools I went to. She's the real deal."

"Meaning you're not? Come on, Mick. That's pretty neurotic."

"Hal, I'm just a cowboy with a diploma, and that's not very impressive at the core, is it?"

Hal shook his head. "Some people think highly of you for solving a murder and eliminating a drug ring. Of course, what do we know?"

"I almost got Jerry killed before I figured things out."

"That man was your friend," Hal said. "You didn't want to believe he was responsible. How is young Jerry these days?"

"He's still searching for the girl who helped us get away. No luck so far, but he keeps trying. Me, I just want to forget about it."

"That will take some doing, Mick. Lowell Palmer and his family were as evil as they come. Good riddance."

"Donny Boy and Frisco got away."

"Still, I submit that's a fair amount of work for one weekend."

"Oh, hush, I'm blushing like a schoolgirl."

Hal laughed, winced again. *What's wrong with him? Is this worse than he's letting on?*

"I'm just pointing out that had young Ms. Barton known the whole story, she might not have reacted so badly last night." The screen went blank. It came back in flickering, colored squares that eventually normalized. "After all, you have been seeing her for some time."

"So you're suggesting?"

"That you just try to remember something. That you are not of some inferior station in life."

"Think I should call her?"

Hal shrugged. "No one has ever accused me of being an expert on the female, but it would certainly seem worth a try."

"I'll think about it. Now what the hell are you doing down in Australia, Hal? I thought you were in Greece."

Hal smiled. "I have far too much money, you know that. My last hedge against the dollar paid off handsomely. Now I must find ways to divest myself of such an embarrassing sum before I am exploited by beautiful young ladies the world over."

"That is one problem I do *not* have. Right now, I would strike out with a crack whore on Sepulveda Boulevard at three o'clock in the morning."

"Ah, sweet memories."

I laughed out loud. "Fuck you, old man. By the way, one of the cops that took our reports last night was a kid named Larry Donato."

"Yes?"

"He's somebody's cousin. You remember me wanting to track down a vice cop named Darlene Hernandez for my Ninth Step, because I thought I should make an 'amends' to her?"

"Vaguely," Hal said.

"God, I must have held you totally mesmerized with my life story, if you've already forgotten."

"Don't get smart."

"I was in a blackout one night, wandering around Hollywood for some damned reason, probably looking to score some cocaine. When I came back to my senses, I was in a coffee shop on La Brea with this pretty brunette who was an undercover vice cop. She was just going off duty. I walked up to her and offered fifty bucks."

"Now I remember." Hal reached across his table for a cup of tea, stirred it. "You were so ashamed when you did your Fourth Step."

I rearranged some papers near the keyboard. "Let's just say it wasn't my finest hour. Anyway, as you'll recall she could have busted me, but she didn't. She had seen me on TV and didn't want to ruin my career. I felt like I should look her up and apologize for my behavior that night, but you said not to."

"I still think that. An 'amends' is a change in behavior. The best thing you can do for the young woman is to keep your life in order."

"And maybe say thank you?"

"If you happen to run into her." He bent forward and grimaced, then shook off the distress. "Damned stomach. Anyway, I don't think I would go out of my way to remind her that she failed to do her civic duty that night. She could have been severely reprimanded for not arresting you."

"Asking for trouble, right?"

"Asking for trouble."

"God knows I keep running into enough. Where are you, anyway?"

"I am ensconced in Perth." He sipped his tea. "It's quite lovely, actually, if a bit cold. It's winter down here."

I glanced out the window at the haze. It was going to be a smoggy day. "I envy you. This summer is going to be brutal. Well, I've got a couple of private clients this morning. I'd best get going."

"Shalom," Hal Solomon said. "You are valued. Be at peace."

"I'll try." I cut the connection, sat for a moment looking down at the desk. *You're not from some inferior class, right?* I dialed Leyna Barton's telephone number. She answered on the third ring.

"Hi, it's me." *That was just brilliant, Callahan, fresh and imaginative.* "How are you feeling today?"

"Mick," Leyna said quietly. "Please don't."

"Don't what?"

She left me listening to a dial tone.

Well, that certainly went well.

I went outside and locked up the house. A battered, dark blue station wagon pulled slowly to the curb; the tailpipe rattled and coughed up one large, black fist of smoke. A short, sturdy Hispanic woman got out and slammed the dented door. Her sleepy cousin drove away. The woman approached me. She had leathery skin and an angular, bony body. She carried a green plastic bucket filled with cleaning supplies.

"Morning, Blanca."

"Good morning, I sorry to be late."

"No problem. I'm just on my way to the gym. How are you doing today?"

Blanca did not meet my eyes. She shrugged. The bucket of supplies rattled. She muttered something in Spanish that sounded like *'God is in His heaven'* and moved to step around me, towards the door. I turned sideways and let her pass.

"Blanca?"

She was all business. "You no set the alarm?"

"I left it off. You have your keys, right?" I opened my car and tossed the gym bag into the passenger seat, turned to face her. "Blanca, have you heard anything from the police?"

Her face went dark and pinched. "No, sir."

"Damn, it's been over a month now, hasn't it?"

"*Si.*" Blanca fumbled for her keys. Her shoulders slumped forward and she looked down at her purse as if fascinated by the contents. I tried to comprehend her pain.

"Please, don't give up hope. Perhaps they will find the boy soon and bring him home."

"I pray to God."

Golden Gym is located near the intersection of Victory and Laurel Canyon. It is a funky, cramped space devoted to hard-core body building and cardiovascular exercise. Several treadmills, spaced only inches apart, face a bank of three television screens. One is perpetually on MTV rap videos, one stays on "CNN Business News," and one runs soap operas all day.

At the back of the parking lot, a large billboard featured radio station call letters—and my face, smiling into a microphone. I found it hugely embarrassing, and it hadn't even gotten me laid.

Inside of the gym there were rows of recumbent bicycles, stair climbers, and efficient and well-maintained exercise machines. One entire corner was devoted to the use of free weights. It was an odd gene pool: haughty starlets and porn actors mingled with trainers, anorexics, and the steroid users with their giant muscles and pimpled skin. I was just one of the minor celebrities who worked out regularly.

I strolled through the glass doors, bright blue canvas gym bag over my shoulder, nodded to the ripped kid at the turnstile. I didn't see Ronnie.

I stuffed the gym bag into an empty cubicle and got on the treadmill. Ronnie Sanders was a tall, handsome black man who had played wide receiver for the San Diego Chargers. He was often late. Sanders had also worked briefly as a social worker. It was nice to have someone to talk to.

Given a choice between generic rap music, "As the Stomach Turns," and business news, I watched the stock market rise and fall while talking heads alternately expressed joy and consternation. Ronnie walked in. He was wearing tight, red spandex with blue piping.

"Ronnie. What a surprise. I should have heard your clothes coming."

"Callahan, my man," Ronnie said. A slap of the palm. "Are you ready to enter the house of pain?"

"I'm not sure I'm ready for 'Sesame Street.'"

Ronnie wandered off to get a plastic mat. I ran for two minutes, slowed to a walk for three, and then left the treadmill and dropped onto my back on the mat. Ronnie stretched my hamstrings.

"Jesus, I *am* old."

"Probably the drinking," Ronnie said.

I heard my right knee snap into place. "Yeah, probably. That also indirectly accounts for the broken nose, the cracked ribs, the bad jaw, and the flattened knuckles. I don't know exactly where the stupidity came from."

"That part is genetics." Ronnie flipped me over onto the stomach and stretched both legs again. He stopped and eyed a livid, reddish mark on my calf. "I've been meaning to ask you. What the hell is this?"

"What?"

"This nasty-ass scar, that's what."

"It's a long story. Some dumb redneck chased me around with a crossbow a few months ago. He got lucky."

"Looks like it hurt like hell."

"It did."

"What happened to him?"

"He stopped breathing."

Ronnie paused for a second, but did not press for details. He slapped me on the back. "Let's get to it."

We hit the machines briskly, both of us used to the cross-training routine. Moments passed in that odd silence only male friends enjoy, although from time to time we spoke.

On the leg press, I said: "Funny thing."

"What?"

"All the psychology classes I've endured, the books I've read, the papers I've written, the shows I have done on relationships, when it comes to women . . ."

"I got a Master's, you got a Ph.D., and between us we don't know dick. Move your feet out a little wider, Mick. That's cool. Now what's been going on?"

I grunted with exertion. "I'm just venting, man. They want you to be strong and tough and protective, right?"

"Right. Until they *don't* want you to be strong and protective."

"And if you are, they get scared."

Ronnie helped me up and led the way over to the bench press. Over his shoulder: "Is this the part where you explain who trashed up your face last night, and why?"

I flopped onto the bench and tested the weight of the bar. "I can't answer the 'who' part. I guess the 'why' was for money. I'm not even sure about that."

"Somebody try to hold you up? Hope it wasn't a brother."

"Beats the hell out of me . . . and by the way, he did." I took a breath and started fifteen repetitions. Ronnie waited for me to finish, gasping.

"You're a little weaker today," Ronnie said. "That's probably from the adrenaline. Your muscles are sore. So what happened, Mick?"

I shrugged but stayed flat on my back. "I don't know. Some idiot in a mask jumped out of the bushes. He had a gun."

"No shit?"

I did another fifteen, grunting and expelling air. "It was over in a couple of minutes. That girl I've been seeing? She watched me break dance with the guy. She says it scared her. Now, she doesn't want to see me any more."

"Man, that sucks."

The last set. "No kidding. I thought she was going to bat

her lashes and call me her hero. Instead, I get dumped on my ass."

"Women," Ronnie said.

"Women."

The workout was brisk and efficient. I was in the shower, dressed, and back outside the front door in a little over sixty minutes. I paused at the counter to buy something to drink that wasn't laced with suspect herbs or diuretics.

I noticed an attractive brunette standing outside the entrance. She wore sunglasses. She was dressed in gym shorts pulled up over a pair of dancer's tights, beat-up white tennis shoes with the laces untied. She carried a bottle of water, some tiny headphones, and a sweat towel. She looked good. Suddenly it struck me that she was staring up at the billboard at the back of the parking lot.

I walked through the doors, intending to be cool, but got a case of nerves. The girl turned to look at me, sunglasses obscuring her eyes. To my utter horror, I blushed.

"I've looked better," I said. *Oh Jesus, that sounded SO arrogant.* She snorted and walked past me, entered the gym through the turnstile, and never looked back. *Smooth, Callahan. Really smooth.*

I walked to the car, feeling self-conscious. I got in the Chevy, turned over the engine, popped in a George Jones cassette, and crossed through two open parking spaces before heading towards Laurel Canyon Boulevard. I passed an old woman in a VW, a black Volvo station wagon, and a man reading the newspaper in a red, wide-body Ford truck.

The light at Laurel Canyon was tricky; it took a long time to change. I was humming along with the music, drumming my fingers on the steering wheel. The red truck pulled up behind me. I finished my drink and waited.

The light changed. I drove straight on ahead, past the

rear parking lot of the department store. The truck waited a moment and followed. I stiffened. *Don't be paranoid. The guy is waiting for his wife to get out of the damned mall.*

I went right, then right again into the next lot. The truck drove past without turning. In the rearview mirror, I saw a large, tanned forearm with a tattoo on it. I caught reflecting sunglasses and close-cut blond hair. It was no one I recognized.

The truck went to the next driveway, turned in, and meandered towards the side entrance. Then I backed out of the parking space. Feeling foolish, I turned around and drove back towards Laurel Canyon. The truck did not follow, but the driver definitely watched me drive away, his face impassive behind mirrored lenses.

I crossed Laurel again, re-entered the parking lot behind the gym, and headed back to Victory. I checked the rearview mirror every few seconds. The red truck did not follow. As I passed the gym, it suddenly occurred to me yet again that my face was on a billboard, thirty feet high. I was a minor television celebrity, for Christ's sake. So what if someone recognized me? I laughed out loud at my own foolishness. Still, I'll admit I glanced in the rearview mirror on and off for a few more minutes.

I saw private clients in a quaint, middle-class area originally developed by denizens of the entertainment industry who worked in and around Universal Studios. It is still called Studio City. I rented a small two-room office in a nondescript, gray office building on Chandler. I pulled into the parking garage below the building, trotted up the stairs, and went in through the back door.

The small, one-person office with waiting room was furnished in beige and forest green colors. It was designed to feel as comfortable as an apartment. A crowded, wooden

bookshelf dominated in the waiting room. I found an Isaac Perelman CD, put on the stereo. I gathered myself, and then opened the outer door. A brunette woman, wearing purple clothing, sat quietly, reading *Premiere* magazine. She looked up and smiled.

"Hello, Janice."

"I heard the music."

"Good. Come on in." I sat in my rocking chair, and Janice assumed her customary position on the smaller couch. "How was your week, Janice?"

She did not make eye contact. "It was okay. You know."

"Actually, I don't know. Why don't you fill me in?"

One tear.

"You're crying, Janice. Are you feeling sad?"

"Yes."

Wait. Give her a moment. I kept my face impassive and eyes kind. After two very long minutes, she spoke again.

"The dream is back."

"Does that surprise you?"

"I don't know. I guess I thought that since we had talked about it, since we kind of understood it, maybe . . ."

"Maybe it would stop happening."

"Yes."

"Did you write it down, as we had discussed?"

"Yes."

"Read it to me," I said. "If something has changed, even the smallest detail, we want to know about it."

But it hadn't changed. A dark man with movie-star looks would creep in the window and force himself upon her. She would resist, but ultimately enjoy the experience. The dream was an unconscious attempt to deal with sexual neurosis, and was a fairly common female fantasy. It was entirely harmless, in and of itself, merely an expression of a

deep wish to be liberated from inhibitions.

Janice seemed incapable of accepting that part of her. She experienced the dream as ego-dystonic, found it extremely disturbing. For a moment I wondered why the dream was now coming nightly, and what might have changed in her life, then smiled as gently as possible, and leaned forward to close the distance between us.

"Janice?"

"Yes, Mr. Callahan?"

No eye contact. "We have been working together for several weeks now. Have you come to trust me?"

"I think so."

"May I ask you something personal?"

Her eyelashes fluttered. She examined her lap as if looking for lint.

"Have you found yourself attracted to anyone in particular, lately?"

Her face turned bright red. Janice nodded briskly. She began to cry.

"May I ask the name of that man?"

But we both already knew the answer.

. . . The boy woke up lying on a square of carpeting; the carpet lay on thick strips of metal. He was blind and deaf, his head covered with thick cloth, perhaps a sack of some kind. There was a gag in his mouth that still reeked of the chemical used to subdue him. He knew he was back inside the van.

He fought back tears and tried to avoid throwing up into the gag. If he did, he knew he would drown in his own vomit.

Loco had very vague images of what had happened during the last couple of weeks. Whatever the man and woman had used to drug Loco had also stolen large chunks of his memory. He knew that he had been photographed because he remembered

the flash of the camera. He knew he had been kidnapped because he remembered the large man with the shaved head and body piercing.

He heard a rumbling sound, something like the coughing roar of a large beast. He cringed, and then realized it was only an engine starting nearby. The floor below him began to tremble and shake. It slowly came to him that he was lying in a vehicle that had begun to move. Loco wondered how far away he was from his aunt Blanca, his home, and his friends. He told himself to be strong. He told himself someone would come for him. He told himself to be patient.

And then he cried.

THREE

"You can get pissed off at somebody you really love?"

"Hell, yes." I was pacing the booth with the headset on, feeling claustrophobic and bored, wishing Leyna hadn't dumped me. "I think it might even be easier to get furious with someone you love. That person is more likely than anyone else to ring your chimes, right?"

"Okay. Thanks. I just wanted to know, because my girlfriend and I fight all the time."

I stopped walking. "Well, hold on, if you argue once in a while, that's fine, but *all* the time?"

A woman's voice, shrill and angry in the background: "Carl, that's just bullshit and you know it!" I grabbed the tape-delay button and cut the offending word. *Got to practice that more often.* The station, which ran on a three-second time delay, had the beeper, and also caller ID, to avoid scatological pranksters. Half of them had their phone numbers blocked anyway. Sometimes technology sucks.

"Carl, old buddy? Sounds like you got your hands full there."

"Yeah," the caller said dryly. "Now she wants to fight about how often we fight. One more question?"

"Sure, go ahead."

"How come every time she reads a self-help book, *I'm* the one who has to change?"

That was a good one, and got its due. I laughed heartily.

"Put her on for a moment, Carl."

"Hello?"

"Hi. This is Mick Callahan, and you are on the air. It sounds like it was frustrating you to listen to Carl talk and not be able to interject."

"Yes," she said, suddenly shy. "Gee, this is weird."

"Being on the air?"

"Yeah."

"What is your name?"

"Gina."

"Well, Gina, what do you two usually fight about?"

"All kinds of things," she said, now seemingly tongue-tied. Her boyfriend was silent in the background.

"What were you fighting about *tonight?*"

"I don't remember now," she said with a giggle.

I did my best to cover the dead air, and my poor choice. "Most couples are not fighting about what they think they're fighting about. There are always underlying issues, generally relating to our childhood experiences."

"Okay."

"You can think of those issues like plates in the earth that shift seismically from time to time and cause earthquakes in the relationship. The trick is to understand one another well enough to see those quakes coming. We have to either head them off, or at least process them in a more adult manner."

"I see," she said.

"Good. Thanks for calling."

"Thank you for the advice."

That was three pounds of uncut, semi-profound bullshit, I thought. *And no matter how you slice it, my country ass is in deep trouble tonight.* I took another caller.

"My name is Gene," the man said. "I was thinking about

51

the sixties. *Free* love, whatever happened to that idea? That we could all just, like, hang out together, get high, and kick back. I really thought that was cool. I mean, the closest thing we have now is that Burning Man Festival out in Nevada. You're from Nevada, right?"

"Right," I said, somewhat cautiously, "from up north, around Dry Wells."

"I just thought you might have gone to that Burning Man thing out there. It's coming up again."

"I know a little about it. As the old joke goes, I spent a year there one weekend. I was pretty blasted at the time, and I had just gotten thrown out of the Seals for fighting."

"For *what?*"

"I know. Kind of like getting tossed out of a casino for gambling, isn't it? Anyway, it's a blur, but the Burning Man Festival kind of represents everything I have tried to change about my life, so I'm not enthusiastic about attending again."

"If you can remember it, you weren't there?"

"I do recall that it's pretty pagan, and originated near San Francisco."

"Look, I loved it. People come together and paint themselves blue, man. They run around naked and create art with just their bodies, or whatever is lying around. You can make a statement. Take 'shrooms or acid, smoke a lot of great weed, all kinds of good shit. Oops."

This time I didn't move quickly enough. The offending word went out over the air. "Careful, I don't want the FCC down on my neck. I don't have Stern's deep pockets."

"Mick, check it out again, might be more fun sober."

"I doubt it. I think I wandered around in shock the first

time, and I was pretty wild back in the day. It just seemed too hippie."

"Huh?"

"Sorry. My stepfather was a real redneck who served in Vietnam. He didn't care much for that lifestyle. I think that rubbed off on me."

"Those were the good old days," Gene said wistfully. "We had our priorities straight."

"Oh, really?" I said dryly. "Is that so?"

"Yeah, we were out to change the world back then. We stood for something. Now look at what's happened."

"I hate to echo a conservative like George Will, who is just to the right of Attila the Hun, but think it over, Gene. Let's take a closer look at what free love and recreational drug use in the nineteen sixties have given us here in the twenty-first century. Ready?"

"Okay. Sure."

I went off on a rant. "We got AIDS and some new forms of sexually-transmitted diseases that are highly resistant to antibiotics. We got pot that is up to twenty times stronger than what John Lennon smoked. We got miles of inner cities devastated by a cocaine and crack epidemic and now also reeling from the abuse of crystal methamphetamine, Vicodin, and Oxycontin. We have truly staggering levels of drug addiction nationwide, a total disintegration of the nuclear family without a logical, disciplined replacement on the horizon, and the genders at war in a way previous generations never dreamed could happen."

"Yeah, but . . ."

"I'm not finished yet, Gene." I got up and began to pace. "We have lost respect for men, for integrity, and to an extent even for the women feminism was intended to defend. Someone explain to me how pornography has liberated the ladies, okay? We have reactionary fundamentalists manipulating some news outlets and trying to turn the clock back. Wars, deficits, apathy. And listen, I recognize that I contributed to this chaos. We all do. Our politicians are sleazy, corrupt, and we no longer revere Congress, the Senate, or the Presidency. And you want us to run off to some festival in the desert to relive the glory years? Come on. That's what we got from the last time around. We got screwed. We're a mess, Gene."

Gene paused. "Okay," he said finally. "But we did get some freaking great rock and roll music."

I roared. "Okay, I'll have to give you that one. We certainly did. And it's also a good thing that we learned to question our government more than we ever had before. Thanks for calling in."

I cut the line, sat in the chair, flipped through some CDs, spoke over the musical introduction. "And here, just for the Hades of it, is a song from Gene's favorite flashback. It is a little piece by Cream, with Eric Clapton on guitar. It's called 'Sunshine of Your Love.' I'm Mick Callahan, and I'll be back with you in just a moment."

The music rocked on and I reached into the small refrigerator near my feet, grabbed a diet soda. The air-conditioning kicked in and a soft rush of cool wind blew past my shoulders. *If that doesn't stir something up, I don't know what will. If it stays dead tonight, maybe it's time for another career change.*

Line one. I took the call during the song. I couldn't hear the voice at first, just noise, the cacophony of competing rock music and some static, voices murmuring in the background. Someone was trying to call from a bar or a nightclub.

"Hello?"

Slurring words, trying to whisper: "I need you."

I glanced at the caller ID, jotted down the number. It was long distance, a 909 prefix, so somewhere out towards San Bernardino, Pomona, or maybe even Claremont. Was this a prank? "Please, speak up. Don't waste my time."

"I need your help," a woman said. She sounded drunk or drugged. "Don't you remember?"

I didn't, not at first. "Who is this?"

She broke the connection, as if startled by something. I frowned, looked at the telephone number, and after a long moment tossed it. Eric Clapton played the last lead licks and the record came to an end.

"Gene, that was for you and your faded, graying hippie buddies. I'm Mick Callahan and I'll start taking calls again in just a moment, but first, a quick word from one of our sponsors." I started a new CD, a short commercial for an expensive skin-care product. I slumped forward in the chair, elbows on the console. After a few seconds I reached into the trash bucket, extracted the telephone number, and put it in the pocket of my jeans.

Line one again. I grabbed it, with one eye on the timer. The commercial was nearly over. "Hello?"

"Is this Mick Callahan?" It was another woman, not the same one.

"Yes. Can I help you?"

"I just wanted to say thank you for sticking it to that idiot who called you about the Burning Man Festival. I saw part of a documentary on it once, and it is a pagan ritual that would be an affront to our Lord Jesus Christ, were He here to see it. Those naked heathens turn my stomach. It says in the Bible that . . ."

I cut her off. "Sorry lady, the commercial is nearly over. Thank you for calling. Let me know when the rapture starts, okay?"

In the nick of time: "Mick Callahan, here. We have just a few minutes left, so I wanted to mention something else that has been on my mind." I looked down at the phones, swearing silently. Nobody, damn it! "We're really busy this evening, and I have so many callers I am going to clear the decks and take caller number five." *Can you guys tell I'm lying through my grinning teeth, here? I certainly hope not.* "I have two tickets to the opening night of the new James Bond movie to give away, so caller number five gets the last question of the night and two hot tickets. Come on folks, hit the phones and let's see who wins."

I played a disc with an out-of-tune version of the theme from "Jeopardy." "Okay, I'm waiting. Time is running out here. Let's get to it. Somebody wants those tickets."

Bupkis, zip, nada.

"How many James Bonds have we had so far?" I asked, desperate to kill more time. "The Stone-Age ones had Connery, then George Lazenby, Roger Moore, Pierce, and the new guy. That's not all? Tell you what, then. The first caller to name *all* of the James Bonds, in precisely the right order, wins a second pair of tickets. The clock is running."

Dead air, deep fertilizer. I played a gag CD that featured a host of Southern-sounding voices chanting: "Shucks, Mick, I don't know" in unison.

The phone lit up. "You're on the air, caller. Can you name them in the correct sequence?"

"Don't you remember me?" It was the drugged girl again. "I'm so sick. I just want to die."

And that's when it finally hit me. I took us off the air. "Mary? Where are you? I'll pick you up."

"I told them I wouldn't do any more porn, so I'm broke. I had to bum quarters to call."

"Where are you? Please think."

"A bar called Oranges, maybe? Something like that. I'm sick. I really fucked up this time. Fancy is going to kill me."

"Who?"

"Fancy." She started to cry.

"Stay right where you are."

I put her on hold, stopped the music. "We're out of time, ladies and gentlemen. Tomorrow night I will trot out the same question, so anyone who wants to do the research can win the tickets. Anyway, what the heck are you doing up so late on a weeknight? Go get some sleep. I'm Mick Callahan, and I'll talk with you again tomorrow evening."

I started the jazz tapes and went back to the telephone. "Hello?"

She was gone. I slapped my hands on the console, dug into the pocket of my jeans for a business card, dialed a cell number. "Larry? This is Mick Callahan."

"Did you think of something that could help us out?"

"Not exactly. I need a favor, a big favor. Can you have somebody run down a telephone number for me?"

"Come on, Mick. You know I can't do that. You're not a cop."

"It's a professional thing, a client of mine. I know she is in a club or a bar in the nine-oh-nine area code. She said something about Orange being in the name."

"Try an operator," Donato said.

"I think it's a pay phone. This is important. I'm not kidding when I say it might be a life or death situation."

"Oh, man."

"Please help me out, here."

"Give me the number," Donato said with a sigh. "I'll mark it as following up on a tip." I read it, heard Donato type something into a computer. "Orange Grove Bar in

Pomona, on Gary and First. Looks like a really cool place."

"What?"

Donato chuckled. "I'm being a smart ass. It looks like the kind of place you want to check out when you have a bodyguard, an AK-47, and some Mace. That's a very sleazy 'hood. You want I should call the Pomona PD?"

"No thanks, Larry."

"Hey, I'm off duty the next couple of days. Call me if I can help."

"I owe you one."

"Stay out of trouble, big guy."

I tried to call the number. The phone rang and rang.

I packed up my things, locked the studio, and ran through the parking lot. I threw my briefcase into the trunk of the car, removed a black case, and took out my Smith and Wesson .357. I grew up with guns, but don't really like them. They have a nasty way of escalating matters.

There were two speed-loaders in the bag, each one filled with six hollow-point cartridges. I slipped some bullets into the chamber and spun it, tucked the gun in my belt. I got in and fastened the seatbelt, fired up the engine, roared out of the parking lot and onto the 101 Freeway.

I opened my cell phone. Jerry was on the speed dial. I got his voice mail and flipped the phone closed. I put both hands back on the wheel and headed for Pomona.

FOUR

The city raced by, a wide smear of colored lights and gray concrete. I drove down the freeway in silence, knuckles white on the wheel, gripped by vivid memories of Dry Wells, Nevada, and how much I owed Mary. I took the 101 Freeway, then the San Bernardino. Only the presence of the loaded gun tucked into the waist of my jeans kept me from speeding.

The drive took less than an hour. I didn't know the area well, but well enough to get onto one of the main drags.

I drove past nice homes with pruned trees and manicured lawns and then down towards the bleaker ghetto neighborhoods, where the middle-class, single-family houses gradually gave way to crumbling apartment buildings, boarded-up rental properties, and vacant lots piled high with trash.

Graffiti popped up, left and right, the usual obscenities and some gang signs I didn't recognize. Broken black men with wine bottles sat forlorn on the gummy sidewalk, brown paper bags in their clenched fists.

In the 1960s Pomona had been bordered by orange groves and rolling hills. Only recently developed, it was relatively free of smog. However, like much of Southern California, it had fallen on hard times towards the end of the twentieth century. Now it was a smoggy swamp of racial tension, poverty, and gang violence known primarily for its yearly hosting of the Los Angeles County Fair. And sure as hell, a tall Caucasian dude was going to get noticed.

I pulled over to the side of the road, parked directly beneath a street lamp, turned off the engine, and checked my watch. It was nearly two in the morning. The sky shook as one large, noisy LAPD chopper flew low overhead, racing east. I shoved the gun into the back of my belt, pulled my shirt out to cover it. I opened the door and hit the street as the droning helicopter faded away.

The funky bar sat sandwiched between a dilapidated joint called the Montclair House and a long, dark alley filled with cracked plastic cans. The neon sign had two oranges sitting in the holes of the capital letter B. The block was nearly deserted. I spotted four nodding needle junkies on a bus bench, leaning sideways. One still had his upper arm tied off with a length of rubber hose. Someone was smoking a joint on a rusty hotel fire escape, and the sickly-sweet odor of marijuana clogged the humid air.

I crossed the street, moving diagonally, my cowboy boots scratching at the asphalt like wooden matches. I walked up to the door of the bar, took a deep breath, and went in.

The Orange Grove was deserted, except for the short, pudgy, balding man in a stained brown apron who was cleaning up. An incongruous white goatee flowered on his warm, chocolate face. He looked up and immediately dropped one hand out of sight beneath the wooden bar. My stomach tightened but I walked closer, expression neutral and hands in plain sight.

"You lost, son?" The man spoke pleasantly enough, but his posture made plain that he had me covered. "I'm only asking because you don't look all that stupid."

"Truth is I'm probably both. I'll bet you can tell just by

looking that this isn't my customary neck of the woods."

"You got that right."

"I'm looking for a girl."

"Who ain't?"

"She's white, around twenty-five years old, maybe five foot seven, brunette, unless she changed her hair around. The lady has got a serious Jones, usually for the sleepy stuff."

"She got a name, this white girl?"

"Sometimes she lets people call her Skanky."

The bartender nodded solemnly, eyes locked solid. He looked down at my empty hands. "Now, I ain't saying it's her, mind you, but a working girl like that been in and out, from time to time."

"Where can I find her?"

"Gotta ask why you want to, son."

"I'm a friend, Pops, not her family or the law. She wants to clean up. She called me, so I'm here. You know how it is."

"I see it from time to time."

"Can you help me out?"

"Long as you swear you didn't get shit from me. Mostly likely she's in a room right next door, bumping her ugly on some stupid bastard didn't go home to his wife tonight."

"I owe you."

"Bullshit, you never met me." The old man relaxed, but only a little. "Now, get on out of here. I got to close up my bar."

I turned. "Maybe there's one last thing you didn't tell me. She shot some porn films and somebody named Fancy was going to try and kill her. You ever heard of him?"

The old man stiffened, brought his hand up from beneath the bar, held a shotgun at stomach level. "Get your lily white ass out of here."

I backed towards the door, palms open, facing the bar. "No offense, Pops. You didn't say a word."

"Goddamn right I didn't." The old man came around the bar, backed me out the door. He locked the place, yanked down the shades, and covered the windows. The neon sign went dark. I heard a sound behind me and spun around.

A drunk was pissing against the alley wall. Someone slammed a top-floor window in the broken-down hotel. That's when I saw two rough-looking, buff young men standing next to my car. They had their hair done up in long, Jamaican dreadlocks and wore black wife-beater shirts, loose, tan pants, and identical, bright red running shoes. Each held a short, ugly piece of iron pipe in one fist. The pipe had been ground to a sharp edge on one end to make one nasty, highly effective street weapon. I tried to offer a brave front and only managed a skeletal grin.

"Hey, guys," I said cheerfully, "I'm just going to go pick up a friend of mine. It would be downright nice of you fellows to watch my car." I strolled over to the hotel. The two kids looked confused.

The lobby of the Montclair House had peeling linoleum, one geriatric easy chair, and four tacky gold couches, patched with black electrical tape. Two old men sat snoring in opposite corners, clutching screw-top bottles. One wore overalls and had greasy hands. The other wore a tattered suit but no shoes, and had a deck of playing cards fanned out near filthy, bare feet.

I walked up to the counter, looked over at the register. The clerk came out before I could pick it up. He was tall, wide, and wore his hair in a quaint 1970s Afro. His forearms were roped with muscles and cobwebbed with ink.

When he spoke, he leaned in and barely moved his lips, an unconscious act that gave his pedigree as pointedly as the jailhouse tats.

"What you want?"

I could literally feel time running out. I pulled out all my cash. It came to eighty dollars. "This is all I've got."

"That's a drag," the clerk said, looking at the money. "But why the fuck should I care?"

"I came for a friend. Her name might be Mary or Skanky. Where is she?"

The clerk gathered up the cash, grinned hugely as it vanished into his shirt pocket. "Thanks. Now, fuck off."

I saw swarms of black dots. I reached over the counter, grabbed the clerk by the thumb and right hand. I twisted the wrist, brought his upper body around, and forced the fingers back and down. The clerk hissed through clenched, yellowing teeth.

"Easy, you're breaking my fucking arm."

"I'm breaking your wrist, to be precise."

"You law?"

"No way, Jose, and that means you are in really deep shit."

"Twenty-one, second floor," the clerk said. I turned the wrist a bit more, felt bones grinding. "I'm not lying, man!"

"Does she have a customer?"

"The john left ten, twenty minutes ago. I'd go kick her out in a minute, anyway. She's probably passed out."

I let go. The clerk grabbed his arm and backed away. He seemed more impressed than frightened. "Thanks for your cooperation."

"Whatever."

The elevator could have trapped me in a confined space, so I trotted up the stairs. The .357 dug into my spine. I peeked around the corner. The red carpet was frayed. The hallway smelled of cigarettes, alcohol, and urine. My heart was thudding like a bass drum as I went flat to the wall, eyes abnormally wide from adrenaline. *Too late to back out. If it doesn't work, you're fish food.*

I found the room, tried the knob, and went inside. There was one lamp, with a ripped shade burned a color like dried feces. Mary was sprawled on the bed, wearing black panties and a bra. I locked the door behind me, checked her arms and legs, found dozens of scars and fresh needle marks. I slapped her, lightly but firmly.

"Mary? It's Mick Callahan. You have to wake up and come with me, right now."

Her eyes opened, slowly focused. Mary was a plain, country girl, with a corn-fed face ravaged by excess. She seemed puzzled to see me. I got her into her dress and shoes, grabbed her purse, and shoved her out the door. She slipped in the hallway and went down, clutching at my pants leg. An old man peeked out from a room down the hall. When he saw the girl kneeling before me, he cackled. I slapped Mary again, dragged her upright.

"Get it together. I need you on your feet, or we're both fucked."

"Okay," she said, eyes clearing a bit. She swallowed, nodded. I took her elbow and walked her back down the hall. We carefully navigated the steps into the lobby. There was no sign of the damned clerk. I almost went for the gun, but reminded myself how often guns escalate violence. Still, it took all my willpower to leave the weapon in my belt.

We opened the front door and stepped out into the street.

The tableau remained frozen for a few seconds: Just the two of us standing before the Montclair House, while across the broken, trash-strewn street stood the kids who had staked out my car. Everyone else had vanished. A light breeze moved dry leaves along the sidewalk with a faint, scratching sound, like someone buried alive.

"You just stay right there, my man."

A very small but strikingly handsome black man in a full-length mink emerged from the shadows of the alley. He might have been a flyweight boxing champion or a rap star: his tiny fingers were festooned with diamonds and gold rings, and his perfectly white teeth gleamed bright in an ominous darkness. *So this little guy is the main man, Fancy. He looks calm, a real predator.*

"Good evening." My voice sounded strange.

"Sir, where in the world do you think you are going?" Fancy said, in a surprisingly rich and cultured baritone. He had an English accent. If it was an affectation, it was well done. "I can't be expected to just let someone waltz on in here and leave with one of my women."

"No offense intended," I replied, as calmly as I could. "She wants out. I'm here to help."

Fancy laughed, uproariously. The two tall bodyguards joined in. "That's rich, and are you perhaps from a church organization, my man?"

"Not exactly."

He shrugged out of the expensive coat, neatly folded it over one arm, and handed it to someone standing hidden in the shadows. Fancy was not only small, his left arm was also deformed or slightly arthritic. It was bent at an odd angle and the fingers were curled.

"I see. So, you are on a mission."

"You could say that." I pushed Mary from behind, forced her to walk toward the car. "I'm not competing with you, if that's what you're worried about."

"What in the world would *you* know about *me?*"

The tall boys with the pipes stiffened, grunted, and moved closer. I paused near my car. "Look Fancy, I know who you are. And so do some friends in law enforcement. Let's just do this peacefully, okay?"

"Threats?" Fancy scowled, chuckled mockingly. "Now you are beginning to irritate. Perhaps I should not allow you to live."

I tried to act unimpressed, but my legs were shaking. "You want to tell these two gentlemen to back away?"

Fancy strolled closer. *A first-class Napoleon complex. He oozes power, lives for it. He is totally accustomed to command.* I felt like a deer that had wandered a bit too close to the lion's den.

"Do I know you?"

I pulled Mary closer. "No, I get that. I just look like someone you're supposed to know."

Fancy gave the girl a wide, alligator smile. "Do you not wish to remain in my employ any longer, darling girl?"

"I don't know," she said sleepily.

"You don't know? Wrong answer."

Fancy snapped the fingers of his good right hand. Instantly the two men by the car moved to encircle me, one on each side. My fingers strayed towards the .357, but then I remembered the figure hidden in the darkened alley. I was being covered from there. I took a deep breath.

"Get in the car, Mary." She stumbled to the passenger side. A few beats of silence followed.

Fancy chuckled. "Ah, Mary the virgin, Mary the whore. Mary is a much nicer name than Skanky, don't you think?"

He snapped his small fingers again. The boy on the right tried to hit me with the pipe. The move was predictable enough for me to fall back on Seal training. I stepped back out of the way, grabbed the boy's arm, used his momentum for leverage, then tripped him and drove him face-down into the pavement. I dropped my right knee on his upper back and cracked some ribs to make sure he'd be out of it for a while.

I grabbed the fallen pipe and moved back towards Fancy, not where I'd be expected to go, and caught the other boy off-guard. He spun, eyes white in his face, and swung at me.

I stepped under the pipe and brought my own weapon up. Metal clanged and echoed down the street. The boy kicked me in the shin. That hurt like hell. I growled. The pipes clanged together.

"Wonderful, gladiators!" Fancy called. "Most entertaining."

The boy closed again, parried my thrust, and raised his weapon. Before he could bring it down, I crouched, then punched once at a kneecap and twice at his diaphragm with the blunt end of the pipe. The boy sank to his knees, wheezing.

It was over.

I pulled the .357. Immediately, clicks echoed all around as weapons were cocked up and down the street. I kept mine pointed down at the pavement. "We don't need to take this any further, Fancy. I just want to help the girl, that's all. This is not about business."

Fancy pondered. "It is always my business, friend. She is one of my very best, certain to star in my next motion picture."

"Do you want money?"

"Oh, please," Fancy said. He waved the withered fingers. "You couldn't raise the money I find in my couch. Let me think on this."

"Take your time." I was having trouble keeping my breathing under control.

"I pride myself on intelligent business practices," Fancy said at last. "Still, one must always change with the times."

"Absolutely, flexibility is a must in any business plan."

"Also, I'm feeling generous tonight. I see no harm in allowing her to retire prematurely."

"Thank you." *For not shooting my sorry ass full of holes.*

"And as for any repeat performance of this evening's festivities . . ."

Fancy moved his good fingers again, and the shape in the alley stepped into plain sight. He was round and compact, a dangerous-looking man wearing a baseball cap and a blue windbreaker. His eyes were deep and haunted, mouth thin and bitter. He carried an Uzi like some men hold a pet.

"I assure you, there will be no repeat performance."

"I'm so happy you see things my way," Fancy said.

I tucked the pistol away. "Well, it's been real. I suppose I had better be going, now."

Fancy gripped his bad left arm with his right. He bowed. "On that we are also in complete agreement."

I got in, started the car, and backed it away, my eyes fixed on that automatic rifle. The man tracked me all the way, sunken eyes hungry. Nearby, the shadows rippled as other gang members moved on again, like an army of the living dead.

The car left the pool of light and re-entered darkness. I shoved the .357 under the front seat. My chest was tight, pulse roaring in my ears. Mary made a coughing sound and leaned against the passenger window.

"Please don't tell," she mumbled.

"What?"

"Please don't tell Jerry about finding me. Not yet."

I did not answer.

"You promise?"

"*Quiet.* Wait a second."

Fancy and his bodyguard finally turned and went back into the alley. I spun the car around and drove a bit too rapidly, back toward the freeway. After a moment, I caught myself and slowed down to the speed limit. A minute later, as if in response, a black-and-white squad car emerged from a side street to follow us for a time.

It worried me some, but the squad car eventually trailed off, reversed direction, and went back to the higher crime district. When my eyes left the rearview mirror and returned to Mary, she had passed out cold.

FIVE

I was sprawled on the couch, scratching Murphy behind the ears. A smoky steel-guitar solo curled through the room before giving way to a Randy Travis vocal. The music did not completely cover the sound of dry retching, a female voice swearing up a storm, the thump of rusty plumbing, and the hiss of another cold shower.

Sunrise began to turn the smoggy skyline a hazy orange. I heard the bedroom door close and a few, careful footsteps. I was up and making coffee by then. When I turned around, a thin blonde woman stood in the kitchen doorway. Suzanne Walton wore a wrinkled blue business suit, flat shoes, and a pair of wire-rimmed glasses. She yawned and rolled her shoulders.

"Mary will be out for a while." She had the warm, honeyed drawl of an ex-Texan.

"Thanks, Peanut. Maybe we should try and catch some sleep."

Suzanne removed her tailored blue jacket, tossed it on the table, and sank into a kitchen chair. She loosened her tie and the collar button of her white blouse and then stuck her tongue out comically, as if panting for coffee. "I am in need."

"I'm on it."

"I can call in sick tomorrow," Peanut said. "It's just some boring old depositions. After that, you'll have to take over your own self, or find somebody else. I'm in court all next week, and there's nothing for it. I've got to be up to speed."

"I'm grateful for whatever you can do."

"As well you should be, cowboy, but I'll call in the favor some day."

I poured some hot coffee with cream and sugar. "How's our girl?"

"She'll sleep some, now."

"That's good."

"She's been into all kinds of sick stuff to get drugs. Did you already pick up on that?"

"I kind of read between the lines."

"It's going to make it harder to stay clean."

"That's why I called. I think she's going to need a woman to talk to."

"Most definitely, bro. She did some pornography, and fairly raw stuff."

"How bad?"

"With everything but barnyard animals, maybe one or two of those. I'm not sure if that was a joke or not."

"Ouch."

"Mary is going to have to live with the idea of her face and body being in video stores, and other people's bedrooms, for the next several decades. This will be kind of like coming out of a long blackout, and she may not be able to handle what happened."

"Maybe she will."

"Either way, she's going to need to talk to a lot of lady drunks before she can love herself again."

"I figured you'd know one or two."

"One or two," Peanut said. "She keeps going on about something or someone burning. Do you know what she means by that?"

"Not a clue." I rubbed my face.

Peanut put a hand on my arm. I flinched at the unexpected contact. "I know you fairly well by now, Mick. You're holding something back."

"Not intentionally." I lie poorly.

"Horse shit. Where did this filly come from? How well do you know her?"

"Not very well. Why, does that matter?"

"It depends," Peanut said. "I deserve to know the truth."

I considered her hours alone with the vomiting, crying girl. "That you do, but this gets complicated."

"Don't be evasive, cowboy. It doesn't become you."

"You really are a lawyer now, aren't you?" I sighed. "You remember me telling you about all that trouble I got into back in Nevada, where a bunch of people died?"

"You were starting the comeback. The only job you could find was in Dry Wells, over Memorial Day weekend."

"A young girl called while I was on the air, and the next day she got murdered. Her name was Sandy Palmer. I got talked into trying to find out what happened. Well, and there was one other dead body I found the night before. Oh, hell, it's a long story."

Peanut shook her head. "You can't even manage to have one boring weekend, can you?"

"Listen, you remember my hacker friend?"

"The one with the burn scar?"

"He got me started in the right direction. Hal helped out. At first we just wanted to see what happened to Sandy Palmer. Then it got messy."

"Mary had something to do with the murderer?"

I told Peanut about how the trail eventually led to a

ranch owned by the Palmer family, and then a ring of drug dealers. ". . . By halfway through the weekend, the speed freaks kidnapped Jerry, and when I went in after him, they caught me and knocked me upside the head. When I came to, we were both tied up in a potato cellar, waiting to get our throats cut."

Peanut sensed what the memory was doing to my pulse rate. She patted my hand.

After a moment, I continued. "Mary was in the gang. She was assigned to watch us. I got her talking and finally convinced her to untie my hands. Well, that's how we got away."

"You owe her." It was not a question.

"Peanut, we wouldn't have had a chance. Later on, a big, crazy son of a bitch named Donny Boy came at me. He was tweaked on crystal. I was going down for good." I swam against the current, lost in a memory. "Donny was mean, a violent sociopath. He just kept wandering around mumbling *'oh boy'* to himself while he hurt people."

"He really scared you, didn't he?"

"He would have scared Godzilla." In fact, he still haunted my dreams.

"And?"

"We got loose. When Donny Boy came after us, Mary whacked him with a shovel. Jerry and I got away. She saved my life twice that day. I promised her if she ever wanted to get clean that Hal and I would help."

"She told me everything else," Peanut said.

"What did she say?"

"You knew each other, but she disappeared for several months. She finally calls you last night, on the air. You drop everything and race your ass down alone into the ghetto, stare down a pimp and some nasty guys with pipes and guns and shit, and take her on home. That about the size of it?"

"Give or take."

"And you act like you still have something to feel guilty about. Callahan, look up 'neurotic' in the dictionary. It has your picture next to it."

A sobbing wail from the other room: "I'm going to be sick again!"

Peanut got up, stretched. She finished her coffee. "Sit your country ass down. This is still my shift. You stretch out on the couch and catch a few winks. I'll look out for the wounded bird."

"Never mind," Mary called. "It's just the fucking dry heaves. Oh, God, I feel so bad."

The retching came again, followed by the sound of water running in the sink. Bare feet stumbled down creaking floorboards and the bedroom door closed again. Peanut shrugged, returned to the kitchen table. She poured herself another cup of coffee.

"I've been meaning to ask you something," Peanut said, "even though I probably know the answer."

"Fire away."

"Do you ever rescue men, or just attractive young women?"

I reddened, considered for a long moment. "That question scares the hell out of me."

"Why?"

"Because I'm a shrink, so the idea that I might be unconsciously exploiting people makes me . . . uncomfortable."

"Exploiting?"

"Favoring young women over men wouldn't be very professional, and it would mean I might be getting some kind of subconscious sexual or romantic thrill out of working with females."

Peanut grinned. "Like me?"

"By the way, do you think L.A. will ever have another pro football team?"

"Funny." She sat forward. "Never fear, Luke Skywalker. I'd suspect you are ever true to The Force. You remember how we met?"

"What's that got to do with it?"

"There are men in the program who would have taken advantage of the shape I was in. I had been beaten up by my husband for so long that kindness was actually a turn-on to me, not to mention the idea that I could be more than just a body to someone. I'm not sure you even noticed."

"Wow, what time is it, anyway?"

"Did you?"

I found something fascinating to examine in the wooden paneling. She laughed at my discomfort. "Relax, Callahan. I wasn't your client. You don't have any professional boundaries to protect."

I grunted. "What was the question again, counselor?"

"Did you realize how much of a crush I had on your sorry ass back then?"

"I thought maybe I could use that to help you."

She raised an eyebrow. "Why, you cocky son of a bitch."

"You didn't place much value on yourself in those days, Suzanne." I shocked both of us by using her real name again. Doing that felt surprisingly intimate.

"No shit, bubba. I had real bad taste in men."

"So if I allowed myself to be significant to you, and then made staying sober a way to please me . . ."

She finished the thought. "I might stay sober long enough to realize that being sober was a better way to live.

So you knew I had a real thing for you?"

"Yeah, I did. But I never looked at acting on it as a real possibility. I just figured I'd tinker with your taste in men."

"Oh, you did, did you?"

"Yup, I thought I could maybe improve on it some."

"Like I said, you're cocky, Callahan."

"I resemble that."

"I've got to let you off the hook, because I know Mary is just another addict to you, except she happens to be a female . . . and this time it's a little more personal. My question was rhetorical."

"It was?"

"I'm a woman who's been lonely quite a while. I could really use me a big, strapping man to hang out with. I gave you my best shot, and I never even got me a goodnight kiss. A girl remembers that."

"Suzanne, look. You're a spectacular female, and . . ."

"Oh shut up, Mick. I'm not done talking yet. Now, I have also seen you go up to the street bums after meetings. Although street bums don't generally get a crush on you, and then do what they're told, do they?"

I smiled. "Mostly not."

"And didn't you let that redneck bastard Tim W. sleep on your couch for a couple of weeks last month, while he looked for work as a truck driver?"

"Yeah, but he went and got high again. I had to throw him out."

She shrugged. "Can't get them drunk and can't get them to sober up either. It's all a matter of choice. I rest my case."

"As Hal would say, you are valued. You're a knockout, and some good man is bound to see that sooner or later."

"Fuck later, make it sooner."

"I'll keep my eyes peeled."

"Go saw some logs. You look like death warmed over. What do you have on your schedule today?"

I groaned. "Oh, shit, that's right."

"What?"

I shook my head. "I have some photo shoots, publicity stuff. The kind of crap I really hate. And now I'm going to look all bloodshot and wrecked. Half of California will think I'm drinking again."

"Can you put it off?"

"I don't know. I'll get some sleep and call them when they're in the office. Maybe I can postpone it for a couple of days. It's the *L.A. Times* Sunday magazine thing. They want to write something about the show."

"Go crash, Mick. I'll just sit here with my eyes closed. When do you want me to wake you up?"

"Give me until ten." I kissed her on the cheek and stumbled out to the couch. The sun disturbed me. After a few moments I went into the bathroom and rooted around in the cabinets, looking for an old, black sleep mask from a Virgin Air flight I'd taken to England. As I passed the kitchen, I saw Peanut fast asleep, despite the coffee, with her long legs up on another kitchen chair.

I went back to the couch, sprawled out, and slipped the mask over my eyes. I still felt restless. My mind saw Donny Boy laughing, and the fierce blade of a sharp hunting knife moving towards my exposed throat. I forced myself to meditate on the image of a calm pool of water. Within a few moments I was under.

. . . In the dream I was a young boy again in the sun-shine of Nevada, riding bareback on a Palomino, clinging

to her pale, streaming mane. I was one with the animal, loping along over hard-packed, white desert soil, moving as if in slow motion through clumps of turquoise sage dotted with yellowing flowers. I felt shoulders baked red by the dry heat and lips parched from thirst, but rode on. The horse faltered and complained. I stroked her thick neck and murmured that there was a small stream deep among the cherry trees at the top of the mountain. Finally we entered the cool shade of the grove. The horse nickered at the sound and smell of rushing water and quickened her pace . . .

"Get your filthy hands off of me! Let me the fuck out of here!"

I sat up, startled, and looked around. I was blind. Panicked, I knocked over the table lamp by the couch before I remembered the sleep mask. I pulled it away from my face and checked my watch. It was eight-thirty in the morning. Mary was going crazy in the bedroom, and Peanut was fighting to keep her there.

"I can't fucking *do* this," Mary screamed. "I can't take the pain. *I'm sick,* goddamn it, don't you understand?"

I stretched and trotted over to the bedroom door, started to open it. Peanut pushed it closed again. "Stay the hell out of here, bro. We're kind of buck naked right now."

"Did you bring anything with you?"

Peanut knew what I meant. "One last pill, so relax. I've got it covered, cowboy. Go back to sleep."

I heard Mary mewling. "Please just let me go. I can't take it. Please."

Peanut said, "Just hang on, sweetie. You're halfway home. I've been there myself, and I'm here to tell you it does get better."

"But I hurt all over," Mary cried. "I can't take any more of this."

"Yes, you can. And you damn well will."

"You have to give me *something*. Please."

"You can have this one last little Vicodin. It will take the edge off the withdrawals, okay? But I'm going to want you to drink some broth with it. Callahan, you still out there?"

"Got it."

Mary sobbed incoherently. I felt a twinge of sympathy but shook off the feeling, walked away from the door, and went out into the kitchen. The harsh morning sunshine hurt my eyes. I yawned, stretched, and threw some cold water on my face.

I made fresh coffee and found a bouillon cube. I started the teapot and boiled some water, made a cup of hot chicken broth, and wandered around the kitchen, killing time. I even rearranged the little magnets on the refrigerator; some were tiny cartoon characters, some bar ads for beer and whiskey, others caricatures of religious figures such as Gandhi and the Buddha.

One said: Experience is what you get when you don't get what you want.

I took out the official business card Officer Larry Donato had given me and stuck it on the fridge, LAPD logo and private cell number visible. I stared at it for a long moment. A passing chill hinted that the number just might come in handy.

Finally, I left a message for the publicist. I yawned as the telephone rang and rang. Finally, the answering machine picked up. I made my voice sound exhausted, which wasn't difficult. I told the tape that I'd come down with a touch of food poisoning and wouldn't be able to do the photo shoot. I hung up and went back to the couch to lie down, feeling like a guilty schoolboy.

"Shut the fuck up."
"Don't talk to me that way, goddamn it."
"I'll talk to you any way I want, bitch."
They are arguing again. Loco can hear them but he does not know who they are or why they are fighting. He swims in and out of consciousness, vaguely aware of being drugged, not at all sure what is happening. The narcotic soothes him and makes his anxieties seem far away and minor. He keeps his eyes closed as they move him into a new position. He falls asleep.

SIX

"You people told me what would happen." The speaker was a young man, disarmingly handsome, with clear blue eyes and a cautious smile. He wore a calm suit and a loud tie and had rolled up to the podium in a state-of-the art wheelchair. At first he had been full of life, telling his drinking story with self-deprecating wit, and the room had been filled with laughter. Now we had fallen silent, sensing what was to come.

The young man said: "You warned me how it would be if I went out again, if I tried to drink and do drugs one more time. You told me it would only get worse, but I didn't want to believe you. For you people who are new, when it comes to our disease, the people in these rooms will *never* lie to you."

Mary was pale, perspiring heavily, sitting stiff in the metal folding chair with a bad case of vibrating knees. She had refused to stand at the beginning of the meeting or to "identify" herself as a recovering alcoholic in her first twenty-four hours of sobriety, but at least she seemed to be listening. She held Peanut's hand. Her lips were thin and her knuckles were white.

"I toasted the New Year. Hell, I'd been clean for four years, right? What difference could it make if I had a few drinks? And then I got behind the wheel and drove home.

"I had two friends in the back seat, both of whom

81

trusted me with their lives that night. Their names were Mark and Barbara. I dropped Mark off safely, God only knows how, but I did. I was driving with one eye closed. You know how you do that? Because the white line is suddenly *two* white lines and you can't stop weaving unless you close one eye?"

A few small grunts of recognition, then the room grew quiet with anticipation. The speaker began to cry. "Well, when you drink that much, and close one eye, you don't have any depth perception. I ran right through the guardrail and down into Benedict Canyon. Barbara wasn't wearing a seat belt, and she was thrown out." The young man's voice broke with grief.

"You can see what happened to me. I was paralyzed from the waist down. I threw away a young woman's life and my own legs that night. After I paid my debt to society, I started paying my debt to Barbara. Now I talk everywhere I can, in and out of the program, about what happened. I want to tell every newcomer, *stay* here. Don't go out there and try it again." He raised his head and stared at Mary, before moving on to the next newcomer.

"Listen, it will only get worse," the speaker said. "And I thank you for letting me be of service. Good night."

Mary sat quietly with Peanut while the others applauded. We rose to join hands and recite the Lord's Prayer. As the meeting broke up, the two women hugged in silence. I walked away to thank the speaker and then stopped to talk to a television actor I'd known for some time. When I returned, I tried to sound upbeat, lighten the mood.

"Is anyone up for some food on the way home? We could hit that pizza joint up the block."

"Sure," Peanut said. We left the little church. "I think

they have a salad and soup bar. We all ought to eat something."

"Hell of a meeting," I offered.

Peanut nodded. "By the way, I love your outfit."

I'd worn ripped jeans and an old XL Rams jersey. "What, this old thing? I've had it for years."

"I believe you, since it says *L.A.* Rams."

We crossed the short parking lot in silence. I opened the car door and Peanut slipped into the back. Mary looked at me, a haunted expression on her face. "That guy really got to me."

"Good," Peanut said from the back seat. "I just hold on to something my sponsor always says. 'I know I have another drunk in me, I'm just not sure I have another recovery.'"

"Amen to that," I said.

Mary turned and looked at me and her eyes were red. "Thank you for everything you've done and for keeping your word. I didn't really think you would."

"You didn't?"

"No."

"Mary, I think it's time I called Jerry. He's been looking for you for months."

She closed her eyes. "Can we wait a little longer?"

Peanut caught my eye. I nodded. "Okay."

"Thank you, for that and for being here."

"You're welcome." Mary took my proffered hand and slid into the front seat. I closed the door and walked around the rear of the car, my eyes searching the parking lot. I still had the nagging sensation I was being watched. *Flashback, maybe? Little people in the bushes?*

The Pizza Pan was a small, family-owned restaurant. It squatted at the far end of a strip mall, with a Laundromat, a convenience store with egregious mark-ups on groceries, and a couple of empty store fronts with FOR RENT signs. The long building backed out into a foul-smelling alley. On the other side sat an apartment building packed with immigrants.

In the restaurant, Peanut filled a plate from the salad bar, sat down for a moment, and then left to use the ladies' room.

"She's really nice," Mary said. "Are you two an item?"

"No, I've known her since she was a newcomer. I helped her find a sponsor. We're buddies."

Mary squirmed in her seat. With her plain face stripped of makeup, and dressed in one of my old work shirts, she looked fifteen years old. "I may have trouble with all the God stuff."

"Everyone does at first. All you need to believe is that it works."

"I think I'm going to be okay, I really do."

"That's good."

Her forehead was damp. She went pale. When she reached for her soft drink, her hand was trembling. "There are a couple of warrants out for me, Mick. Did you know that?"

"No, I didn't. Why?"

"Some shit I pulled, but one is a felony. Does that mean I am going to have to go to jail?"

"Don't get ahead of yourself. All that will work out, somehow. The important thing now is to get clean and stay that way, one day at a time."

"Okay," she said. She held her stomach and bent forward, perspiration running freely down her face.

"You going to be okay, girl?"

"Just more withdrawal stuff, but this too shall pass,

right? I love all these little AA sayings. I feel like shit. It's kind of like having the flu, you know?"

"Yes, I do know."

"That trouble with the law . . ."

"Like I said, we'll worry about all that later."

Peanut returned from the restroom, slid into the booth. Mary mirrored the movement a second later. She started towards the restroom.

"I thought you ladies always went together," I said.

"We generally do."

"Peanut, I think she's rehabbing, just talking the talk. She says she'll be fine, now."

"What do you think?"

"She's going to rabbit."

Peanut trotted over to the ladies' room door. It was locked. I heard her call Mary's name. I went out the front door and down the alley. A window in the brick wall was yawning open. Mary had climbed out and fallen into a pile of trash, mostly smashed fruit and cardboard boxes. She got to her feet and tried to run just as I reached her. I grabbed her wrist and pulled her close. She smelled of sweat, garbage, and fear.

"Easy, let's just go home."

Mary cawed. "I can't do it; you got to get me something to take the edge off, Mick. I can't do this. I got to score."

"Wait a bit, just a few minutes longer."

She struggled again. I picked her up and carried her down the alley and over to the car. We got in and slammed the door. Peanut peeked out the front of the pizza joint, signed that she would get the food to go.

"I'm sorry," Mary said. "I'm sorry."

"It's okay." I stroked her hair. Suddenly she grabbed my face in both hands and kissed me full on the mouth. At first

I froze, then gently pried her lips and fingers away.

"Not a good idea." I smiled to soften the rejection.

"Why not?" She was breathing hard.

I decided not to mention Jerry for the moment. "Because sex can be a drug, too. The brain gets opiates and endorphins and dopamine from attraction and orgasm. If we junkies can't have one kind of drug, we usually go for another."

She cried again. "You just don't understand."

"Yes, I do, better than you think."

I held her for a while. Peanut returned with the pizza and some salads in Styrofoam containers. She arched an eyebrow. We rode back to my house in silence. Mary, arms folded over her chest, raced up to the porch, then into the guest bedroom. She slammed the door. Peanut and I exchanged glances.

Finally, Peanut shrugged. "So, go to work."

She knocked softly and went into the bedroom. I heard them talking. I tossed the worn Rams jersey on a chair, showered, and changed clothes for work. When I went to get my briefcase, I stopped near the doorway, uncertain whether or not to knock and say goodbye.

"It's who he is," Peanut was saying. "It's not personal."

Mary, crying again: "He makes me feel ugly."

"That's not because of him. I felt the same way."

Mary stopped, startled. "You did?"

This is pretty low, Callahan. Move out. But I stayed anyway, and eavesdropped.

"He's strange that way," Peanut said.

"He's gay?" Mary asked, incredulously. "I don't believe it."

Peanut laughed. "He is most definitely not gay, but he is kind of old-fashioned. Maybe that's why he used to get drunk. It let him fool around a bit."

"I don't understand."

"Girlfriend, you don't have to understand. Just count yourself lucky. He won't hit on you, because that's all anybody else has ever done."

"I still don't get it."

"He doesn't either, but I do," Peanut said. "He's a one-man rescue operation for damaged females. My guess is that's because he can't remember his mom. She died when he was little."

I blushed, listening in the hallway. *Pretty right on. It stings, so it's probably true.* I tiptoed backwards, made loud footsteps approaching the door, and knocked.

"I'm out of here."

"Okay," they said, in perfect unison. They dissolved into giggles as I walked away. One of the truly scary things about women is that they seem to understand each other so completely.

I locked the front door, threw the briefcase in the car, and drove away. As I got on the freeway, I turned on KZLA and listened to Dolly Parton sing about growing up in Appalachia.

I had felt something for Mary when she kissed me, a rush of emotion I found hard to define, something strong and vibrant, yet not of this time and place. It wasn't exactly lust, although somewhat erotic. It was a sensation I'd felt before, with other women I'd known, but seldom with one who'd become a lover. Perhaps it was pity, mixed with some kind of urge to protect, just as Peanut had suggested. It also felt quaint and not a little grandiose.

Peanut is right, of course. I've spent my adulthood symbolically trying to save my dead mother's life. And my recurring struggle with violence was probably an attempt to construct a positive meaning from having been physically abused by my stepfather.

Maybe I'm the one who needs some lessons on the nature of love, I thought. *Like Buddha says, the student becomes the teacher.* The two women staying in my home seemed to have an enviable way of communicating. They listened. To my eternal embarrassment, I am far better at lecturing than listening.

Moments later I was on the air again, holding forth like someone with something to say. The first two hours of the shift flew by, and the phones blinked like homes dressed for Christmas. I was comfortable and in my element, anchoring the debates and cracking wise.

"Okay, okay. Let's just say, for the sake of discussion, that you're right. Let's say a womanizer like you is promiscuous because he truly loves women."

"Damn straight," the caller said.

For the hell of it, I left the "damn" alone. I was pacing again, working myself up. "Just loves women to death. Hey, in fact you can't keep your mind or your hands off them, right?"

"No matter how hard I try," the man bragged.

"I see." *You're a smug prick. I think you're covering up for something. Like maybe a really tiny dick or some homo-erotic fantasies you can't allow to surface.* I figured this call was more about the dude blowing his own horn than anything else, so he was fair game. I bored in.

"Okay. What about all the hurt feelings from betrayals and lies? How do you account for emotional fallout? Would you call that part of it loving, too?"

"I can't be responsible for everyone else's reaction."

I pounced. "The best definition of integrity I ever heard is from a guy named John Kabat Zinn. He calls it 'obedience to the unenforceable.' Integrity means being a man, instead of a lying piece of dog crap who can't be trusted to go to the corner grocery store without trying to hump something."

"Hey, wait a second . . ."

"Thanks for calling." I dropped back into my chair. "But if that's all you have to offer, don't bother to again." I cut him off and let a dial tone hang for dramatic effect.

"Listen people, there are all kinds of excuses for having affairs, and both men and women do it. But the bottom line is you're lying, and you're betraying your own honor. And dishonestly is most definitely *not* love. End of lecture. This is Mick Callahan, and I'll be back with you in a few minutes after these brief words from the good folks who pay my meager salary."

I started a station ID linked to four minutes of commercials, leaned back to stretch. My beeper went off. Puzzled, I checked the digits and saw it was my own number. I dialed with one eye on the clock.

"Peanut?"

"I think someone is in the back yard."

"Tell me about it."

She was tense, speaking in a whisper. "I heard something moving around out there, something big."

"Are you sure it wasn't Murphy?"

"This was bigger than a cat. At first I thought maybe a dog had gotten into the yard, you know? But when I peeked out the side window, I saw that the gate is closed."

"Could Mary have gotten outside?"

"She's asleep in her bed. Mick, I'm really scared. What should I do, call the police?"

The commercial was running down. *Goddamn it, Mary has felony warrants.* "No, don't call the police yet. Hang on just a second."

I went live. "I'm in the mood for a little music. I'm going to play one of my favorite songs while I pick the next topic." I started a song that turned out to be an old Nat King Cole. "Peanut, you there?"

"I'm in the kitchen now, sitting on the floor. I haven't heard anything. What if it's that pimp, come for Mary?"

"How would he know where I live?" But I knew the answer. He had someone follow me home from Pomona. "There is a number on the fridge, a cop named Larry Donato. He's off duty tonight, so see if he can come over. I am going to call you right back."

"Okay."

She severed the connection. I programmed the computer to play some extra music, broke in on the Nat Cole song as I stuffed things into my briefcase. "This is Mick Callahan, and I have to stop a little early for personal reasons, but I'll see you again tomorrow. Until then, here's some cool jazz."

I burned rubber out of the parking lot, hit the freeway on-ramp, and dialed my home number. There was no answer. Frustrated, I changed lanes like a madman, but for no apparent reason the freeway was a parking lot.

I left the highway and roared down Victory, even clipped a parked car while beating a red light. Eventually I screeched to a halt in front of my home. The lights were on and the front door was standing open. I slipped around to the trunk, opened it, and reached inside for the .357.

"You know that's against the law?"

I spun around. A tall man, about my own size and build, stepped out of the shadows. He wore nothing but a pair of dark Bermuda shorts and tennis shoes with no socks. I went for the gun.

Officer Larry Donato laughed. "Whoa! I'm one of the good guys, remember?"

"Jesus, you scared me. Are they okay?"

"They're okay," Donato said. "No maniacs in sight. Quite a harem you have in there. Which one's yours?"

I grunted. "Neither, pal. The tall one's a good friend, and the other girl is somebody we're trying to help."

Donato smiled. "I am really glad to hear that, because I just asked Suzanne for her phone number."

"Damn, you work fast." I felt a small twinge of jealousy that caught me off-guard. *Wow, that's mature, Callahan.* "You treat her right, or you and me will be dancing some night."

Donato grinned, a bit wickedly. "Big brother?"

"Absolutely, I have a proprietary interest in that woman's happiness and safety. Speaking of which, how the hell did you get here so fast?"

"I live two off-ramps away. I was watching the game. I just threw on some shorts and I brought these." He reached down and produced his badge, a long flashlight, and his snub-nosed .38. "Just to be on the safe side."

"Thanks. Seems like I'm going to owe you quite a few favors."

"No shit. A lot of trouble to go through for one damned autograph."

"Yeah, but you got Suzanne's phone number."

"There's that."

We started towards the house. Donato said: "Hey, do you want to maybe tell me what the hell is going on?"

"Actually, it's probably no big deal."

"And you have some swampland you want to sell me."

"I'd tell you if I could, and I really am grateful."

"My cousin Darlene? The vice cop who busted you and cut you loose that time? She said you were trouble. I should have listened."

"Maybe you should have."

Donato grinned. "Okay. I needed to make a heroic impression, so I've already been around the yard twice. Want to come with me the third time?"

I followed him into the house. We closed and locked the door. Peanut was curled up on the couch, dressed in pink pajamas and sipping some water from a tall plastic cup. I noticed that she sat up and primped her hair when she saw Donato coming. I got that vaguely sick feeling again. *Physician, heal thyself.* I stopped and patted her on the shoulder.

"I think that boy wants you, Peanut."

"He's nice," she said. "You don't mind?"

"Don't be silly. Now, what happened?"

"I guess it was nothing. I'm sorry if I worried you, Mick."

"Don't be ridiculous. I'm glad you called. Mary still sleeping?"

"Like the dead."

"Mick?" Donato, from the yard. "Can you come out here a second?"

"I'll be right back."

I stepped out onto the porch, waited for my eyes to adjust. Larry Donato was standing in the far corner of the yard, shining his flashlight on the ground. "This look right?"

The area around the telephone line was trampled. The panel was open, but the wires had not been cut. I frowned and scratched my chin. I needed a shave. "I don't know, maybe somebody from the phone company? Nothing is damaged that I can see. Is the line still working?"

"Like a charm," Donato said. "I already checked. But look at this." He moved a few feet away. The pale light from his flash illuminated the succulent garden at the back of the property. "Jesus, now I'm freezing my ass off for some reason."

"Look at what, Larry?"

"Where was it . . . over here?" Donato held the light steady. I got down on one knee. Something looked ominous. It was a circular, burned patch of grass, perhaps eight inches around. In the center of it lay a small black stone. The stone had a stick-figure scratched on it.

"I saw you got a lot of Oriental shit on your bookcase," Donato said. "So at first I thought that maybe this was a meditation thing, but didn't you say the asshole that jumped you had a tattoo?"

"Yeah, and it looked something like that. A stick-figure surrounded by flames." I touched the grass. The burned blades crumbled beneath my fingers. I sniffed the cinders and palmed them. They were still quite warm. "It's a burning man, sort of like at that festival."

"What does it mean?"

"I don't rightly know, but the lady wasn't hearing things, Larry. Somebody was out here."

"This some kind of voodoo shit?"

Voodoo? I thought of Fancy and my stomach clenched. "Maybe."

Donato knelt at my side. "You're pushing my limits. I'm an officer of the law, remember? Now, I'm always happy to help out a beautiful woman, but I need to know what's going on."

"Turn out the light, Larry."

He did. The night closed in around us. We continued by starlight. "I don't know much. That girl I went to get, out in Pomona? That was Mary. She had a pimp, a rich, powerful, bad-tempered dude. This may be a message."

"Saying you're not out of reach?"

"Look, nothing is really broken or out of place, nobody got hurt, and I can't prove anything. And what do you want to bet there are no fingerprints on this piece of stone?"

"No bet."

"I need one last favor," I said.

He saw it coming. "No."

"It's simple. Please don't say anything to anybody. Just sit on this for a few days."

"Let's see now," Donato said, "and you're not going to tell me why because . . . ?"

"Because it's better you don't know." *I don't want you complicit in helping someone evade a felony warrant. That could end your career.*

"You know, I plan on making some serious moves on Suzanne, so I'm going to find out eventually."

"Later, Larry."

"Oh. Well, fuck you too, then." Donato sighed, got up, and jogged into the house, calling back over his shoulder, "I *am* freezing my butt off. Give me something to drive home in, and we'll call it a night."

I went inside, grabbed the XL L.A. Rams jersey from the back of the armchair, and tossed it to Larry Donato. He slipped it down over his shoulders. Peanut was standing at the kitchen sink. Larry winked at her.

"Suzanne? I'll call you in the morning. Maybe we'll go grab something to eat, okay?"

"Okay." Peanut blushed, busied herself with tightening her robe.

"Callahan? One more thing." Donato opened the front door.

"Sure."

"Don't ask me to keep any more secrets, okay?"

"I won't. Thanks." I followed him to the door and

watched him drive away. I went back inside. Peanut had gone into the bathroom, probably to avoid being teased about Donato. Another emotion had replaced the pang of jealousy. *Damn it, I envy them. The way they look at one another, the things they're both thinking and feeling right now.* It had been many years since I'd allowed myself to fall in love.

I went to the bathroom door and tapped. "Sleep well."

"You too," Peanut said. She was busily brushing her teeth. I went back out into the living room, stood in one place for a long moment, thinking about Leyna Barton, then shook off the maudlin mood and went to the kitchen.

I opened the cabinet and removed a can of cat food, clicked my tongue, and listened for paws on wooden floorboards.

Silence.

I opened the back door and called for Murphy, but saw no sign of the old dude. Perhaps startled by all the activity, he refused to come in.

I checked that all the doors and windows were locked and tried, with little success, to sleep. Then I noticed that the red light on the bedside answering machine was blinking. I listened to the morose voice, and then replayed the message again. Jerry had phoned me from Nevada.

I did not return the call.

SEVEN

"Is anyone here in their first thirty days of sobriety?"

The leader was a short, rotund woman in a red pants suit. She had silver hair and a grin-inducing, squeaky voice. She looked around the room, and eventually her eyes came to rest on Mary. After a few seconds of silence, she blushed and got to her feet. Peanut was sitting beside Larry Donato, who had come along out of curiosity. We all applauded along with the others.

"My name is Mary," she said, for the very first time. Her voice trembled. "I am an alcoholic and a drug addict."

It was another warm night. Mary was well scrubbed, and seemed healthy again. She wore a bright yellow dress, very little makeup, and a ribbon in her hair. She was a completely different person. This was a change I'd seen often in my years in the program, but had never completely gotten used to. A few minutes into the sharing, the leader chose her. Mary reddened, but spoke clearly and forcefully. "I feel like I have learned a lot in the last couple of weeks, but I'm on pretty thin ice. I still want to get high a lot of the time."

"Hey," a woman said, "you're not the only one."

Laughter. "You guys tell me not to think about anything but staying clean, but it's hard not to be afraid of my past catching up to me. There are a couple of people I never want to see again, some legal problems, that sort of stuff.

And some of the things I did . . . well, I would rather not remember."

"Just the wreckage of the past," a man whispered, half to himself.

"But some of these people are bad. Scary. Does anybody know what I mean?" A few people nodded. "But I guess I will just have to keep taking it one day at a time, or I'll never get my thirty days. Thank you."

She sat down to applause. Peanut leaned past Larry Donato and squeezed her hand.

But some of these people are bad. Scary. I felt uncomfortable and glanced up. A heavily made-up girl wearing sunglasses was staring right at me. I almost waved but caught myself. She looked familiar at first, but then I couldn't place her. She broke eye contact, turned, and walked out of the room. *Probably someone else who's seen the billboard,* I thought. *Take it easy.*

As the next person shared, I got to my feet and went to the lavatory. The room had gray tiles with black grout and smelled of antiseptic. I threw water on my face and washed my hands. Someone else entered the room hurriedly; more footsteps followed, and my survival instincts kicked into high gear. I turned carefully, while reaching for a paper towel.

Three men dressed in business suits. One wore sunglasses. The tallest was a skinny man in his thirties, with auburn hair and a light dusting of freckles. He stayed by the door and quietly slid the lock into place. My pulse jumped up a notch. The shortest, a stout, middle-aged man who was nearly bald, stood next to the one in sunglasses and kept his arms folded over his chest. *Laurel and Hardy.* I felt giddy. *What was it that Mary had said about the past catching up to her?*

The third man removed his sunglasses, folded them, and tucked them neatly into his pocket. He closed the distance to the sink, washed his hands daintily, and dabbed his face with a wet towel. He had clear, intense hazel eyes and neatly-combed blond hair. He turned, his face only inches away from mine. His breath smelled of mint.

"I fucking hate California," he said softly. "The appalling heat. The foul odor of smog."

"So, leave."

"I want to, Mr. Callahan, truly I do."

"That happens all the time." I manufactured a wide smile.

"What does?"

"That radio guy. I guess I look a lot like him. People come up and ask me for autographs and stuff. Silly, huh?"

Something slammed into my kidney. I moaned and sagged forward. Four strong arms caught me from behind. I measured the distance to the third man's testicles, but held myself in check. *Who are these people?*

"Guys, that was very rude."

"My name is Fields, Mr. Callahan," the dapper man said. "Agent Jack Fields of the Federal Bureau of Investigation, Baltimore Division. I work with a group called the Innocent Images Initiative. I am also a liaison with the U.S. Department of Justice, Criminal Division, with respect to Child Exploitation and Obscenity."

"Your mother must be very proud."

Knuckles struck my other kidney. This time I kicked out at Fields, but the agent had already stepped to one side, and I only managed to knock over the trash container.

"What the hell did I do, what *is* this?"

"Knock it off," Fields said. He frowned at his subordinates. "There's no need for that yet."

"Yet? That's comforting. Do you mind if I ask to see some ID?"

"Not at all." Fields opened his calfskin wallet, flashed an FBI identification card listing his name and phone. I committed the number to memory.

"Agent Fields, what the hell are you hassling me for, especially at something as benign as an AA meeting?"

Fields began trimming his nails. I noticed that he wore a new Rolex. "I wanted to ask you a few questions in private, and it would have been inconvenient had you decided to have an attorney present. This way we can have a candid, off-the-record conversation. Are you reading me?"

I just stared. "So far. Go on."

"You turned up in a surveillance photograph, and that fact disturbed me."

"Why is that, Agent Fields?"

"A public figure like you should be very careful about the company he keeps, Mr. Callahan. If a photograph like this were to fall into the wrong hands, especially after our investigation is finished and the subject goes to trial, the implications for your career prospects would be dire."

Now I was genuinely curious. "Would you mind letting me see the photograph you're talking about?"

Fields slid a brown envelope from his jacket pocket. I started to reach for it, but the other two men still held my arms from behind. Fields opened the envelope and slid a couple of eight-by-ten color prints into his hand.

A tall man was standing in the shadowy street, holding a gun pointed down at the ground. He was talking to a small, handsome black man with a withered left arm. Fields showed me the second shot, and in this one my face was visible.

"Fancy."

"So you admit you're cozy with the little prick?" It was one of the agents behind me. Fields shot the man an annoyed glance.

I sighed. "Cozy is not the word I would choose."

"What word would you choose, then?" Fields relaxed a bit. "Please do define this relationship. I shall be most attentive."

"*Quid pro quo,*" I said. "First, was this picture taken by a camera on some kind of timer?"

"Why do you ask?"

"Because I want to know if you saw what happened a few seconds before and after the photograph was taken."

Fields studied me without expression. Finally he answered. "This particular photograph was taken by a camera hidden in a deserted building. It takes a shot every sixty seconds, and then forwards each image to our central computer. Satisfied?"

"Yes, and don't worry. All you missed was me getting into a scuffle with the two street punks Fancy sent after me."

"And why was that?"

"First have these honor students let me go. I think you and I can do some business."

Fields nodded. The other two agents released me and stepped back. Someone knocked on the restroom door. The short, bald agent said, "Out of order, man. Somebody took a dump and it backed up all over the place. Sorry." The footsteps went away.

I continued to address Fields. "A girl Fancy was pimping and using in porn called me for help. She wanted to get sober. I went out to get her."

"And?"

"That's it."

"How old is this girl?"

"I don't know for sure, but she is well into her late twenties, maybe even thirty."

"Can I talk to her?"

"Not yet; she's newly sober and shaky. She already tried to run once. I want to give her a fighting chance."

"And what if I say I am just going to talk to her anyway?"

I shrugged. "I have an LAPD officer sitting in the next room. There are also several attorneys present. A couple of them are friends of mine, and one does personal work for the Mayor. I will have the local law involved, and her ass covered up, in less than thirty seconds. It will take you months to get her in for a deposition."

"You're a prick," Fields said, a small hint of admiration in his tone. "Just so you know, according to our latest information Fancy is probably aware of that hidden camera. That may be the only reason you're not pushing up daisies."

"Gee, does that mean I owe you one?"

"You think you're bad, don't you?" Laurel said. "He thinks he's bad."

"Me? I'm a pussycat." I kept my face pleasant. *Child Exploitation and Obscenity. What if this ties into Blanca and her missing nephew?* "Now you answer me something, Fields. Are you trying to tell me that Fancy makes and distributes kiddy porn over the Internet?"

"I'm telling you he is under suspicion," Fields said. He reached into the envelope for some other photographs. "Take a look at these."

A small African-American boy was naked, crying, apparently being fondled by someone wearing panty hose over his face to distort his features. I thought of Blanca's nephew

Loco again. *Damn, could it really make sense that it was Fancy who ordered that boy kidnapped? The man who kidnapped Loco was described as white. Weren't all of Fancy's boys black, or was it maybe just the ones I saw?*

I looked down again. Another photo showed a nude Oriental-looking girl wearing eyeliner and lipstick. A third showed a prepubescent white boy and a heavily made-up little girl kissing and fondling one another.

I gave the photographs back to Fields. "You've made your point." *But I need to know if you're for real before I tip my hand. Why slap me around in a toilet, if you're who you say you are?*

"Good. You don't need any further motivation?"

"No."

"Then let me inform you of something else," Fields said. "I take my work seriously, Mr. Callahan. I take it *very* seriously. You might say that I am on a bit of a personal crusade here. If I can prove what I suspect is true, your Mr. Fancy is going to go down in a big way. Would that bother you?"

"No. This crap is as distasteful to me as it is to you."

"Then I need your help. What do you know that we don't?"

An awkward silence followed. *He's bargaining. He is a self-centered and ambitious man. He won't believe me unless he thinks there's something in it for me, too.* "Look, I think we can work something out."

"How?" Fields asked.

"You know I do radio, so you probably know I used to do investigate reporting. I want to get back into it. I've been talking to a network about doing a new television show."

"So?"

"You help me, I help you. I want you to feed me a solid

exclusive on your investigation, smashing a ring of child pornographers. Do we have a deal?"

Fields studied me. "Maybe we can do business."

I nodded. *And just maybe I'll buy enough time to decide what to do, and how to approach this if Fancy does have Loco.*

"How did you get onto Fancy's operation in the first place?"

"For more than a decade, there has been one primary ring operating in the United States." Fields coughed daintily, as if offended by the restroom's odor. "They are gigantic, and no one seems able to touch them. A cynic might say that it's because they have some friends in high places. I'm a cynic."

"Me too."

"Our sources tell us that now a second production and distribution ring has popped up, and this just in the last several months. It's a small-time operation but seems to have caught on fast. And because of that, it already has a great deal of capital. It is growing rapidly enough to be a serious concern."

"And you think this new guy is Fancy."

"Do you know the work of Stephen Whitelaw? He is at Buchanan International Security, the software firm near Glasgow, Scotland."

"I remember reading something about him. He was trying to find a way to track what he called the dark side of the Worldwide Web."

"Correct. It was his people who tipped us to a second U.S. ring, and how rapidly it was growing. Father Rinaldi did the rest."

"I have heard of a Father Fortunato Di Noto. Do they work together?"

"No, but it was Father Di Noto who inspired Father

Rinaldi. These gentlemen are a great help to us. They work with our agents by going online, pretending to be teens looking for older lovers, or pedophiles looking for kiddy porn. When they identify a contact, they pass the information along."

"And you put the ring out of business."

"If we can find them."

"Because finding the website alone isn't enough, right?"

"Right," Fields said. "In fact, that's just the beginning."

"How does it work?"

The second guy, Laurel, butted in. His voice was thin and reedy. "Let's say there is a website that has illegal content posted on it. We track it down, but then we find out it's just a mirror site, a relay point. There can be a load of them, in fact, hundreds of illegal mirrored sites, coming from only one source. Someone has hacked into a gated community and used the server that the residents use for shared bandwidth. Are you following this?"

"Mostly." *Jerry, where are you when I need you?*

"The residents get their own IP address and access the Internet," Hardy said. "The IP is a static domain, so the numbers don't change. This perv gets into their server and uses the residents' IP numbers to post his site. Since they only use the bandwidth for Net access, and not hosting, chances are they don't even know anything is going on. After a few months, he folds his tent and goes somewhere else to do business."

"What about collecting the money? Same idea?"

"More or less." Hardy knew his stuff. "Any smart hacker can pull it off. They create endless dummy corporations to launder the cash, until it finally it ends up in the Netherlands Antilles or the Cayman Islands. There somebody skims maybe twenty percent and passes the rest on to our guy back in the States."

"How much money?"

"Multi-millions, each and every year."

I was saddened by the amount. "It's that large a problem? I knew it was bad, but that's a lot bigger than most people realize."

"Let me put it this way," Fields said. "In nineteen ninety-eight, we had something like seven hundred cases of online pedophilia that we investigated. By two thousand, there were nearly three thousand. As of two thousand and one, there were five thousand, and so on. So, this year we expect to be humping around twelve thousand open files."

"Jesus," I said. "And any therapist will tell you that pedophiles are virtually impossible to treat."

"He's been gone quite a while, Jack," the taller agent said. "Someone is going to notice."

Fields looked away, then back at me. He picked imaginary lint from his sleeve. *Fussy about his appearance, very vain.* "I'm going to trust you," he said. "And we are going to share information. For the time being, we won't bother the girl. How much time does she need?"

"A couple more weeks."

"But when you are willing to let her talk to us, you will get in touch. Agreed?"

"Agreed."

"Here is my card." He handed it over. I verified that the ID number matched the one on the badge. "Keep it on you. Do you have any reason to think you will be hearing from Fancy in the near future?"

I think I already have. "Let me put it this way," I said carefully. "He knows who I am and where I live. I'm afraid he could still be after the girl. If he does contact me, I will call you at once."

"Do you want protection?"

I shook my head. "I have friends. Besides, he already found your camera. I think he'd spot you a mile away."

"So much the better."

"But if you're right about Fancy doing kiddy porn, then what do you think he will do to her if he thinks she is already talking to the FBI?"

Fields sighed. "Point taken. We may be watching you anyway, Mr. Callahan, if only from a distance. May as well get used to it."

"I already am." *Because that explains a lot of paranoid feelings I've been having lately, doesn't it?*

Fields gave me a strange look, but let the remark pass. "Come on gentlemen, let's leave Mr. Callahan to the company of his fellow alcoholics."

I stepped back with another Cheshire smile. "Hey, and don't let the door hit you in the ass on the way out."

Fields turned away, but with a smirk. "Why delay, when we can go outside and enjoy so many carcinogens in the malodorous air?"

"Yes, why delay?"

Hardy slid the lock open. Fields went out first. I resisted a heavy temptation to repay little Laurel in kind for those two kidney punches.

"Agent Fields?"

"Mr. Callahan?"

"Doesn't the FBI have a height requirement, or has that been suspended?"

"Very fucking funny," the little man said.

"Hey, *I* thought so."

They left through the side exit. I took a deep breath and rubbed my sore back. I threw cold water on my face again, and waited for the tension to subside. *Just when it can't get any worse, it does . . . and what the hell does Mary know that she's not telling me? Was Blanca's nephew taken because of her connection to me, and by Fancy's boys? But why, since we hadn't even met yet?*

I arrived back at the AA meeting just in time to join hands for the finish. Larry Donato and Peanut were stroking each other on the arm during the prayer. I almost told the young policeman what had happened, but decided to keep silent. I didn't want him in trouble if things hit the fan.

I drove my three friends to a nearby coffee shop for dinner. I kept looking over my shoulder for a plain sedan, but saw nothing out of the ordinary.

"So you washed out while you were on probation?"

I tore into my salad and spoke with food in my mouth. "Yeah, I did BUDS and jump school, made it through the whole deal by my fingernails. I still hate going anywhere near the beach."

"Me too."

"So, I never got to actually wear the trident, because they drummed me out while I was still on probation."

Donato seemed amused. "What happened?"

"I got in a fight with an officer," I said, weary of telling the tale. "It's a long story."

"What are you guys talking about?" Peanut was toying with her food, staring at Donato. *She's totally gone. Well I'll be damned. At least she's got good taste.* For her part, Mary kept her eyes on her plate, ate mechanically.

Surprisingly, Donato had no questions at all about the meeting. I found myself carrying the stilted conversation. Peanut and Donato seemed lost in one another, in a hurry to leave. When we arrived back at my house, Donato made a show of saying goodbye, but it was patently obvious he intended to see Suzanne again shortly. I felt another highly embarrassing and completely unwarranted twinge of jealousy.

After helping her pack, I walked Suzanne out to the driveway. I had an absurd urge to try to compete with Donato but shrugged it off, settled for a kiss on the forehead.

"Thanks for everything, girl."

Peanut grinned. "Thanks for letting me be a part of this. I think Mary has a decent chance."

"I hope so."

"You're like my big brother," she said. "What do you think of Larry?"

"I think Larry is a very nice guy. It's a tough world to be alone in. I wish you both well."

She gave me a long, tight hug. She looked up. "You're a good man, Callahan. Do you know that?"

"Sometimes," I said. "Other times it slips my mind."

"You need to see a shrink about that neurosis."

"Probably a good idea."

Peanut turned, trotted over to her car, a white Ford Mustang ragtop. She waved, slid behind the wheel, and drove away. I stood in the cool evening air, considering my options. There weren't many good ones. So, it seemed foolish to involve others until I knew more. I decided to wait for events to unfold. I went back inside, closed and locked the door.

Mary was in the shower. I went into the office and took out the card Jack Fields had handed me. I punched the number into the telephone and waited. Since Baltimore is hours ahead of Los Angeles, I got an electronic message, which identified FBI headquarters. I punched in the extension number listed on the card. A man's voice came on, asking the caller to leave a message. It was the same voice. Jack Fields was legitimate.

So, do I tell him about Blanca's nephew Loco now, or wait?

I put the phone down and the card back into my pocket. I walked out into the back yard, whistled, and clicked my tongue.

"Murphy? You out there, Murphy?"

No sign of the cat. I went inside, locked all the doors and windows, and closed the blinds and shutters. I made some tea in the kitchen, put George Jones on the stereo, and sat down on the couch. *Why would Fancy have it in for me? Have we met before, maybe when I was drunk? Did I do something years ago to injure him, something I don't even recall? And what will that mean for little Loco, assuming things are connected?*

Mary came out of the bathroom, wearing one of my over-sized robes, rubbing her hair dry with a white towel. She sat down on the opposite end of the couch. Somehow, she managed to be attractive and plain at the same time. *I'll make the decision tomorrow.* I pushed thoughts of Fancy to one side and composed myself, smiled, and Mary smiled back.

"She's nice," Mary said.

"Peanut? Yes, she is."

"Why do you call her Peanut?"

"Tell you the truth, I don't really know. It just sort of popped out one day and she laughed, so I kept on using it as a nickname. It doesn't mean anything in particular."

"Officer Donato is nice, too. Larry."

"Yes. He sure is."

"Thank you again, Mick," she said suddenly, impulsively.

"You're welcome."

Her robe opened slightly, revealing a shapely breast. A long, uncomfortable silence followed. Finally I downed the tea and got to my feet. "I need to get some sleep. I'll see you tomorrow morning. We'll go to the gym."

"Okay," she said shyly. "Good night."

I tossed and turned for two long hours. It was a hot, sultry night, and I was suddenly fearful and tormented by ambivalent feelings. I wanted Mary. I'd tried not to think about Jerry, but couldn't help myself. I came up with some decent excuses: *She doesn't seem to want to see him anyway. She's not a client of mine, so there are no rules here. And I've been alone for a long time.*

But I knew better. I understood both intellectually and emotionally that Mary would never be able to perceive me as an equal. My status as a celebrity and participation in her early recovery gave me a highly idealized image, and therefore an unfair advantage. I understood these things well; I just didn't want them to be true.

This would have been a good telephone call for my show. Hey, Mick: Is it loving to sleep with a girl a good friend of yours has a thing for?

No.

Well, how about someone who is lonely when you're under extreme circumstances like this? Hey, you both could use a little comfort and consolation, right? Huh?

I don't know.

Well, how about this one, then. Is it loving to withhold your love from someone who wants you, just because she might regret it later and doesn't know any better?

Well . . .

What would be the best thing to do, or not do, Mr. Callahan?

At about two-thirty, I finally began to nod off to sleep. Only a few moments later a smooth, naked female body brushed up against me. I felt warm feathered breathing on my neck, light and experienced fingers creeping down under the covers.

For a few moments I swelled, gratefully succumbed. *This is wrong, this is wrong . . .* When her lips touched my sex I arched my back and moaned but forced myself to push her away. Her mouth tried to reach for me again, but I pulled her up next to me on the pillow. Mary began to shake and to cry.

"Why not?" she asked, whining plaintively.

"We can't. It wouldn't be right."

"Because of Jerry?"

"That's one pretty damned good reason."

"Yeah, but it's those things I've done, too, and because I did porn for Fancy. No, man is *ever* going to want me, now."

"That's not true at all." But in truth, I wondered, in a place so buried it could barely be acknowledged, if that *was* part of the reason. I didn't like the thought.

"Why?"

"Look, people need to leave newcomers alone in the beginning. Like I said before, sex can be a fix, too, just like drugs. In a way, it's even messier. This is a line a man and woman can't retreat from, once they've crossed over."

"We don't have to tell Jerry anything. Who would be hurt?"

"You would," I said truthfully. "And me, because I know better."

"Saint Mick." She giggled and pretended to grab for me. I twisted away, but this time she was just joking. "Hey, I felt some evidence that I did turn you on."

"Trust me, you have nothing to worry about on that account."

"Your loss, then." She spoke lightly but her voice had gravel in it.

"That's right, my loss. Now go get some rest."

Later, when I checked on her, she was snoring. I went back to my room and sat in the dark, pondering a pimp, a burning man symbol, a little boy gone missing, an FBI agent I couldn't trust, and an enemy I did not yet understand.

EIGHT

*. . . Crouched in the darkness, unable to see. I smelled
something rank nearby, something rotting away, didn't
know where I was, but my hands were balled into fists and
my heart was hammering at my rib cage. The metallic
taste of adrenaline filled my mouth. I was waiting for
something to happen, but did not know what. My right
leg had fallen asleep, so I shifted position in the dark. I
could hear someone struggling nearby, and the ragged
breathing of a frightened woman. Mary? Part of me
wanted to comfort her, but I was too afraid to move, so I
reached out in the blackness and touched her shoulder.
What was that?*

Footsteps, someone approaching from above.

*I swallowed, sat back on my heels, and waited. Sud-
denly the sky seemed to burst open with the sound of
cracking wood, and a massive pair of doors swung up and
away. A gigantic shape stood there, a young man with a
Mohawk haircut. He was roped with muscle, marked by
tattoos and multiple body piercing. Donny Boy whispered,
"Oh boy, oh boy . . ."*

I woke up. Someone was moving around in the house.
I rolled out of bed onto the floor, drenched with sweat.
Damned dreams. As my mind cleared, I recognized the
small footsteps. She'd cleaned up her share of messes

113

during my drinking days. She was family.

"Good morning, Blanca."

"Hello," she replied. "You like coffee?"

"Please."

I stumbled into the bathroom and splashed cold water on my face. The bulk of the nightmare was always the same. I would be back in that potato cellar in Dry Wells facing Donny Boy, or brawling somewhere drunk, or up against my stepfather, but always fighting for my life and just about to lose. I shook the dream away and went back into the bedroom. *There's no point in telling Blanca anything about Fancy, not yet. I don't want to get her hopes up, get her more upset.*

The sun had just come up, and the sky was shifting from pink to blue. I changed into tattered gray jogging clothes, stretched out on the floor, and limbered up. I stopped in the kitchen to grab some bottled water and started out the front door. Blanca was on a stool, dusting the mantle over the fireplace. I wanted to tell her I'd stumbled onto something and almost opened my mouth, but froze. *There's no proof. And she would flip out if she knew anything about pornography or Fancy.*

I tried to smile, but Blanca looked away. She had been crying.

"Blanca, you okay?"

"It's nothing," she replied, in her heavily accented English.

I moved closer. "Still no news?"

The tears flowed. *Jesus, should I let her know?* Blanca shook her head. "No news, they say little hope."

"There is always hope, Blanca, always. Is there anything more I can do?"

"Oh, no, you have done so much for my family already."

"Not enough." *I have something else in mind. I wish I could*

114

tell you about it. "I really thought my talking about Loco on the air would stir something up, but there are so many missing kids . . ."

"*Si.*"

"Well, I'll think of something else. I'm working on it."

Blanca sniffed. "He is such a good boy." Her sister, an addict from the barrio who had since overdosed, had given her son Loco over to Blanca's care. Blanca had brought her intense, handsome little nephew to my home on a couple of occasions.

"Are you sure there's nothing else I can do to help out?"

"No, no," Blanca said. "You have made that reward already, from your own money." I'd offered five thousand dollars over the air, the week the boy was taken. Nothing much had come of it. Blanca straightened up and returned to work. Said: "It is now in the hands of God."

"I guess it is."

It must be nice to believe that. Just saying it seems to calm her. I patted her shoulder, threw the gym bag over my shoulder, and turned to go. Blanca moved into the kitchen and began to wash some dishes. I stopped at the front door. *I'm going to tell her that I have a lead. Give her just a little hope to go on. What could that hurt?*

"Blanca?"

"*Si?*"

Damn it, I'd be opening a Pandora's Box of questions, most of which I wouldn't dare answer. Again, my nerve weakened. I reversed direction and went to check in on Mary in the guest bedroom. "Nothing, I was just wondering why Mary wasn't up."

The bed was neat, the room empty. She was gone.

I swore under my breath and Loco left my mind for a moment. "Blanca?"

"*Todavia aqui.*"

"Have you seen the young woman staying with me?"

"Not this morning, *señor.*"

I ran to my room to get the keys and cell phone, trotted out to my car. The day was already warm. I got in, slammed the door, started the engine, and dialed Peanut. She answered, sleepily, on the third ring.

"She call you?"

"Who, Mary? No."

"She's gone."

"Oh, shit."

"She's on foot, so I'm going to drive around a bit. Maybe catch up with her before it's too late."

"Take it easy, Mick," Peanut said. "Remember, you can't force this." Her accent made it *"caint."* "Mary has to want it. She has to be willing to do the work."

"I know. Sorry I woke you."

I shut the phone, squealed around the corner, heading towards Fulton. Impulsively, I drove down one of the side streets. Someone had cut down a large tree, and several bundles of wood were piled beside a bright green rubbish container. I cut over to Coldwater Canyon, shading my eyes against the rising sun. I saw someone running, a young girl who looked away and then back again.

Mary was jogging down the sidewalk. I drove up to pace her. She saw me, grinned, and waved. I pulled over, feeling foolish. She came towards the car willingly, opened the passenger door, and hopped in.

"I'm on my second mile," she said. "You wanted to go to the gym this morning, right?"

"Uh, right."

116

"Well, I was feeling good, so I thought I'd go for a jog first. Wow, what a terrific morning!"

"Yes, it is nice, isn't it?"

"Is something wrong?"

I studied her carefully: Freshly scrubbed face, no makeup, dark hair pulled straight back, large, soft brown eyes that seemed empty of guile. She was not a woman of classic beauty, but very attractive. She blushed under the close examination and looked down.

"What is it?" she asked.

"I'm just a little sad. My housekeeper's nephew was kidnapped a few weeks ago, and it turns out he's still missing. She's pretty upset."

"That's too bad." Something flickered in her eyes. *Was she lying? But if she knew something about Fancy being involved with kiddy porn too, why wouldn't she say so?*

"They called the cops, right?"

"Sure. It didn't help."

"That's a drag."

"Mary," I said, as casually as possible, "was Fancy into anything . . . strange? Like, other than garden variety pornography, I mean?"

"I doubt it," she said firmly. "He's scary, but straight as hell. He wouldn't touch anything too kinky. You're asking because of that kid?"

I shrugged. "Just thinking aloud."

She touched my face. "You don't look so good. What's wrong?"

"I thought you were running away. I was worried about you."

"I wouldn't do that," she said. "Not now. Although the truth is, I probably *should* just get the hell out of here."

"Why?"

117

"Because you've been so kind to me."

"I don't understand."

Mary crossed her arms over her chest, the classic posture of someone keeping secrets. "I'm just trouble, Callahan, I always have been. More trouble than you can handle."

"Mary, what is it that's burning?"

"I don't know what you mean," she said. She was lying again. *That's twice now.*

"When you were sick and coming down off the drugs, Peanut told me you kept talking about something burning. She said whatever it was, it seemed to scare you. What was she talking about?"

"I was sick," she said. "Who knows?"

"You ever hear of something called the Burning Man Festival? It's held out in Nevada?"

She pursed her lips, shook her head. "I don't think so."

That's three lies. What the hell is she hiding? I decided to change course. "I had another nightmare about Dry Wells this morning. It happens every now and then. I think we're back in the cellar with that big, crazy speed freak coming in after us."

"I know."

"It's all such a jumble, now, with the Palmer family, my friend Loner, everybody dealing drugs and Bobby Sewell in on it. That was one hell of a long weekend, Mary."

"Yes."

"Do you still think about it?"

"More than you could know. And it fucking freaks me out every time."

"But you don't know what Peanut was talking about, when you said something was burning?"

"I don't have a clue."

I held her gaze for one long count. *She's not going to give an inch, at least right now. I wonder if she's somehow involved with whatever's going on?* The thought truly disturbed me. I bought some more time. "I'd be dead, if it weren't for you."

Her lower lip trembled. "And I'd be dead, if it weren't for you, so I guess that makes us even."

"Jerry really wants to see you again, Mary. He's been very upset, very worried. I think it's time we called him."

"Wait just a little longer," she pleaded. "I'm not ready."

"Mary, look . . ."

"Mick, *please* wait, okay?"

"Okay, another day or two. But I need to know why."

Mary studied her fingernails, but her eyes looked far into space. After a time, she said: "He cared about me when I was nothing but a coke whore. I want to be as together as possible, before I see him again. Can you understand how I could feel that way?"

It seemed like the truth. "I understand."

I leaned back and rolled the window down. A pregnant Hispanic woman in a white dress was pushing two other babies in a stroller. She entered the crosswalk, saw me, and nodded pleasantly.

"Mary, are you hungry?"

"Not yet, I had an apple."

I measured my words, spoke again. "We'll eat later, then. Look, somebody from the FBI approached me."

"Oh, God."

"Don't worry, I haven't told him anything, not even your name, but I'm running out of excuses. I'll probably have to contact him, if he doesn't look me up first. I'm going to ask you one more time. What is it I don't know? Is this about working for Fancy, or something else?"

Mary didn't say anything, but her face changed color

again. It went white with fear. "Jesus, all you ever think about is Fancy and Donny Boy and the cops! Can't we talk about something nice?"

"Let me in on what's going on."

"Look, I got myself into some real trouble this time. And I'm trying to think of a way out."

"Then maybe I can help."

"Maybe you can, Mick, but not just yet."

"What is Fancy up to? What does he want with me?"

"Give me one day, Mick," she said urgently. "Twenty-four hours, that's all I'm asking. I have to think things over, and very carefully. I have to be sure I'm doing the right thing."

"I don't understand."

"I can't just go off half-cocked. Trust me for one day."

"Do you think you're in real danger?"

She grimaced. "We both are."

"And that's the real reason you don't want me to call Jerry yet, isn't it?"

"I want to protect him. I'm sorry I'm bringing so much trouble down on you, Mick. Really, I am."

"Don't be. I can take care of myself."

That line sounded artificially macho, even to my own ears. Fortunately, she ignored it. "Listen, I love Suzanne, but I actually felt relief when she finally went back to work. I was afraid something bad would happen to her too, and after she had been so kind . . ."

"I have to idea." *We give her the day, but then that's it.*

"What?"

I took her hand. "Look, you've been clean for two weeks now, right? So maybe tomorrow we'll just move you to a women's sober living house. Nobody will know where. And then I'll get in touch with Jerry to let him know you're okay."

A pause. "What would it be like in sober living?"

I smiled. "We can drive by a place I know and check it out. Usually it's two or three women to a room. Everyone goes to AA meetings and works to pay their own way, but the rent is reasonable. There's a curfew. Drinking or using gets you thrown out on the spot, but other than that it's pretty comfortable. And it's one step closer to being out on your own."

She leaned into me, one hand on my thigh. She ticked my hair. "Okay. But can't I just stay with you for a few months?"

I moved her hand. "Don't, Mary."

"Why not?" she whined.

I tensed up, searched for the right words. Mary took her hand away and laughed. I suddenly realized she was teasing again. A smidgen of self-esteem had returned, enough to let her crack a joke at her own expense.

I grinned. "Smart ass."

"Got you, Mick."

"Yeah, you did."

"Are we going to work out, or just sit here in the car all morning?"

At Golden Gym, Ronnie stretched her out carefully, droning on in his way about drugs and toxicity and health food cures. Meanwhile I jogged on the treadmill. Then the big trainer worked us both simultaneously, smoothly transitioning from one machine to the next, chattering all the while. He seemed half-smitten with Mary, which did her ego a great deal of good.

I paused to refill my water bottle and stood for a moment, watching them from across the large, mirrored room. Her body language was totally different. She seemed composed and confident, and it was now impossible to ignore Mary's lithe figure and bright smile.

I scanned the gym and noticed several other men had zeroed in to watch. A few of the regular women seemed annoyed. Feeling a bit guilty, I drank cold water and considered the situation. I studied Mary carefully, but finally dismissed the idea. *Back off for Jerry. She's not a client, but close enough.*

We spent a long, leisurely few hours at the mall, watched a movie, and ate lunch at a small Italian restaurant called La Pergola. I found myself at ease in a way I hadn't been in a long, long time.

"Let's go in there," she said suddenly. It was a loud video arcade intended for bored teenagers. I protested, but Mary won out. We wasted thirty dollars and more than an hour blowing things up and racing virtual cars side by side. Blanca had left by the time we got home, and the little house smelled of furniture polish and air freshener.

That night, Mary accompanied me to the studio. She fell asleep while I was still on the air. While packing up, I paused for a long moment to watch her. She was now dressed in one of my old, blue workshirts and a pair of swim trunks and she lay curled in a ball on the floor, using the yellow pages as a pillow. She looked like the fifteen-year-old who'd first run away from home.

I woke her gently, and half-carried her to the car, all the while sniffing the wind and eyeing the brush like a suspicious predator at the watering hole. I drove home carefully, tucked Mary into the guest bed, and locked up the house.

" 'Night," she mumbled.

"Mary?"

"Huh?"

"Twenty-four hours, Mary. That means we talk to-morrow, okay?"

"Okay."

"Good night."

"How concerned are you?" Hal asked later, from the video monitor. His lips were perfectly synchronized for a second, an effect so rare it seemed almost comical. Suddenly his voice crinkled like cellophane and got louder. "Tell me."

"I'm very concerned." I reached forward and dialed the speaker volume down. "Can I get you to have your people do a little nosing around?"

"About?"

"Well, this Burning Man thing in Nevada, for starters. It's pretty well known, so it won't take them long."

"What do you want to know about it?"

"Beats the hell out of me; it just keeps popping up. I don't know if I told you this, but I went once, years ago. It is kind of a half-naked, sixties-style art festival. It cumulates in the group torching of a forty-foot stick-figure."

"That sounds fascinating." Hal coughed. "I must re-member to put it on my itinerary when next in the wilds of Nevada."

"I had so much fun, I lost a couple of days. But one of the things I *do* remember is freaking out and hitting some innocent people."

"So?"

"So at least one of them was a black girl, who was maybe in her twenties at the time. Look, this is a bit of a long-shot, but please check out whether or not this Af-rican-American pimp named Fancy, or perhaps one of his relatives or associates, has ever somehow been involved with that festival."

"Will do. You don't have any cognomen other than Fancy?"

"No. Could be first, last, or just a nickname. But maybe a cross-reference on computer will tie him into the Burning Man."

Hal smiled. "I'm way ahead of you, young stallion. I shall see what we can discover about your festival. And what was the name of that gentleman who purported to be an FBI agent?"

"I already called the bureau and the office number he gave me," I said. "It was definitely his voice on the voice mail. Of course, that call could have been rerouted somehow."

"Certainly."

"The name was Jack Fields. I didn't get names for the other two. He's probably legitimate, but see what you can find out, okay?"

"Are you starting to wonder if the disappearance of your housekeeper's nephew was in any way targeted at you?"

"That's exactly what I'm worried about."

"Let us hope you're wrong."

"Let's hope. Thanks, Hal."

"I will have a couple of employees jump through hoops. I'll get back to you in a day or two. How are things otherwise?"

"You mean with Leyna Barton? She still won't talk to me."

"That is a pity. Perhaps she'll come around."

"I don't know if I give a damn."

"Pride goes before a fall."

"I'm serious. To tell you the truth, I always had the feeling she was looking down her nose at me, like I was a bug under glass or a noble savage."

Hal donned his reading glasses and shuffled some papers. His mind seemed to wander. He grimaced, signed something, and looked up again. *He's not himself. He's really distracted.*

"I know I'm getting boring, Hal, but are you feeling all right?"

"Certainly."

Not true. "Are you sure?"

"Of course I'm sure," Hal said. "Back to Ms. Barton. So, perhaps it is all for the best, then?"

"Perhaps."

"Or perhaps you are merely rationalizing a stinging defeat."

"Fuck you."

Hal laughed. "In the meanwhile, you have a beautiful, deeply-wounded young creature on the premises. Has that particular situation tempted you in any way?"

"Remember what you told me a long time ago? I asked you how to stay out of trouble with women, and you said that if I didn't go to the shoe store and hang around all day, I was not likely to buy myself a pair of shoes."

Hal nodded. "So, you have been staying out of the metaphorical shoe store then, despite the fact that it is located in your own guest bedroom?"

"Indeed I have, and you know what?"

"What?"

"It's a drag being the good guy all the time."

"Tell me about it." Hal winced and held his stomach. "Damned gas pains again. I must away, stallion. Take care."

The screen went dark. He was keeping something from me, I felt sure of it. I sat thinking for a few moments, then dialed Jerry's telephone number, but stopped on the last digit. Then I punched the final number, but didn't let in ring. Instead, I broke the connection and lowered my head. I was trapped in a maze and wild beasts were chuffing hungrily all around me, just out of sight.

. . . Loco came to his senses. He was looking into the eyes of a little girl. Her face was heavily made up, and she was wearing false eyelashes. He was lying on top of her. She, also, was clearly drugged and very confused. He felt someone push his head down her body, towards her little belly. He cooperated, but his mind was fighting to clear itself.

He looked up. The room was empty, save for a videocamera on a tripod, a bed, and a fake wall with an artificial window. He raised his head higher, and tried to struggle.

"Quiet him down," someone said in English.

Loco felt a sharp sting in the flesh of one buttock. He fell asleep again.

NINE

"You got rocks in your fucking head or something, Jackson?" The raven-haired Latino woman was leaning over the speaker phone with one hand on a stack of papers, the other flat on the desk. She was in her thirties, tall, strong, big-breasted, and obviously fit, and she wore a 9mm and a badge on her belt. "I told you not to talk to my goddamned witness."

"I was trying to help," a man said, his voice tinny from the speaker. "Hey, I'm sorry."

"Oh, you helped all right," the woman said. Her tone was razor-sharp. "You helped her decide to go back to Mexico." She pronounced it correctly, *MEH-hee-co*. "Nice going. Just like a man."

"Maybe it'll still shake down okay. I'll back the hell off, and she'll talk to you again, okay?"

"Bullshit," said Sergeant Darlene Hernandez. "Her lips are tighter than a gnat's asshole."

I was wearing a sticker that said "Guest," although I doubted anyone would have mistaken me for a cop. I stood silently, and watched her with genuine admiration. She shuffled through some wanted posters, found what she wanted, and tore it up. Darlene wore tan slacks, a tight, white blouse, and dark, flat shoes. She seemed aware she had an audience, but probably assumed it was one of the other LAPD detectives.

"Okay." The man sighed, exasperated. "Well, what the fuck do you want from me?"

"I want you to consider going into some other line of work," Darlene said. "I think you'd make a great fireman."

She broke the connection and then, feeling eyes on her back, turned to face me. It took her a while, but then she focused. Her smile flickered and widened.

"Well I'll be goddamned," she said softly, "it is the star himself, my own, personal Hugh Grant."

I blushed and forced a smile. "Your cousin was supposed to have told you I would be stopping by. He left my name for a guest pass."

"The one that's half-Italian, Donato?"

"Yes, ma'am, Larry."

"He didn't tell me anything," she said flatly. "Or if he did, I forgot."

"I hope this isn't too much of an intrusion."

"Oh, not at all," Darlene said, deadpan. She came around to the front of her desk and perched on the edge. "I had nothing else to do today except babysit some pampered, boy-toy celebrity."

"Ouch."

"Get to it, Callahan."

"Can I buy you a cup of coffee? I mean, since we're off to such a good start here and all?"

Darlene Hernandez cocked her head like an angry parrot. "Jesus. Why in the world would I want to go get a cup of coffee with you of all people, Callahan?"

I considered. "Okay then, how about a chili cheeseburger?" Her mouth twitched. Encouraged, I pressed my case. "But only if you're done roasting my nuts over an open fire."

"A chili cheeseburger? Okay, that's better. Just let me

grab my coat and sign out."

The Hollywood Police Station is on Cole Avenue, on a side street, flanked by several craftsman cottages. Black and whites pull in and out constantly, both solo and clustered in formation. Darlene Hernandez set a blistering pace. The crowded, pale green halls of the police station were filled with cuffed perpetrators and scurrying detectives. She shoved the patrolmen out of the way, or proceeded as if they were expected to scatter like pigeons.

She marched me out the front door and down the concrete steps. I had to struggle to keep up with her. At the foot of the steps, she stopped abruptly and I ran into her from behind. She looked back over her shoulder and flashed a sarcastic, thin-lipped smile.

"Back off, or at least kiss me first."

"Where exactly are we going, Sergeant Hernandez?"

"You can keep calling me ma'am."

"Ma'am."

"Follow me."

I grabbed her elbow, chuckling. "I already jogged this morning. Why don't we try walking instead?"

"Don't put your hands on me." She wasn't joking.

I immediately let go. "Sorry. No offense intended, Sergeant."

A pause. "None taken. Let's move."

"Why so fast?"

As we set out down the sidewalk: "Some of us work for a living, Callahan. That means we only get an hour or so for lunch."

"Why, that damned near breaks my heart. We media stars get six or seven one-hour breaks every day, and that's just to fuss with our makeup."

"I'll bet you do."

"And we are going . . . ?"

"There's a great burger stand three blocks down, kind of a family joint, with chili to die for."

"I'll defer to your expertise. Can we talk as we go?"

"So, talk."

"Okay. But I want to get something out of the way first."

"What?"

"I don't really remember that night. I'm grateful for what you did, but I was in a blackout or something."

"When you hit on me, you mean? Offered me a measly fifty bucks for a blow job?"

"Look," I said, wincing, "I'm really sorry."

She laughed. "Which part? Asking for a blow job, or only offering me fifty bucks?"

I stopped in my tracks. "Christ, woman, cut me some slack, will you? I'm trying my best to apologize."

"Fine. Apology accepted."

"I partly came here just to thank you."

She turned. Two small children in blue uniforms ran through the crosswalk. She waited for them to pass before responding, and by then she had softened. "Look, Callahan. You were bombed out of your mind, right? And I had already spent the last eight hours walking around Selma Avenue in high heels and teased hair, with my tits hanging out, trying to act like a hooker. I was not in the mood for more paperwork."

"What happened?"

"You really don't remember?"

"I really don't remember. I just remember afterwards, that you poured me into a cab."

Darlene grimaced. "I was done for the night. You came stumbling along looking for your car, and you saw me. I was getting ready to ask if you thought you should be driving smashed like that, when you hit on me. That was it."

"Except you didn't arrest me, and you should have. You took me to a coffee shop, showed me your badge, talked to me for an hour, and then got me to take a cab home. Why?"

Darlene thought for a moment. "My back-up had left, except for Tommy Riley. You probably don't remember this, but he and I argued about arresting you. I told him to take off."

"Like I said, why?"

"You seemed so unhappy." She studied my face. "I watched you on the tube sometimes, and I knew it would be all over the papers. I felt kind of sorry for you and I didn't see how taking you off the air would be best for anybody, all right? But I'll tell you something, if the rest of my crew had still been working, you would have gone down."

"You know I'm clean and sober now?"

She nodded. "I read that somewhere. And Donato said he ran into you the other night. Somebody jumped you and your date, right?"

"I still don't know exactly what that was all about. That's the final part of why I came to see you."

Darlene started walking again. I moved to her side, dropped into step, and looked down. "I really did want to thank you for keeping what happened that night a secret."

"You're welcome."

With a straight face, I said, "Of course, you did go and run your mouth to your big, no-good, half-wop cousin."

"Hey, screw you Callahan! I could have made a wad by taking that story to the tabloids or something. I did you a good turn, and you know it."

"Damn, you're feisty. I was just pulling your leg. Is this the place you were raving about?"

A splintered, white wooden sign said "Willie's" in bright red letters. An emaciated old man in an apron was crouched over an immense, grease-splattered grill. He was frying what seemed like forty pounds of raw bacon. A large metal pot stood on one end of the blackened stove. It was filled to the brim with thick, dark, reddish chili.

"Trust a cop," Darlene said. "Best food in town."

We sat on tall wooden stools, ignoring the acrid smell from the exhaust of passing cars and the odor of the thick layer of morning smog. The chili quickly overpowered the air pollution. It did smell good, thick with onions and peppers and rich beef stock.

Later, she said, "The guy is a pimp? I hate pimps."

I swallowed a bite of the burger, grunted with pleasure, and downed half a can of soda. "He's a pimp, and there is also a chance he's involved in kiddy porn in some way."

Darlene shook her head. Twin red dots appeared on her cheeks. "What the hell is it with you men?" She was smiling, but she didn't mean it. "There's nothing terribly complicated about sex, but men come up with every conceivable perversion and just keep on going. How much is enough?"

"No offense intended," I said. *Screw it; what the hell do I have to lose?* "But don't you think lumping me, and most of the men I know, in with a group of child pornographers is pushing the tired feminism rhetoric just a bit too far?"

The air was thick. We measured each another a bit differently. Finally, Darlene said, "Maybe. The jury is still out."

I put down my cheeseburger, like a man lowering his weapon in a street brawl. "I'm sorry I happen to have a penis, but I didn't come here to argue with you. I came here to ask for your help."

"What kind of help?"

"I just helped a girl who wanted to get sober. She's someone who did a lot for me when I got in all that trouble up in Dry Wells, Nevada."

"I read about that. Some people got killed."

"It was a close call, but fortunately I wasn't one of them."

"Go on." She squinted, bit, and chewed.

"This woman, she's got a pretty sordid past."

"Okay." Darlene wolfed down more of her hamburger.

"Part of it involved making some porn movies for this pimp Fancy."

"So?"

"So he may be after her. Both of us."

"Based on what?"

"First, somebody tried to rob my date and me the other night. That's when I met Larry Donato. Then someone may have been stalking this girl and another lady friend of mine who was staying with me. They were alone at my house, and I was at work."

"Fool me once, shame on you," she said. She looked intrigued. "Fool me twice, shame on me. Is that how it goes?"

"Yeah, well, fool me three times, then. I was at an AA meeting and three guys in business suits cornered me in the john. They pushed me around a little."

Darlene used a finger to bend her nose to one side. "Mob?"

"I doubt it. In fact, one of them flashed me what looked like genuine FBI identification. He asked about a pimp named Fancy. That's who I took Mary from in the first place."

"Fancy and the Feebs? Now, this *is* getting interesting." Darlene finished her burger and licked her fingers. She wiped them on a napkin and nodded. "And you got the name and badge?"

She produced a pen from her slacks and I recited from memory. I watched upside down as she scribbled the names and the FBI identification number. "And you want me to nose around?"

"I'd be most grateful if you would. The truth is I don't know anyone else I can ask."

Darlene belched with no trace of embarrassment. "I can already tell you a little about that asshole Fancy. He's done a lot of delightful things in his time, but nobody has ever been able to make anything stick. He was born and raised in London. He's smart as a whip, genius-level IQ, and by the time he came to the States he was already rich."

"He dresses like it."

"Fancy runs a pretty serious operation out of Pomona, reaching as far east as San Bernardino. The street says he sells low-level dope like grass and Vicodin, but his main thing is pornography."

"From there?" I asked. "Jesus, it's not as if that business is underground anymore. Why bother?"

"That's a good question," Darlene said. "Some people figure it's because the kind of porn he's making is too nasty even for the Italians who run the San Fernando Valley. Others say it's just because he started to give them a run for their money, so they drove him out of the area. I'm inclined to believe the latter, but who knows?"

I finished the food and wondered if my hands would ever feel clean again. "You seem pretty on top of Fancy. Why is that?"

"Memos circulate. Everybody knows he's raking in the cash hand over fist, but no one can figure out exactly how and from what end of the business."

"Or why he's out in Pomona, if he's so successful?"

She nodded. "Or why he's out in Pomona."

I signaled for the check. Darlene allowed me to pay it. She stood up. "Ready?"

We began to walk back towards the Hollywood station. "What about the kiddy porn thing?" I asked. "Do you know anything about that?"

"Besides that it's despicable?"

"That may be too mild a word."

"Jesus, Callahan, even cons hate pedophiles."

"Has anything come across your desk lately that I should know about? About kiddy porn, I mean?"

She considered. "Not much, actually. There is a Father Fortunato that's been getting a lot of attention lately. Have you heard of him?"

"Yeah. He's the guy who is concentrating on the Internet side of things. Fields mentioned him, and someone else named Rinaldi."

"Everybody knows there has been a fucking explosion in child pornography because of the Net. They busted some rabbi in England a couple of years ago. He was actually wholesaling the stuff. Maybe this Rinaldi is involved with some of the people who are fighting back."

"I guess so. What do you hear about who is behind it, supplying the real money and the muscle?"

We stopped at the crosswalk. An Oriental woman, wearing a yellow slicker and carrying a STOP sign, escorted four more uniformed children through the traffic. Someone honked angrily. The old woman glanced down to make sure the children were not watching and flipped him the finger. Darlene looked at me and laughed.

"Only in L.A." We started walking again. "Look, Mick, I have read that there has been one main group financing and peddling child pornography around the world for several years, now."

"Any names?"

"Nope. They funnel huge sums of money to front groups, even outfits like NAMBLA, and they are wired into high places in several different countries. It is a well-oiled machine of money and influence. It is presumed that the heads of the organization are probably pedophiles themselves."

"Who are notoriously unrepentant."

Darlene snorted. "How unusual for a man, to be always convinced he's in the right."

"Funny, I thought that was women," I muttered. Fortunately for me, she didn't hear.

"These perverts, they actually think that cultural sex hang-ups are the only reason they can't molest all the little children they want."

I caught such a wave of repressed rage, my step faltered momentarily. I looked down at Darlene again, hoping to read her expression, but her face was chiseled in stone.

"Darlene, Fields mentioned that there might be some relatively new group muscling in on their territory, somebody with money of their own, ruthless enough to be giving the big boys headaches. Have you heard anything about that?"

She shrugged. "I think I saw something in some memo. You're thinking it may be Fancy and his boys?"

"Maybe."

"I keep pretty good records, so I'll go back and take another look."

"I'd appreciate that. And I meant what I said about thanking you for covering me that night, even if you did tell Donato."

She deadpanned. "Hell, I had to tell *somebody* that I met Mick Callahan and he asked me to blow him. That was quite an event."

"Actually, I was hoping to have the incident engraved on my tombstone."

Darlene laughed, softened further. We walked in silence for a moment. "One last favor?"

"Jesus, Callahan. Donato warned me about this. And just when I was starting to like you."

I stopped and held her gaze. "My housekeeper's nephew got kidnapped maybe six weeks ago. That's bad enough, but now all this talk about Fancy and child pornography is starting to make me feel sick. I want to satisfy myself that his disappearance has nothing to do with me."

"Aren't we being just a wee bit paranoid?"

"Maybe, Darlene, but Blanca has been with me since my drinking days. She is really torn up about this. I don't want the boy to just fall between the cracks. If I fax you some stuff about that case, would you look into it?"

"What do you expect me to be able to do?"

"Just ask around. Maybe there's some way you can nudge that investigation along, or keep it alive so that it doesn't die under a stack of papers. He's just a nine-year-old kid."

"Do you know how many kids . . . ?"

"Yes. I do. But this one is special to me. His name is Manuel Garcia, and his nickname is Loco."

She sighed. "Oh, hell, I didn't have anything else to do this weekend." She thought for a moment. "So you like Fancy for that kidnap, too?"

"That's a real long shot, but what the hell."

She considered that. "You're right. What the hell."

We arrived at the Hollywood Station. Darlene squinted

up into the sun and then examined my face as if panning for gold. "You look good, a damn sight better than you used to. How long you been sober?"

"A couple of years now. I plan on staying that way."

"Good for you, Mr. Callahan." She shook my hand briskly, quite formally. Then I realized that two patrol officers in a black-and-white were staring at us, ready to tease her mercilessly if they saw one sign of weakness. "You give me a couple of days, and then call me. Okay?"

"Okay, I will, Sergeant. Thanks again."

I watched her hips as she walked up the steps and back into the building.

TEN

"Six hundred thousand dollars is serious money."

"Indeed it is," J.C. Kramer said. He kept smiling, but his face had gone pinched and pink. My deal was going south faster than the NASDAQ in 2001.

"So, of course," Darin Young said unctuously, "I'm sure you realize we would have some serious liability insurance concerns that we would need to address."

I asked, as innocently as possible, "Like what?"

"Oh, come on. Your reputation precedes you, Mr. Callahan. That business in Nevada, for example, was quite messy."

"I thought there was no such thing as 'bad' publicity."

I was in trouble. The thin, well-manicured network VP had already fired me once, for missing an audition, and had only agreed to see me again under pressure from above. Darin was arrogant and narcissistic in the extreme. He was also in his mid-twenties.

Now, this is a combination guaranteed to give me fits.

I looked at my new agent, J.C. "Judd" Kramer. He smiled weakly and tried to intervene.

"Darin, I'm sure you realize that the Nevada papers referred to Mick as a local hero. After all, he broke up a drug ring and solved two murders almost single-handedly."

Darin Young smiled and picked at his teeth. He looked like a well-fed shark. "Mick here also physically assaulted some townspeople and nearly got himself killed in the process. Gentlemen, the truth is that the cost of that pilot episode would actually be chump change. If we go ahead with a syndicated television series, we will be risking millions. We need to know that Mr. Callahan has his instinct for adventure under control."

I reined in my true reaction. "I've been sober for quite a while now, if that's what you're referring to."

Young pursed his lips, looking like nothing so much as an auld English fop. "You would be prepared to guarantee your sobriety in writing?"

Kramer interrupted with a cautionary wave of his hand. "Wait a minute. And just how could he do that?"

"Drug testing, perhaps, on a random basis?"

"Listen, you little . . ."

The snarl escaped before I could contain myself. Kramer kicked me under the coffee table. I nodded, fell silent.

"That temper of yours is also of some concern to us," the executive said. "I don't know that we want to deal with that."

I forced a tight smile. "Just don't piss me off." Then I laughed. Kramer laughed too, but a little too loudly.

Darin Young just chuckled. "I also have it on good authority that the backstage behavior on your former show was less than desirable. In fact, an anonymous executive from that production company suggested that we build in a very severe clause with respect to moral behavior."

"That's enough." Judd Kramer got to his feet. "Come on, Mick. I guess this meeting is over."

I remained seated, took a long, slow breath, and let it out again. *Never let a narcissist put you in an adversarial position. Play on his vanity and his need to feel superior.* "Hold on a moment, Judd." I was opting to play "good cop." "I can understand Mr. Young's posture, here. I was given a wonderful opportunity. I was blessed with decent ratings, and I managed to fail in a quite public way. He wants to know that history will not repeat itself."

Darin Young blinked. "That's exactly right."

"As a matter of fact, I think it takes a great deal of courage to just come right out with matters this delicate, with no beating around the bush. I respect your honesty, Darin."

"Thank you," the executive said. He began to preen, straightened his cuffs and smoothed his already-perfect hair. "I'm glad you understand that my position is difficult."

"Oh, certainly," I said. "Sit down, Judd."

Baffled, Judd Kramer sat. He groped for words and settled for something harmless. "Where were we, then?"

"Mr. Young was voicing his concerns over my reputation. It seems I am known for being hot-tempered, abusing drugs and alcohol, and some other unspecified forms of moral turpitude. I assume he is referring to my former propensity for collecting groupies."

Darin Young bowed forward. "Exactly. More to the point, for pursuing your . . . well, shall we say 'recreation' while on company time?"

"Alcohol removes inhibitions, Mr. Young. That's one of the main reasons people drink it. And that kind of loose behavior tends to go along with alcohol and drug abuse. I don't drink any more."

Darin Young made a steeple with his fingers. *He probably read somewhere that this makes him look wise. Maybe in one of those cheesy books on body language.*

"May I be candid with you, Mr. Callahan?"

"But of course. Let's all be as direct as we can."

Young stood up slowly, making a theatrical production out of gathering his thoughts. He clasped his hands behind his back and slowly paced by the picture window that faced the studio lot below.

"Some of our executives have a legitimate interest in the possibility of bringing you back to television, Mr. Callahan. I, however, have expressed serious reservations from the very beginning. This is because it is a brand new world out there. What worked a few years ago may not work today. You understand what I am driving at?"

You want your fingers in the pie. That's what you're driving at. You're just not sure how to play me.

"Certainly."

"But let me think for a moment here," Young said. He put his fingers to his temples, as if lost in deep contemplation. Judd Kramer was sweating this out, and his panicked look begged me not to laugh.

You little shit. You want to have it both ways. If the show succeeds, it will be because of your involvement, and if it fails, you warned everyone from the beginning that they shouldn't do business with me. This is a classic case of "cover your ass."

Young finally turned to face me. "Gentlemen, let me put it to you this way. Meeting with you today has stopped me at the fifty-yard line, and I am going to reconsider this project."

"Gee, thanks." This time I barely concealed the sarcasm. Judd Kramer was already on his feet, right hand extended.

"Great, Darin. Why don't you just think things over? Take as much time as you need, just get back to us before the end of the month."

The King had spoken, and we were now free to go. I could not bring myself to shake hands, so I waved on the way out the door. "Nice seeing you again."

"Likewise, Mick. Thank you for coming."

The weighted silence lasted past the receptionist with the fake breasts, down the carpeted hallway, through the lobby decorated with movie posters, and into the padded elevator. Just as the doors were closing, I turned to Judd and guffawed.

"That pretentious little shit? No way am I working for him. He's probably not even toilet trained."

Someone behind us snorted. I turned and saw two female office workers at the rear of the elevator, likely leaving for lunch. They both giggled.

"Sorry."

"Don't be," one of the girls replied. She had red hair and wore thick glasses. She clutched a diet book in one hand and a bag of potato chips in the other. Her friend was a slender Asian with a dour face.

We rode in silence to the parking lot. As the girls walked away, the Asian girl turned my way. "Quick question?"

"Huh? What?"

"*Which* pretentious little shit were you referring to?"

Another burst of muffled laughter. Judd, who was driving, beeped his key chain. We found the brand-new silver Lexus. I slid into the plush upholstery of the passenger seat. I was still fuming.

"Take it easy, damn it," Kramer said. "At least wait until we're out of the fucking parking lot before you have a meltdown."

"Did you see that little putz?"

Kramer started the car. Rock and roll music blared. "I saw him. And by the way, I thought you handled that whole thing brilliantly. I was about to stage a walkout."

"It doesn't take a rocket scientist to realize he just wanted us to kiss his ring. Oh man, Judd, I don't know if

I'm ready to start all this crap up again."

Kramer pulled out onto Riverside Drive. A Mercedes nearly clipped his bumper. He honked, and a gray-haired man in Armani shot him the finger. "Not ready for this? Now he tells me. Look, Mick, you told me you wanted to get something rolling, so I got something rolling. Don't flake out on me."

"I know, I know. And I do appreciate your taking me on after all the bad stuff you've heard about me."

Kramer shrugged. "It wasn't all that bad, to tell you the truth. People over at the agency just said you were self-destructive. Like that's some kind of strange news for Hollywood."

"Want to get a coffee?" I felt thirsty and tired. "There's a place over near Lankershim that makes a great ice-blended mocha."

We pulled into the chrome and glass shopping center in the newly-revitalized NoHo Arts district. I jumped out, got in line, and ordered two drinks while Kramer looked for a place to park. As I counted out change on the counter, I glanced up. The kitchen area was rimmed with mirrors. I caught a glimpse of someone watching from the sidewalk. It was a stocky, well-built blond man who wore sunglasses, a black T-shirt, and pale blue jeans. His arms were covered with fading tattoos. My heart kicked and my stomach went cold. I paid for the drinks and walked back outside.

The silver Lexus pulled up. "Hop in," Judd Kramer said. "I can't find a goddamned parking place anywhere. We'll drink them in the car. I should be getting back to the office soon, anyway."

I reached inside and handed Kramer his coffee drink. "You go on ahead, Judd. My car is only a few blocks down the street. I'll walk. Thanks for putting up with me."

"You sure, Mick? It's hot as hell out here."

"I'm sure. I'll call you at the beginning of the week and we'll put our thinking caps on. We need a plan B, just in case Young doesn't come along for the ride."

"Okay, then. Have a good weekend."

"You, too." I slammed the door and waved. Kramer slid out of the lot and into traffic. I sipped the frozen drink, gathering my thoughts. As usual, until I knew exactly what I was dealing with, I didn't want anyone else involved.

I strolled back to the sidewalk, into the shade, and leaned on the window, half-facing into the coffee lounge. I sipped the drink and waited. After a few moments I saw the man again, behind the wheel of the red pickup truck. The same one he had driven the day he tried to follow me home from the gym.

I walked down a side street, moving in the direction of my car, back where I'd first met Kramer. The man tailing me would have no reason to be suspicious.

He wants to get me alone. I began to cast about for a weapon. Expensive homes lined both sides of the street, all with well-manicured lawns and bushes. Towards the end of the block was an alley that ended at the back of Los Lobos, a famous Mexican restaurant. Some of the trash containers were metal.

I made a great show of finishing the drink and searching for an appropriate place to deposit the empty cup, then abruptly jogged towards the alley and angled across a lawn with hissing sprinklers. Behind me, I heard the driver gun the truck engine from reflex. I knew the alley was a dead end, and chances were so did the other guy. I kept my eye on a flight of concrete steps leading up to the back of the restaurant.

I bobbed, danced, and jumped as if pretending to play

basketball and sailed the cup across the alley. It bounced off the rim of a can. I raised both arms as if in frustration and bent to pick it up. The truck eased into the alley behind me, engine purring. I tensed to run up the steps if the vehicle came closer, but the engine shut off and the alley went silent.

When I turned around, the blond man was leaning on the truck, powerful arms folded over his chest. His face was a blank wall, and he still wore the sunglasses. I showed my empty hands.

"I think you've been looking for me. Well, here I am. What's on your mind?"

Watch out! The man shifted his weight slightly and appeared to be reaching behind his back, so I brought the metal trash container up and around and charged. He brought his hands up just in time, blocked the blow with his forearms. The alley echoed with a crunching sound.

I pulled back and struck again. This time the blond man gave ground and backed into the driver's door. The container scraped some red paint from the hood of his truck. The man swore, ducked under the can, and drove me backwards onto the floor of the alley. I kicked up with my knees and tried to roll the man back over his head. The can cut off my leverage. *Think, you stupid bastard,* my stepfather said. *Get up off your ass.*

I slammed the can up into the man's face. His dark glasses flew off and his nose sprayed blood. He already had bruises around his eyes, as though he had recently suffered a beating. I elbowed the trash container away and tried to grab at his hair, but it was too short. I settled for thumbing an eye, then grabbed an ear and twisted.

The man screamed and slammed a fist down. It connected. I shook my head, jaw throbbing, and twisted the ear again. I felt the sensitive flesh begin to tear. The man struck again, but I moved out of the way at the last second. The fist struck asphalt, with the full force of his blow. The man screamed and fell backwards, nursing his fractured knuckles. I got up and looked around. No one was watching. I went down onto one knee. Both of us were panting.

"I want to know why you're following me."

"Jesus, my hand is broken," the man said. "I need a doctor."

"Talk to me, or I'll break something else."

"You fucked up my life," the man said. His breath carried the crisp stench of bourbon. "I just wanted some payback. Jesus this hurts."

"I don't even know you. How did I fuck up your life?"

"You remember Donna Edwards?" the man asked. I pictured a zaftig waitress who picked at her face, wore a lot of makeup, and couldn't seem to stop talking. I didn't answer.

"You saw her for a couple of months," the man reminded me. "You told her I was bad for her."

"Well, I must have had a reason to say that."

"We used to fight all the time. God this hurts! But you told her to get away from me, that I was some kind of batterer, or something. That was bullshit, man. She hit me more often than I hit her."

I sighed. "So you thought you would just follow me around and kick my ass to get even?"

The man started to cry. "I really loved her, man. I miss her. How can I get her back?"

The guy was drunk and in great pain, so I weakened. "I think you need to stop drinking."

"I miss her so much," the man said, ignoring me. He put his face into cupped palms, smeared fresh blood on his cheeks. "You don't know what it's like. You ruined my life."

I got to my feet and examined the torn knees of my jeans, waited for the crying to slow down. "Listen to me. You need to get some help a lot more than you need to kick my ass."

"I tried to stop drinking before," the man said. "It didn't work."

"You have to talk to people for it to work. You can't just sit there."

"I know I have a problem. I know."

"If you want to get her back, that would be the best way."

"If I do, will you tell her for me?" the man asked. He looked like a lovesick teenager.

"The truth is that I haven't seen her for several weeks. I wasn't her regular therapist. So, if you think you can send a message through me, you're wasting your time."

"Shit."

"Listen, man, get your life together."

"Do you think she'll take me back?"

"Beats me, but you'll be better off, I guarantee it."

"What should I do when I get clean again?"

"Then I guess you write her a letter, or something. But sober up or you lose, buddy. Beyond that, I can't help you." I started to walk away, then stopped, turned. "By the way, have you been following me around on and off for a week or so?"

The man nodded. "I'm sorry."

"Forget it." I walked briskly away, feeling guilty and relieved all at the same time. "And hey, you might want to see a doctor about that hand."

ELEVEN

My countdown was on the money. I slipped the final CD out of the player, started up the computer, and rolled the station ID all in one smooth motion. "This is Mick Callahan signing off for the night. We'll be playing smooth jazz from now until dawn, and I will be back with you again tomorrow night at the same time. Until then, sleep tight."

I popped a soft drink and rubbed my eyes. I was in no hurry to drive home. I went through some business correspondence, threw out some solicitations, even read some fan mail. One woman seemed to think I was the Second Coming of Jesus, but another the reincarnation of Adolph Hitler. There was no accounting for taste.

I opened my laptop, booted up, and read the news postings on the Internet service. I checked my e-mail and found one from Hal Solomon.

Young stallion:

First, thank you for once more providing some brief escape from the turgid, trance-inducing rhythms of a wealthy retirement. I have been driving my people almost as crazy as if they still reported directly to me, rather than to that moron to whom I sold my holdings. I think they still love me, or at least they seem to understand my boredom. How many times in a week can one play a mediocre game of golf?

In truth, it is highly stimulating to once again feel a sense of purpose. As we discussed, I have put some of those overpaid former minions to work researching the decadent festival. Video will be streamed to your hard drive upon your request.

Incidentally, I have consulted a local physician to explore the source of my continuous flatulence. The man is a moron.

Take care,
Hal

I did not access the streaming video, since it would take longer to download and play on the smaller machine. I closed the laptop, packed my briefcase, and shut down the studio.

When I stepped outside, the air was heavy with humidity and one solitary jet aircraft winked soundlessly beneath the surface of a pocked, gray moon. I searched the parking lot with my eyes, walked briskly to my car, looked around again, and slipped the key into the trunk. I tossed my things inside and locked it, opened the door, and got in. The car complained and the engine refused to turn over. I tried again, wondering if it had been tampered with.

It started.

I drove out of the parking lot, still checking in every direction but chiding myself for a bad case of nerves. After all, that mysterious feeling of being followed had just been explained. I changed lanes on the freeway, trying to catch someone following, but failed.

When I pulled into my driveway, the side gate was slightly open. The hair on the back of my neck fluttered. Hadn't I closed it before leaving? Perhaps Mary had come outside to water some plants. I slid out of the car and moved quietly through the shadows to the side of the house.

I was suddenly illuminated in a bright pool of light and jumped back a step. The motion detector had kicked the porch light on. I located a metal spike from below the rose bushes and pulled it out.

I eased quietly into the back yard, stopped at each window to check that it had been properly latched. I tried the back door, and it was locked. I walked around to the north side of the house. I could not help tensing up as I approached the corner. I peeked around the edge of the building and then stepped out onto the cement sidewalk, makeshift weapon in hand.

The yard was empty.

Feeling foolish, I reversed my steps to put the metal spike back where it belonged, and then let myself in the front door.

"Mary?"

Not a sound. She's probably just asleep. I closed the door, locked it, and armed the alarm system. I crept down the hallway. The hardwood floors creaked. I gently opened the guest room door and peered in. There was a lump under the covers. I walked closer to listen for the sound of breathing.

Mary whined softly in her sleep and rolled over, her dark hair fanning out across the pillow. Again, she looked fifteen years old. Feeling foolish, I backed out of the room and closed the door. I kicked my boots off and stretched, then dropped into the executive chair.

I booted up the computer, flipped on the large color monitor, and dialed up the files Hal Solomon ordered. They told me Burning Man was an annual experiment in something euphemistically referred to as "temporary community," where the humans involved would *become* the entertainment they wished to see. The latest versions of the festival seemed to revolve around something called a "theme camp," arrived at by consensus among coteries of participants and acted out in costume. Small camp after small camp spiraled out from the center of the makeshift town itself, which was created where the four-story wooden figure of a man, based on those used in ancient pagan rituals, would be raised and eventually burned. I vaguely recalled seeing the figure on fire many years before, when I'd attended.

I squirmed as the video proceeded. I saw several nude people, their bodies painted green, yellow, and purple, dance through the barren Nevada desert. A few wore masks, and for a split second, I cringed because one had been painted black. Meanwhile, people were pitching tents in the middle of nowhere, and time-lapse photography showed a small "city" springing up.

Someone had spray-painted a sign that said: "Welcome to Black Rock." What appeared to be a full bacchanal began and flourished. A number of apparently gay men were dressed as a macabre version of nuns. They had long plastic penises hanging out of their black habits and they hooted as a group of topless women danced by wearing hula skirts. One woman with a stunning figure rolled around naked in blue mud, playing with her nipple rings.

As I watched, a dark part of me remembered how much the old Mick loved this kind of irreverence. As I'd told Hal, I had virtually no memory of having attended the festival, other than the fight that resulted from taking mushrooms while blind drunk. I'd had sex with someone, perhaps the black girl I'd accidentally struck, but everything else was a blur.

A narrator informed me that a hidden camera had been

used to record the footage. Generally the press was no longer allowed at the Burning Man Festival, except as full participants. Some pieces of a production shot before the ban were also attached. I watched them as well.

Burning Man was always held the week prior to and including Labor Day. The event had begun in 1986, when a broken-hearted man named Larry Harvey decided to mark both the solstice and the end of a passionate love affair by burning some stick-figures on Baker Beach in northern California. The action was blatantly illegal, but several onlookers and some of Harvey's friends found it amusing.

So, they did it again the following year. Some observers thought the festival was a reaction to the economic excesses of the Ronald Reagan 1980s; some just considered it a throwback to the solstice celebrations of pagan religions.

By the third year or so, the crowds had grown from dozens to hundreds and finally thousands of people, and the Park Police demanded that the stick-figures not be lit for safety reasons, but the crowd had insisted. The police cracked down and the festival was banned.

The following year found the entire festival transplanted to the emptiness of Nevada. That was where the video had been taken. I slowed the film to enjoy some of the scenery.

The most striking visual was the majestic emptiness of that four-hundred-square-mile alkaline expanse known as Nevada's Black Rock Desert. I had been born and raised in the northeastern part of the state, up in the Dry Wells area, and had not spent a great deal of time exploring directions other than south, towards Elko and eventually Reno, before moving to live in Los Angeles. Only someone born in the desert can fully appreciate both its terrible beauty and stunning emptiness.

At first glance, the footage made me feel homesick: the

magnificence of the yellow-flowered, harsh, turquoise angles of a clump of sage only apparent when seen in full contrast to the nothingness within which it grows.

As the film went on, and the macabre Labor Day festival began, something disturbing happened. It was obvious that the vast majority of the participants were harmlessly acting out their resentments of social norms, customs, and societal prohibitions. This was anarchy, nudity, and drugs, plus Halloween costumes, nothing more. But for me, it was also an unpleasant trip down memory lane.

What had been somewhat fun years ago now seemed sad and even destructive. I only saw that humans had invaded a barren, gorgeous wasteland with their beer cans and fires and guns and cars and airplanes and somehow scarred it, polluted it with their obsessions, desperate death anxiety, and egoistic need to rebel. I saw myself in those humans, and it did not leave me comfortable.

I could see some logic to the so-called performance art involved and even find myself able to identify with the often expressed, and somewhat valid, concerns about the potential geopolitical economic impact of free trade and corporate monopolies on developing nations. But the positive intent was too often marred by the presence of drugs and mindless sex. That took the edge off the sentiments. Bettering the world by tearing it down was an old idea, and it had never worked.

The Black Rock Arts Festival, as the Burning Man is also known, prided itself on keeping a neat and environmentally friendly camp. Portable toilets abounded, as did collection areas for plastic and tin. Many of the participants went to great lengths to clean up afterwards. Yet for me there was something dualistic here. On one level it was harmless fun, adolescent rebellion. On another, it seemed obnoxious and self-centered.

On the video, several people began shooting automatic weapons at paper targets while being pelted with water balloons. A voice indicated that firearms had since been banned from the festival. I turned the video off and sat back in my chair. After a few moments of contemplation, I checked the time and called Hal Solomon.

"Somebody is toying with me."

Hal's silver hair rippled on the monitor. He tilted his head. "What makes you say that?"

"Because these days the whole event takes place in a place called Black Rock City." I explained the night Peanut had called Larry Donato. "That burned area in my back yard had a small black rock in it."

"I see."

"That was a personal message of some kind, Hal. Something the cops weren't supposed to understand." I rubbed my temples. "But from whom? And was it intended for me, or for Mary?"

"Didn't you tell me that the man who attacked you after work wore a spray-painted Halloween mask to hide his features?"

"Yes, he did."

"Well, do you think that was just a coincidence, or could it also have something to do with this eccentric festival?"

"It seems connected, and I am starting to have a very bad feeling about all of this."

"That strikes me as a sensible response," Hal said from the monitor. "Of course, there is one other possibility." His face dissolved into multicolored pixels and then reassembled.

"What is that?"

"You have irritated a lot of people over the years. Perhaps someone from your drugging or drinking days, or even from that long-ago night you went to the Burning Man Festival, is newly out of prison and hot on your trail."

"Maybe," I said. "I keep dreaming about this black girl . . ."

"My word." For a brief moment Hal was in perfect focus and his lips were in synch. He leaned to one side and clutched his abdomen. His face was as closed as his fists.

"Hal?"

A moment passed. Hal grunted and shook himself. "I suppose it is time to come clean."

"About what?"

"My drinking career has caught up with me. It seems I have substantial scarring around the bile duct, causing lingering digestive problems and pain. In short, I have been diagnosed with chronic pancreatitis."

"Damn. Hal, that's very serious."

"Indeed it is. It appears my poor, exhausted little internal organ does not produce enough digestive enzymes. The self-created obstruction must be removed surgically."

I touched the screen with my fingers. "I'm so sorry. When are you scheduled?"

"Soon. We are working on it, stallion. We are working on it."

"Will you keep me in the loop?"

"Most certainly, and do be sure to tell your clients that however fun the party may be, the bill always comes due at some point."

"Believe me, I do."

"Let us now return to whoever may be after you. Could it perhaps be a former drug dealer you owed money to? It would be relatively easy for someone to find you and follow you home from the station to establish where you live. Do you still have the gun?"

"Yes. It's in the closet."

The synch slipped again. Hal shook his head, a bit sadly. "Perhaps you should keep it handy?"

"Hal, Jerry still lives up north, right there in Nevada. He has been looking for Mary for months, but she won't give me permission to tell him she's here. I think she's protecting him in some way."

"And she knows more than she's letting on?"

"I *know* she does, and I'm going to try to pin her down about that tomorrow. Listen, about Jerry?"

"Yes?"

"I wonder what he knows about this festival. Can you send the footage on to him? Just ask him to take a look and tell you what he thinks."

"Yes again. Shall we also ask him to call you?"

"Not yet, I don't want to have to lie to him again. Please just add a note that I said I'll get in touch later today or tomorrow. I think it's time I had a real heart-to-heart with Mary, and not just about Jerry. I think she's used up her grace period."

"Get some sleep." Hal massaged his belly.

"I will. And you take care of your poor, abused stomach."

"Pancreas."

"I stand corrected."

"Good night."

I switched off and sat back. It was nearly one-thirty in the morning. I stretched and went into the bathroom, brushed my teeth, went to the bedroom, and turned out all of the lights except the one nearest the bed. I flipped on the bedside clock radio, put the volume down to a low level, and then found some Merle Haggard playing on KZLA.

"Where you been all this time, my darlin' . . . ?"

What would the world be like without Hal in it? That was not something I wished to contemplate. I had just stripped off my shirt and started to remove my jeans when something rustled in the bushes outside the bedroom window. I froze.

Seconds later, the sound came again.

I stretched flat in the darkness and turned out the light, waited a few moments, then slipped out onto the floor. I crept over to the closet, slid the wooden door open as quietly as possible, and took down the gun case. I opened the zipper and removed the .357 from the nylon case. I slipped in a speed loader with hollow points, put the case back up on the closet shelf.

I gently clicked the cylinder shut and edged down the wall into the hallway, both hands on the gun, barrel pointed down towards the floor. The boards creaked. The radio station switched to an old record by Emmylou Harris, *"You've got it coming to you honey . . ."* I stepped over the floor heater-grill and into the kitchen.

I could see the entire yard. Someone had set off the motion detector, and the porch light glared out into the bushes. I let my eyes roam over the shadows, probing for any unusual shapes.

After a time, I dropped into a low crouch and moved briskly across the kitchen floor.

I went to bent knees by the silverware cabinets and took a deep breath. I reached for the handle to the back door and then stopped, thinking it would be better to wait for the lights to go out again. *How long were they set for? Was it two minutes, or five?*

I could just call the police, but if Fancy and his posse were outside, there would not be time enough for help to arrive. I also debated waking Mary, but didn't know what I was up against. Why terrify her if I could handle this alone?

The noise came again, and, after a few seconds, another time. It sounded like footsteps in that patch of ivy that grew up and over the side fence.

I started to open the back door and then stopped. The burglar alarm system was on. If I opened the door, it would raise holy hell, Mary would be awake, and the neighbors alerted.

I turned the porch light off, so it wouldn't respond to movement, and slipped back out into the living room. I punched in the five-digit code and disarmed the alarm system, then slipped out the front door and down to the side gate.

I stood quietly for a long moment with eyes closed, then opened them. The moonlight was sufficient. I walked carefully down the sidewalk with the gun pointed up towards the sky this time, peered around the corner, and pulled back. Nothing happened, so I stepped out into the back yard.

The sound.

I dropped into a crouch and thumbed the hammer back just as a small ball of fur jumped high in the ivy and landed again.

"Murphy? Goddamn it, where have you been?"

The old gray cat had been trying to catch something in the ivy, perhaps a lizard. He saw me, cried out in hunger, and ran over to thread himself between my legs. I eased the hammer down, shook with relief and unused adrenaline. I grabbed the cat, fed him well, and finally went to bed.

. . . His eyes were covered and his hands were tied behind his back. The vehicle was moving. Loco felt the metal vibrating

159

under his flesh. He forced himself into a sitting position. The drugs seemed to be wearing off; perhaps his captors were being lazy and didn't want to bother to stop to inject him again.

He decided he must be in some kind of van. It hit a bump and he almost lost his balance. His splayed fingers grabbed the metal floor for purchase, and he felt something. His heart kicked as it rolled away from his right hand, then back again. He grabbed the splintered wooden handle. He groped it like a blind person.

It was an old screwdriver.

The boy carefully adjusted his fingers and tried to wedge the screwdriver into the tape that bound his wrists. He sawed back and forth, back and forth, his heart feeling hope for the very first time. After a few moments his hand began to cramp. He paused, as another thought occurred to him. His fingers explored the metal panels behind and below him, and eventually found the heads of screws. He used his fingernail to be sure, and found that the heads of the screws were normal, not indented in an X pattern. He wriggled his fingers.

The van hit another bump, and he almost lost the screwdriver, but this time he held on. It took several tries to wedge it into the head of a screw and begin to turn. Confused, he at first turned clockwise but then remembered what to do. He cautiously backed against the wall, found the screw beneath his bottom, inserted the screwdriver, and moved his hands.

The screw began to turn.

TWELVE

. . . I was hiding in the barn, studying a pair of notched, worn hooves. One huge brown leg moved up, shook some flies away, and then came down again. The exhausted old plow horse broke wind. A man appeared in the doorway, a tall, lanky farmer in a battered tan cowboy hat and torn blue overalls. His wide shoulders were peeling from sunburn, thick knuckles stained with dark green grease. The knees of his jeans were swirled with the dried blood and white feathers of recently slaughtered chickens. Daddy Danny Bell! Then it was not my stepfather any longer, it was Donny Boy from Dry Wells, and he was whispering, "Oh boy oh boy oh boy" over and over . . . "Trouble's coming, Mick." . . . Wait, that was not Donny Boy, that was my stepfather . . . I'm dreaming. I have to wake up now.

"Jesus!"

When I finally came to my senses, I was tangled in the sweat-soaked sheets and one foot was hooked under the bedside table. The morning was humid and fierce, as only the San Fernando Valley can be in mid-August. I grabbed a plastic bottle of tepid drinking water from the table and downed half of it.

My bad dreams usually involve alcohol in some way, but are also often prompted by memories of my stepfather. I stayed flat on my back for a few moments, willing away a

161

terrible sense of futility the dream had engendered. What had my unconscious been trying to communicate? *Trouble is right behind you, Mick,* Danny Bell said.

I knew another therapist would call it mildly delusional. I recognized the superstition and wishful thinking. And yet in some way this was real. Daddy Danny was trying to warn me about something.

I slid out of bed and onto the floor, stretched myself, and did crunches until my stomach muscles felt like a rack of hot coal. I drank the rest of the bottled water and went into the bathroom to shower. When I looked at myself in the mirror, I tapped my broken nose and winked.

"You look like shit."

I turned on the radio and got into the shower, covered myself with soap, sang along with Allison Krauss in squeaky falsetto. I probably sounded like Minnie Mouse straining for an orgasm.

The shower helped. I shaved quickly. I would normally have done that the night before, but I'd been too tired. I went back into the bedroom, towel around my waist, and got back into the same pair of jeans and boots. I pulled on a fresh black shirt and went into the hallway.

"Blanca?"

She had yet to arrive. I peeked into the guest bedroom. The bed was neatly made, the white curtains were drawn, and the bedside clock radio was playing. Mary must have gotten up early again, probably to go for a run. I went to the kitchen to make coffee.

Murphy chirped a greeting from his post on the worn couch and came to be fed. I scratched his ears. "You about scared the hell out of me last night, feline." I poured some overpriced dry food that claims to help aging male urinary tracts.

The coffee smelled wonderful. Several birds were arguing on the back fence. I amused myself by watching Murphy watch them. The old tom's hunting instincts were aroused; his tail twitched nervously as he cackled with excitement. And then I suddenly felt uneasy again. The dream redux: *Trouble is right behind you, Mick. Wake up!*

The telephone rang. I grabbed it immediately.

"I assume this isn't too early, since you don't party anymore."

"No, it's not too early."

"Good," Darlene Hernandez said. "You remember that enormous, unwarranted favor you asked me for?"

"Sure do."

"Well I did it. And Mick, you owe me big time."

"Another cheeseburger?"

"Chiliburger, and that's for starters. First, you were right. Your Agent Fields does check out as legitimate. He got his B.S. from some tiny college in upstate New York, J.D. in Law from Penn State. He's single, seems square as a postage stamp."

"He's a little old to be single. Never married?"

"He dates occasionally, but he's never been married. He does live pretty large, got a nice house and a fancy car."

"I noticed an expensive watch, too."

"Yeah, but I poked around, and it turns out he inherited some family money from a rich grandmother. Like I said, he seems legit. He goes to church on Easter, doesn't even smoke."

"Just a guy who's obsessed with his job."

"So it would seem. Fields has been with the FBI for more than twenty years. He started out as a liaison with the ATF on some gun trafficking case or another, and worked on organized crime for over ten years."

I leaned over the sink. "Ten years? Isn't that a long time?"

"Not necessarily, but it can be pretty draining. He must be one tough cookie. He personally cracked himself a narcotics ring or two. After that, Fields requested a transfer to his present position, and that was a little more than four years ago." She stopped, as if reading from her notes. "He is now a liaison with the U.S. Department of Justice, Criminal Division, with respect to Child Exploitation and Obscenity."

I paced the kitchen. A sparrow landed on the windowsill and pecked mindlessly. "Anything more personal on him?"

"Some stuff, not much. What's bugging you?"

"Actually, I can't explain why, but he really bothers me. He dresses like a movie star, for one thing."

"Like I said, he inherited around two million, or at least so they say."

"But keeps on working?"

"He reads pretty driven, Mick, and let's just say that his departmental rep is pretty consistent with the attitude problem you described."

"He's kind of a hard ass?"

"And that's probably because he's no spring chicken. The FBI has a lot of new meat moving up in the ranks. He needs to make something happen, or his career will stall for good. Anyway, the word is that he's gotten totally preoccupied with tracking this new, unknown gang that's started moving kiddy porn from somewhere out here on the left coast. I mean, like he's *way* pissed off."

"He's pissed, all right. I got that loud and clear. Okay. Thank you, Darlene; now, what about the other gentleman?"

"Fancy's real name is probably Fredrick Newton Wainwright."

"Good lord."

"I shit you not," Darlene said. "Fredrick Newton Wainwright. He was born in Jamaica, but raised by his prostitute mother in some of the funkiest areas of England."

"Is he here legally?"

"Seems that way," she said. "His mother married an older American when he was about fourteen and brought him over. They lived in Denver, then San Francisco, and finally Los Angeles."

"The nickname?"

"Apparently got it here, I suppose because of the English accent and the way he dresses and talks. This guy is scary, okay? He may be physically small, but he's got a well-hung rap sheet."

"What kinds of charges?"

"Assault and battery, pandering, armed robbery. There's a lot more in the file, but nothing they could make stick. He has some kind of deal with the Crips, but nobody knows exactly what. Maybe he pays them for protection. We know he is deep into the porn business, too, production and distribution. This dude is *way* wrong."

"Fields said he ticked off the mob at one point."

"They drove him out of L.A. after a brief, bloody war. Both sides lost a few soldiers. Different detectives at different times have been on his ass for everything from robbery and assault to murder one. You'd best be careful."

"I didn't plan on inviting him over any time soon, but thanks for your concern."

"And last but not least . . ." She rustled some papers. "The stagnant investigation into the disappearance of one Manuel Garcia, a/k/a Loco, age nine, has just resumed. I

165

happen to know the D2 who originally caught the case, so I asked him to move it back to the top of his slush pile. Like I said, you owe me."

"Big time. And what about the chances the missing kid has anything to do with Fancy?"

"All I can see is we certainly can't rule it out." She chuckled. "And on a personal note, thank you for getting my Italian cousin out of the topless bars. He's completely smitten with your friend Suzanne."

"Peanut."

"Larry just won't shut up about her. Now, Donato has been a dog for years, so it's fun watching him get some of his own. She won't hurt the poor child, will she?"

"Not a chance. She's the best."

"That's cool. And how's our newly sober girl doing?"

I sat down at the kitchen table, sipped some coffee. "Mary? She got up before me. I think she went out for a morning run."

"Sounds like you've been a pretty positive influence."

"She had a pretty positive influence on *my* life. She allowed me to continue breathing."

"You're a decent guy, Callahan. I didn't grow up around decent guys. It's kind of a nice surprise to meet one."

"It sounds like there is a story there."

"Maybe I'll tell it to you sometime."

"Okay, I'd like that."

After a beat, Darlene said: "I never asked you. Is she attractive?"

I blinked and then smiled. *I'll be damned, she likes me.* "Not really, and she's like a client, Darlene. I wouldn't notice, anyway."

She laughed. "Bullshit, counselor. You might not do anything about it, but you'd still notice."

"Point taken. Darlene?"

A little hitch in her voice? "Yes?"

"I think what I owe you is dinner or something."

"You don't owe me anything," she said briskly.

Oops, that sounded terrible. "What I meant to say is that I would like to take you out to dinner. Or lunch. Or something."

"'Or something' sounds nice," she said. "I have some vacation time coming."

I was stunned. "So, let's do it. Where were you thinking of going?"

Darlene Hernandez laughed. "Don't sound so enthusiastic, Callahan. I was just kidding. Dinner would be fine."

"Oh."

"For a therapist, you sure don't know much about women, do you?"

"No, I suppose I don't, not outside of therapy rooms."

"Maybe you should try practicing what you preach."

"Let's not get carried away."

She chuckled. "This may surprise you, but we occasionally have discovered an alcoholic or two in the police department."

"You don't say?"

"Once they sober up, they seem to all be clueless about dating and sex," she said teasingly. "Why do you suppose that is?"

"Somehow, I have lost control of this conversation. I think I had best hang up, now."

"Why, Mick Callahan, you're a total coward!"

"I resemble that remark. Thanks a bunch."

" 'Bye."

I put the phone down gently, smiling to myself. I whistled as I washed the coffee cup and fished the car keys from the pocket of my jeans. The telephone rang again.

"Total coward speaking."

"Mick, they're going to kill me."

My mind went into high gear, gathering bits of information. *I think I hear a freeway. She is on a cell phone, keeps cutting in and out.*

"Black," she said.

"What?"

"Tent" came through the static, and then what sounded like the word "city." The reception was terrible. Mary was somewhere else, not nearby. She was frightened and in pain. It sounded like she was trying to whisper, moan, and sob all at the same time. "Please come get me," Mary said. *"Please."*

And then the phone went dead.

THIRTEEN

"Why didn't you call me before?" Jerry stood in the living room, twisting a dark Yankee baseball cap in his small, sunburned hands. The ugly, triangular burn scar that covered the side of his face was pulsing, dark with angry blood. He paced in concentric circles, and the wooden floor squeaked in syncopated rhythm. "You knew I'd been looking for her for months, man. You *knew* that."

"Mary asked me not to call you. She said she wanted to have it together before she saw you again. She was protecting you. I'm sorry."

"Maybe she doesn't care about seeing me again," Jerry said.

"I doubt that."

"Look, we have to find her, Mick." His voice broke.

"I know."

Jerry looked away. He went into the den. "I love your little house, but why do you still have such a piece-of-shit computer setup?" He ran his experienced hands over the entire system, his thick black eyebrows twitching wildly. He wore dirty blue jeans and a red cowboy shirt. He adjusted the baseball cap and turned it backwards. I could see his obsessive mind working. He was happy to see me, but still angry and upset.

"Jerry, listen . . . I'm really sorry."

Jerry ignored me. "You need to pop for a better system, dude."

"Money can be a finite thing, Jerry. Those of us who come by it honestly tend to run out now and then."

He shook his head and grinned. "Then you need to find another way to make it, man. Anyhow, I have elected to take pity upon your sorry ass. I come bearing gifts."

"Say what?"

"Like I said, we have to find her. I assume we'll be working with old Hal again? We will have to video-conference with him from time to time?"

"I suppose, but I already have a . . ."

"Good," Jerry said, blithely interrupting. "That's why I asked you what you had humming around in here before I drove on down. I just happen to have a few cool upgrades out in the bed of my truck."

"Jerry . . ."

"I brought a few items, things that got lost on their way to the warehouse, if you know what I mean."

"But . . ."

"No buts about it," Jerry said. He rubbed his scar absently. "This shit is way cool. It will synch the picture up to the sound almost perfectly, and it can store what he sends us without jamming up your files. All I gotta do is stick a satellite receiver on the roof and run a few cables, and then outboard a piece or three and we're in business."

"Jerry, we won't even be staying here, except for tonight. I figured to take off first thing in the morning."

"So? Won't take me but a couple of hours, good buddy," Jerry said. He was already opening his toolbox. "You'll be in business for real. We'll just take my bad-ass laptop with us for everything else."

"Can I get a word in, here?"

Jerry didn't look up. "Sure."

"Don't you want to know what's going on?"

"Oh, you're finally ready to tell me?"

"Touché. Now, sit."

Jerry folded up the toolbox, sat on the small sofa beneath the window. He peered out into the smoggy red sunset and closed the drapes, slid the toolbox under the computer desk, and spread his hands. His thick eyebrows twitched like caterpillars. "So, fill me in."

"What did I tell you so far?" I sat down. "I don't remember."

"You said Mary called and you took her in," Jerry said. "You gave me some line of shit that she didn't want you to tell me she was here."

"She didn't want me to call you, Jerry. You think I'd make that up?"

Jerry shrugged casually, but his lips were thin. "Mary's a pretty girl, man. You never know."

"That's bullshit."

A long silence followed. My face reddened. I turned away to gather myself. *You are lower than whale shit, Callahan . . .*

Jerry said: "Then after a couple of weeks she went missing on you, like all of a sudden. You told me to get my sorry ass down here, and that maybe there's this pimp involved, and some missing kid named Loco."

"My housekeeper's nephew."

"Right. And then you said I should get my hands on a top-notch digital camera and a pro sound boom."

"You did that? Good."

"I had the store call Hal Solomon and he covered it." Jerry seemed to pull himself back together. "That camera set him back nearly five large, man. It's one hell of a piece of gear. I haven't even had time to screw around with it yet. Mick?"

"Yeah?"

"It is awful good to see you."

I shook his hand. "It's good to see you too, Jerry. I screwed up, and now I'm damned sorry. I should have just called right away and told you Mary was here."

"She really asked you not to?"

"Yes."

"I guess it don't matter now," Jerry said. "Because here we are. What do you need me to do?"

I eyed Jerry carefully. "We went through a lot the last time we were together. We almost got ourselves killed. This one could end up even worse. Are you sure you're up for it?"

"I'm up for anything, Mick," Jerry said. "I want to find Mary. You know that I had a thing for that girl, even before she saved our butts. And I owe you something, too."

"You don't owe me." A sense of déjà vu followed; memory reminded me that Darlene had used the same phrase. "But I do think we both owe Mary a great deal."

"I heard that. What do you need me to do?"

I booted up my computer. "I want you to take a look at this footage of the Burning Man Festival. You've heard of it, right?"

"Sure. Hal e-mailed me some shit and I answered him. I don't think I copied you on that."

"Well?"

"Well, the thing of it is that I didn't know anything, except that it happens every year. No offense, Mick, but what the hell?"

"Bear with me, Jerry. Take a look at this video then, and we'll talk. Look, I was at this thing once, years ago, in a drugged stupor. That may or may not have something to do with what happened to Mary. What I know so far is that this festival, or someone who is planning on being there, has something to do with why she vanished."

"So it really matters that I see it. Okay."

"Jerry, get on it. We don't have much time."

Jerry looked puzzled. "And the camera . . . ?"

I stood, hooked my thumbs in the belt of my black jeans, and leaned against the wall. "I'm taking some vacation time. The station will play reruns. You and I are going to pretend to make a documentary about that festival. That way if anybody recognizes me, it will make sense why we're there."

"Okay."

"You're now a camera operator."

"Cool."

"It will also give us some cover with the local law, or even a badass FBI agent, if we happen to run into him. Don't ask, I'll explain later. But what we're really going to try to do is find out what the hell happened to Mary."

"Dumb question?"

"Shoot."

"I assume you already called the cops?"

"Of course I did, both officially and unofficially."

"And?"

"Officially, they told me that people go missing every day. That Mary may not have even given me her real name. That there wasn't anything they could do, especially since I didn't even have a photograph to give them. They said both she and the little boy were probably gone for good."

"And *un*officially?"

Someone knocked on the front door. Jerry jumped, startled. He wriggled his thick eyebrows. "Who's that?"

"'Unofficially' just got here."

Larry Donato stood under the porch light, wearing my old L.A. Rams jersey. "You look great in that," I said with a straight face. "Do you plan on returning it anytime soon?"

Donato grinned. "I'll wash it first." With feigned innocence, "You do know my lovely cousin, don't you?"

"Hello, Darlene."

Darlene Hernandez seemed to be wearing larger earrings and a bit more makeup. She wore a neat beige pants suit and flat shoes. For my part, I was glad to see her, even under these circumstances. I saw her dark eyes widen slightly at the burn scar on Jerry's face, and admired her for how well she concealed the reaction.

For his part, Jerry didn't much care for cops. He forced a feeble smile, introduced himself, and then headed straight for his truck to collect my new gear. He never looked Larry Donato in the eye, which was probably a good thing.

"Damn," Donato said quietly, once Jerry was gone, "what the hell happened to that kid's face?"

"He was in a foster home when he was a boy. A psychotic woman burned him with an iron."

"Christ."

"Anyway, come in."

"Mick, how the hell are you?" Donato asked. "Peanut said you sounded like you were in a world of hurt. It took me fifteen minutes to talk her into staying behind at my place. What's up?"

"What's up is that I'm going to get Mary back, but in order to do that, I'm going to have to track down and talk to Fredrick Newton Wainwright."

"Oh, shit," Darlene said.

"Fred is actually a pimp and porn maker known as Fancy."

Donato sagged. "*Fancy?* You've got to be out of your fucking mind."

Darlene began pacing the room, hands behind her back. "You're not telling us this, you realize that."

"Of course not, I would never tell two sworn officers of the law that I was about to embark on a dangerous and probably highly illegal rescue mission and spill a drop of blood or two. I would never say that, if that's what you mean."

"Good," Darlene said, "because we would be in all kinds of trouble if you told us something like that and we failed to report it."

I went to the icebox for sodas, called back over my shoulder: "All I am telling you is that I am taking some vacation time to shoot two privately-funded documentaries with the help of my old friend Jerry."

"Documentaries?" Donato was baffled.

"Yes. That's the kind of work I used to do, back when I did television instead of radio."

"Two documentaries," Darlene said. She was already with me. You had to love this woman.

I brought two colas and popped the cans. Darlene accepted one.

"Two documentaries. One about prostitution, actually a certain group of streetwalkers out in Pomona, to be exact."

"The other?"

"The other will be on the next Burning Man Festival out there in the flats of Nevada."

"Okay," Donato said. He took a drink. "I think I get you now. What does the Burning Man have to do with any of this?"

I sprawled on the couch, boots up on the coffee table. "I'll be damned if I know, but somebody keeps sending me

175

messages that point that way. First, someone called my
show and brought it up. Mary said something about
burning and a tent city when she called."

Donato nodded. "And then there was that burned spot
on the ground, with the black rock in the middle."

"Same as that guy's tattoo."

Darlene sat next to me. I told her more about the night I
first met Larry, and about the assailant and his tattoo. She
put her drink down on the table and hunched forward.
"Mick, in all seriousness, why the hell are you telling us all
this?"

"Because I want you to help me, because I need to find
Mary, and to see if any of this leads to the missing boy."

"You know we can't do that," she said.

"No?"

"Not on the books."

I smiled. "You told me you had to do some undercover
stuff as a hooker once, right?"

Darlene shrugged. "So?"

"So take your vacation time. Hal will pay you to come
along with me, under the guise of helping me to shoot these
documentaries."

"How much?" Darlene asked, a bit mischievously.

"Oh, come on," Donato said.

"No, really. How much?"

"Five grand a week."

"Five grand?"

"You will be an official advisor to the two productions,
and also provide security. Two thousand five hundred per
project. We will keep it all aboveboard, do a letter agreement for your records, and pay IRS on your behalf, the
whole deal."

Darlene wavered. "That's a nice-sounding number, and

I would like to help you find the girl, but—"

Donato interrupted her. "It isn't worth throwing away your career. Come on, Darlene, think for a minute. What's going to fall on your head if this all blows up in a big way, if there's some shooting involved?"

Darlene nodded. "He's right, Mick. No can do."

Jerry came back with some cardboard boxes. He was pale, except for the rippled scar. He looked straight ahead as he passed Donato and Darlene on his way to the office. I waited, but neither cop spoke again.

After a few moments, I sighed. "No way, huh?"

"No way, Mick."

"I understand, but what *can* you do to help me out, then? Anything?"

"I'm screwed either way," Larry Donato said. "If I help you, I could get nailed; and if I don't, Peanut won't ever speak to me again."

"Or sleep with you, anyway," Darlene said.

Larry stuck out his tongue. "Okay, I can feed you information, off the record. I can call in a couple of favors on the sly, maybe run some license numbers, petty shit like that, but don't put me in any worse position than that."

"Fair enough, and I want you to know I really appreciate everything you've done since my date and I got jumped that night."

"Just who was this date, by the way?" Darlene purred.

"Right now, Larry," I said, acting as if I hadn't heard her, "the best thing you can do for us is just nose around about Fancy's porn business. I know where he keeps some of his girls, but that's about it."

"Will do."

I turned to Darlene. "You really think it would get you in trouble, if you moonlighted as an advisor on a legitimate documentary?"

Darlene eyed me. "How legitimate are we talking?"

"Darlene," Donato protested. "Come on!"

I smiled. "I'm not bullshitting you. My sponsor Hal is a pretty wealthy man. He has made millions with a media company, and still advises its board. That's who is putting up the money for us to do this. Everything will be on the books, just like I said. You'll be covered in the contracts and with the IRS."

"I'm with you now," Darlene replied. "And if anything were to happen to go wrong with a legitimate news project . . ."

"We would certainly have the right to defend ourselves," I said, finishing her thought.

"And that weird kid?"

"Jerry? He's an electronic genius and a world-class computer hack. I know how his mind works. He'll be Stanley Kubrick with that camera in less than an hour."

Donato stood up. "Darlene, you can't be serious. You could lose your badge for getting involved in something like this."

She batted her eyelashes. "Why Larry, a girl has a right to moonlight a little after hours and on vacation, doesn't she?"

Donato shook his head. "Don't do this."

Darlene chuckled, sighed, and shook her head. "He's right, Mick. Actually, I can't. No hard feelings?"

"No hard feelings." I took her hand and squeezed. "I had to ask, though. You can understand that, can't you?"

"I wish I could help out," she said. "But like I said, Larry is right. This is my career we're talking about. My pension."

"Say no more. I get it."

We heard sounds coming from the other room: Raucous cheering and then the loud blaring of rock music. Jerry had finished tinkering with his computer and started playing back the streamed video of the Burning Man Festival.

"Jerry, you want to turn that down some?"

The music got louder. I laughed. "Let's go out on the lawn, it's probably cooler anyway."

I got up, opened the front door, and stood to one side so that Darlene and Donato could leave first. Night had fallen, but the porch lamp was off. I flipped the switch and the front yard turned into an odd blend of light and shadow.

Donato stepped out onto the porch and stretched his tall frame. Suddenly he stiffened and twitched. A millisecond later a POP came from somewhere far away. I felt my stomach flip over. Donato grunted, as though he'd heard something funny, fell against the porch post, and then rolled out onto the cool evening grass. Dark blood flowed out from the side of his head and ran down onto my L.A. Rams jersey.

I grabbed at the back of Darlene's blouse, but she was already moving, flinging her open purse away, going down the lawn with a 9mm in her hand, screaming at the top of her lungs.

"You motherfucker!"

Another shot blew a bathroom window out and showered us with fragments of broken glass. Tires squealed. Darlene quickly assessed the situation and saw that she could not safely discharge her weapon. She swore under her breath and lowered the gun. She turned and ran back.

I was already crouched down beside Larry Donato. Darlene knelt on the opposite side and chanted under her breath: "Face is red, raise the head; face is pale, raise the tail." She checked Larry's color in the dim light. He was

179

flushed. We propped his head up slightly to keep him from choking on his own blood.

"Easy, Larry," Darlene whispered. "Hang on."

Jerry appeared in the doorway, eyes wide with fear. I yelled at him. "Move! Call an ambulance!"

FOURTEEN

"Can I get some more coffee?"

"In a minute," the detective said. He was a balding, bony man wearing a cheap brown suit that shined at the elbows. His fingers were yellow from tobacco use, and his hands trembled with fatigue, or maybe a Jones for booze. He finished writing and closed his spiral notebook. "Now, when I go outside again and talk to your friend, he's going to tell me the same story you just did, right?"

"He's going to tell you he was inside my house. He came out when he heard the shot and found the three of us down on the lawn. That's all he knows."

"What the hell happened to his face?"

"Tough childhood."

"Okay, you have my card?" The detective seemed bored, yet tense. I decided he was probably desperate for a smoke.

I nodded and tapped my shirt pocket. I had already forgotten his name. "I've got it right here, and if I think of anything else, I'll call you."

"Right." He got to his feet, hands searching his pockets for a mangled pack of cigarettes. He called to his partner: "Jack, you about done down there?"

The one called Jack looked Hispanic. He was solid, intense, and had a neatly-trimmed moustache flecked with gray. He was still at the end of the long, white hall, seated backwards in a metal folding chair, listening intently to

181

Darlene's version of events. Darlene had stopped crying and seemed furious again.

"Jack?"

Jack waved a hand, as if annoyed. "Yeah, Gardner."

"I'll be right outside," Gardner said. That was his name, Dave Gardner. He stuck out his hand and I shook it. "Take it easy, Mr. Callahan. Sorry about your friend."

"Thanks."

"He's a cop, right? You know what that means?"

"It means you're going to move heaven and earth to figure out who capped him."

"You got that right," Gardner said. "And we'll make the bastard pay for what he did, before we bring him in, too."

"Good."

Gardner glanced at Darlene. "She holding up okay? Sure is a beautiful girl, especially for being on the job."

"Gardner, do me a favor. Tell Jerry to just hang around here when you're done talking to him, okay?"

"Sure thing," Gardner said. He walked away to smoke.

Valley Presbyterian was the closest top-notch hospital with a decent trauma center. The paramedics had arrived within minutes, and, with the neighbors watching, they gently patched Larry Donato, slipped an IV in, shifted him onto a gurney, and rolled away, siren screaming.

The police had placed yellow tape up and down my yard and taken over the premises. We watched numbly as they searched the street for any spent shell casings. They found nothing. One of the neighbors vaguely remembered seeing some kind of a large van or small motor home, painted a dark color, but that was about it.

We spent the evening in the hospital, grabbing catnaps and answering the same questions over and over again. I'd worried about getting every little detail right, until I remembered that the cops always expect small discrepancies. I said nothing of his conversation about finding Mary or confronting Fancy, only that I'd been discussing hiring both Donato and Darlene to work on documentaries. I relied on a quick exchange of words that had taken place before the paramedics arrived, and believed that Darlene would take the approach we'd agreed upon, but not knowing for certain made me anxious.

I rubbed my tired eyes and broke a five at the coin dispenser, went to the automated coffee machine, and made two more cups of espresso with sugar. I kept one eye on Darlene as she dully answered the other cop's lengthy questions.

I sipped one of the watery coffees and waited. A handsome young doctor with wavy brown hair walked briskly through the swinging doors. He stopped to strip off a pale green gown splattered with droplets of blood. He knelt by Darlene and spoke to her softly, patted her arm, and strode away.

Finally the cop called Jack got to his feet, handed Darlene Hernandez his card, and left the building to look for his partner. Darlene leaned forward on the plastic chair, let her arms and head fall forward into a slow stretch. I walked over and sat down.

"Any news?"

She looked up. Her eyes were puffy. "He's still in a coma, nothing has changed."

"I'm so sorry." My voice broke. "He was wearing my shirt, and I can't help thinking . . ."

"Don't say it. Let's just not say it, okay?"

I looked at her and then looked away, offered the second espresso, and she gulped it down gratefully. "I can go and see him if I want. They moved him to ICU on the third floor."

"Do you want me to come with you?"

"Yes," she said. "Please."

We walked silently to the elevator. As the doors closed, the Muzak began to play an insipid version of an old Beatles classic. I felt for her hand and squeezed it. After a long moment, Darlene squeezed back. The elevator stopped on the second floor. The doors slid open and an old woman got on, closely followed by two adults who looked stricken. Suddenly, all three began to weep inconsolably. They meant to descend to the ground floor to go home and had gotten on the wrong car. Time seemed to slow to a crawl, and the elevator felt claustrophobically small.

At the third floor we had to squeeze by the grieving family. I pulled Darlene by the hand and led her into Intensive Care. The scrubbed floor tiles and bare walls were all shockingly white, and most of the beds were discreetly screened off by curtains. Some of the exposed patients were shriveled and so stuck full of needles it was difficult to look at them.

A tall African-American woman in white stood behind the counter. She had narrowed eyes and held her clipboard like a weapon.

"Larry Donato?"

"You on the list?" The nurse eyed us like a customs agent looking for dope.

Before I could say anything confrontational, Darlene showed her badge. "He's my cousin."

The woman nodded. "Fifth bed down on the right, honey."

Darlene marched on ahead, heels clicking on the tiles, but when she arrived at his bedside and heard a machine wheezing in spurts, she hesitated. She looked back at me with an expression that was both childlike and sorrowful. I stepped in closer, took a breath, and gently moved the curtain out of the way.

Larry Donato had a tracheotomy tube sticking out of his neck, and the area around the incision had turned a reddish shade of brown. A plastic mouthpiece had been jammed between his teeth, perhaps to assist in the event of a seizure, and his lips were pulled back in what appeared to be a permanent grimace of pain. The bullet hole had been bandaged. His handsome features were badly distorted by the damage caused on impact. The machine was helping him breathe.

Darlene whimpered and bit her hand. I held her upright. She reached out and touched one exposed arm, ran her fingers lightly over the IV needle and the surgical tape holding it in place. One tear fell on the metal gate that surrounded the bed. She needed time, so I waited. Darlene breathed deeply, stepped back, and regained her composure.

"Let's walk," she said.

The nurse barely glanced up as we went by, except to say: "Go get some sleep, honey. Someone will call you when there's news."

The elevator opened. Peanut stepped out. She was wearing red sweats and tennis shoes with no socks. She was red-eyed and trembling. When she saw us, she sobbed and hugged me.

"God, Mick, what happened? Who would want to shoot poor Larry? Was he on duty?"

"No," Darlene answered. "We were just leaving Mick's when it happened. I'm Darlene; we spoke on the phone."

"Hi Darlene," Suzanne Walton said. "Thank you for thinking to call me."

Darlene's eyes filled. "He's crazy about you."

The women held hands. Peanut cleared her throat. "Can I see him?"

"He's down the row," I said softly. "I'll come with you."

"Mick, I want you to come outside with me." Darlene hugged Peanut. "Take some time alone with him, honey. We'll be back in a few minutes."

We rode down to the lobby level in a different kind of silence. Darlene looked around, saw a security guard, and snapped: "Wait here."

My body felt stiff, so I ran in place for a moment and did some pushups on the pale blue wallpaper. Darlene returned with three cigarettes and a book of paper matches. She walked past me, without saying anything, through the large glass doors and out into the nearly empty parking lot. She fired up a smoke and paced, her arms tightly crossed over her chest.

"I didn't know you smoked."

"I quit. Did you know that I never intended to be a cop?"

"No."

The patio area had been decorated in a vaguely Oriental fashion. I found a concrete bench near a planter and sat down. Bugs were dancing under a nearby faux lantern, and we watched them for a moment. I knew she was not finished. Darlene took another long pull on the cigarette.

"My father was a cop," she said. "So was his brother. Larry's father met Larry's mom when she was on the job in Chicago. It's a real family tradition for some reason. Cool, huh?"

I saw no need to answer.

"It changed my dad, almost destroyed him, but I was certain nothing like that would happen to me. I just figured this would be a way to make some decent money while I decided what I really wanted to do. And I was naive enough that it sounded like fun."

"Chasing the bad guys?"

She grimaced. "Exactly, but the first day on the firing range, when I was holding that big piece of impersonal metal in my hand and trying to blow a hole in a target shaped like a human being, it started to sink in. Do you know weapons?"

I shrugged. "I have a .357 I keep around."

"You ever take it out?"

I dodged the question. "Naturally, I grew up around a lot of guns in Nevada, and some of our neighbors were bow hunters."

"And in the service?"

"They damn near make you worship weapons in the Seals, so I have a healthy respect for what they can do, but the truth is I am pretty ambivalent about guns. They take away a lot of options in a fight."

She wrinkled her brow, finished the first smoke, and lit the second off the orange butt. "I do not understand that concept."

"I had a stepfather who used to beat the hell out of me and made me fight other kids for money."

"You told me all that the night I busted you."

"Oh. Anyway, I learned an awful lot about fighting and how to drop into a neutral state of mind when using force. I learned how to be impersonal about it during matches, and to think clearly. Danny also taught me that most of the time the idea was to stop the fight by winning, not to kill, but that guns push it over the line. When a gun gets pulled, somebody usually dies."

"He was right," she said.

I caught something in her tone. "Go on. Tell me what you were about to tell me before I interrupted you."

"I was maybe nine or ten weeks out of the Academy," Darlene said. She sat down next to me on the bench. She stared straight ahead, out into the darkness. "I had a partner, a lazy old fart named Jenkins. We were getting some coffee at a little stand, kind of like the one you and I ate at last week, but this one is way down in the 'hood. Radio goes 'two-two-seven, two-two-seven, four-one-one' and the address. It's a home invasion thing. It's like two minutes away.

"Jenkins was a bad cop, the kind that will sit on his butt and let someone else get there first. Me, I was new and thought I had something to prove. So when he didn't move fast enough, I slapped the coffee out of his hand. That pissed him off. We got in the car. I drove, and left rubber for half a city block trying to ride to the fucking rescue."

Darlene paused. She smoked in silence for a moment. "I don't talk about this all that much," she said cautiously. I waited, allowing the tension to build, eyes locked on hers.

"Jenkins took his fucking sweet time getting out of the car. I guess I should have expected that. Big bag of shit comes stomping out onto the porch, carrying a pillowcase full of stuff. People inside the house start screaming how he took everything they own and we have to do something and we have to stop him.

"The guy takes off like a track star, bag swinging at his side. Got his knees pumping halfway to his chest and I take out after him, screaming he should stop because I'm the police.

"I'm strong, but I'm not fast. He's going down the back yards and the alleys, and he's got things he has to jump over, see, trash containers and old bicycles and tires and shit. I can bob and weave through them a little easier. Somewhere along the way, the porch lights start going on and the whole damned neighborhood starts getting into this.

"He's hauling it over fences, dragging that sack behind him, and I'm huffing and puffing but staying pretty close behind. Naturally I turn a corner and look over my shoulder for my back-up, and there's nobody in blue watching my sorry ass. No sign of Jenkins."

Darlene paused. She eyed the third cigarette, thought the better of it, and tossed it away un-smoked. "We're kind of going around in circles, actually, although I didn't know that at the time. The local news was on it live. Fuck, it felt like the whole damned town was watching. A helicopter pops up overhead, shining that spotlight down and it's just like the movies. Except I have a stitch in my side that's white-hot and I'm ready to puke and scared half out of my mind."

"I don't blame you," I said quietly. "What were you carrying back then?"

"I didn't like the 9mm at the time, so I had a Smith & Wesson Model 66, .357 Magnum, brushed stainless finish with night sights and Pachmeyer combat grips."

"Serious weaponry."

"Anyway, I wind down and I'm about ready to give it up. I say fuck it and turn back towards the squad car. I'm moving down the sidewalk, and I'm starting to let up, you know?

"And there he was, like magic. He just appeared, all of a sudden. I saw his gun. I don't know how it happened exactly, but I pulled my 66. I had it up, hit my stance, and fired two rounds into his chest before I had even made the decision. He fell back a step, kind of leaned against a fence,

189

and looked down at the mess that had been his chest like he was amazed. And then he dropped like a bag of sand."

I reached out, touched her hand with the tips of my fingers. She started to cry, but was determined to finish. "Up close, I could see he was maybe seventeen years old. Oh, he had a gun. He was going to kill me. It was a righteous shoot. But just like that, I had ended a life."

"It feels unresolved," I said. It wasn't a question, just a fact.

"Sure. But not because of what I felt, because of what I *didn't* feel. I kept waiting for a wave of guilt, or shame, or rage, or something like that, to come over me. I just sat there and looked at the body.

"The spotlight found us, and so did the neighbors, and then eventually my so-called partner. I just waited, shaking from adrenaline but not even crying, just trying to sense something that wasn't even there. And do you know what I was really feeling, looking down at that poor kid?"

"No," I said, although I *did* know.

"I was glad it wasn't me."

I rubbed my knuckles. "Makes perfect sense. That's what I've heard from everyone I've ever talked to who's lived through something like that."

"Clients?"

"A couple of Vietnam vets I worked with, and one guy who had to kill the kid that ripped off his liquor store."

"Wow."

"Anyway, my stepfather, when he wasn't pounding on me, used to tell me things about Vietnam. He said that when it comes down to it, nothing matters but survival. Forget the movies and the stories you've heard. Push comes to shove, you will kill, and that's the end of it. Your friend dies; you leave him there and keep going. You just want to live through it, and come out okay, that's all. You just want to be able to go home. The feelings, they come later."

"That's the truth. Mick?"

"Yeah."

"He was pretty bad, huh?"

"Daddy Danny? He was pretty bad, but I think he meant well. In his own twisted way, he was convinced he was doing me a favor by toughening me up. I can see my inner turmoil in the way I dream. Sometimes he's a monster chasing me, and sometimes he sits around giving me advice, sometimes both at once. It's strange."

"Unresolved?"

I laughed. "That's right. It's unresolved."

Darlene stood up and began to pace. I just waited her out again and tried not to stare at her body. *Can't you show a little class?*

Finally, Darlene said, "Is your offer still good?"

For a moment, I was confused. "Oh! Of course it is, and Hal is good for the money. The checks will clear."

"I don't care about the money, but it has to look legitimate."

"It will. Why did you change your mind?"

"I think we need to find out if Fancy is keeping your housekeeper's nephew and a bunch of other kids as sex slaves. That, and because I think he ordered the shooting."

"Darlene, look . . ."

"I'm not done yet. And also because until I got to know you better, Larry Donato was the only decent man I had ever met."

I couldn't think of anything to say to that.

"And I need your word on something." Darlene walked in close and looked up.

My heart fluttered. "Okay."

"I'm going to help you find Mary, Callahan. I'm going to help you find that kid, too, if he's with Fancy. But I need to know you will stick to the cover story, no matter what."

"No matter what."

"Hal's company hired me to moonlight on my vacation time, because we're friends. I will be advising you on a couple of documentary projects and providing security. That's it, right?"

"That's it."

"If we get in any trouble with that bastard Fancy, if it comes out that he ordered the hit on you, I am going to swear on a stack of Bibles that I didn't know there was a connection."

I stood up and stretched. "We shall take our secret to the grave, Deep Throat. I have to ask you something, okay? Do you blame me for what happened to Larry? I'd understand if you did."

Darlene crossed her arms over her chest and paced in a small circle. She kept her eyes on the cement. "I did for a while, not now. Are you blaming yourself?"

I hesitated. "Yes, in a way."

"Well don't. Mick, one last time I want your word you'll perjure yourself, whatever, to back me up all the way. I really don't want to lose my career."

"Then maybe you shouldn't do this. It's a big risk."

Darlene stopped pacing and looked up. Her eyes were puffy, but dry. "Now I want to, because I'm calm."

"I don't understand."

"I'm Latino," Darlene said. "And revenge is a dish that tastes better when it's served cold."

I gave her a hug. She remained stiff at first, but eventually relaxed.

"Do we have a deal?"

"We do. And remind me not to piss you off, okay?"

. . . *The boy was hungry.*

Loco smelled hot soup. He opened his eyes and realized they had decided to feed him again. The food came intermittently, at odd times of the day or night, which only added to his confusion.

Anxiety flooded through him, and he felt in the back of his pants. They had not discovered the screwdriver. It was still there.

Loco sighed with relief. He looked around. He was still in the van, but now only his legs were bound. He realized he'd been lucky. If he'd tried to cut the bindings on his wrist, they might have noticed. He turned and looked down. The three screws controlling the bottom of one metal panel were still loose. He grinned and turned back around.

The tray sat on the metal floor. It held one large piece of bread, some broth in a plastic bowl, and a glass of apple juice. He ate and drank rapidly, his eyes darting about, chewing like a small animal stealing food from a trap.

Someone will come for me, he told himself. Someone will come.

Meanwhile, he knew that time was running out. He knew that the evil ones had decided to kill him. They no longer even tried to hide their faces. The one who brought him food now had a strange way of looking through instead of at him, as if he were already dead.

FIFTEEN

"Excuse me, miss?"

"Buzz off," the girl said. She was a pallid, pimpled white teenager wearing heavy jewelry, torn cut-off jeans, and an egregiously padded bra. She spat on the ground, turned on her slightly wobbly high heels, and strode away. I motioned for Jerry to stop filming.

"Somehow I think you need to come up with a warmer, more effective approach," Jerry deadpanned.

"Well, we'd best do it soon."

Jerry's baseball cap was now on sideways, for no apparent reason. His eyebrows danced. He shifted the camera to his right and rubbed his lower back. "This goddamned thing is getting heavy."

I caught a slight slur on the word "is," and it troubled me. Had he been drinking again?

The Pomona Valley night was sultry, perfumed by trapped smog, the street air thick with the pheromones of unrequited addiction and sexual desire. Flashy, indolent crack dealers were doing a brisk business in the alleys, and skinny addicts prowled the burgeoning shadows with flickering, orange pipes.

Hour after hour, dozens of cars, all sizes and models, rounded the corner one after another. A driver or passenger would buy drugs, or arrange for a sexual favor, and the vehicle would slowly drive off again.

A bleached blonde in white shorts stepped out of a doorway and stood watching. She wore a plain, white blouse, which seemed odd, and something about her struck me as familiar. Jerry was also staring, briefly puzzled, but the girl did not react to us or wave. After a few moments, she went back inside the building.

"I thought I knew her for a second."

"Probably from one of your many late-night binges. Heads up."

A buxom black girl in red hotpants and a white halter came waltzing around the corner, swinging some ample hips. A middle-aged, balding man in a battered black Ford was following, chattering like a wind-up set of teeth. They were negotiating.

"Aw, don't be that way," the man whimpered. He had the sad, wrinkled face of a bulldog. "I'm all worn out and I need me some sugar. That's all I got, I swear. *Shit!*"

He saw me holding the microphone like a low-rent "60 Minutes" guy, saw the camera in Jerry's hands, backed up with a squeal of brakes, and sped away. The girl swore and stomped the sidewalk. She shot Jerry a withering glare.

"Excuse me, ma'am," I said pleasantly. "Can I talk to you for a minute?"

"The fuck you doing down here, you lily-white, ugly-assed, broken-nosed, muscled-up, giant, honky mother-fucker?"

I laughed and applauded. "Hot damn, that was a string of invective. Girl, you're a poet. What's your name?"

She arched a brow, somewhat mollified, and sized me up. "Dolly," she said, strutting towards me. Even the words felt well-lubricated. "They call me Dolly."

"Dolly, look here, I'll pay for your time."

"That's entrapment, officer," she sneered.

195

"I'm not a cop, I'm a television guy. And I will pay."

She eyed me with suspicion. "Like how much? My time is expensive, you know. I ain't no common street ho'."

"Any fool could see that," I said unctuously.

"Goddamn right."

"Would twenty dollars be sufficient?"

"Twenty dollars don't even buy your ass the right to order me a tropical drink, boy. Damn, you a cheap bastard."

I pretended to consider my options and then enunciated carefully. "I'm on a limited expense account, Dolly. How about fifty bucks?"

She sidled over, ran her practiced hands up my pants leg, and purred. "Just what did you have in mind, honey?"

Jerry was caught off-balance. All elbows and eyebrows, he stepped sideways to try for a better angle and banged the camera into a metal telephone pole.

The girl jumped, scowled, and turned her back on him. She leaned close, tickled my bare arm, and whispered, "This geek got to be there to watch, Daddy?"

"Sure does," I chirped, feeling totally ridiculous.

"That camera thing got to be on, then?"

"Well, you see, it's like this. We're making a documentary," I said, and moved her educated fingers away from the crotch of my jeans. "But don't worry about a thing. We'll go back and cover your face up later on, before it's done."

"Make it look all blurry and shit?"

"Absolutely. All blurry and shit."

She held out her hand. I paid her, and the money immediately vanished into her ample bra. "Okay, handsome." She ran a finger over my broken nose. I tried not to think of where that finger had been. "What you want to know, then?"

I waved Jerry closer. "Just talk to me, tell me about how

you came to be a working girl, things like that."

"Shit, honey. Why you wanna know?"

"It's my job, nothing personal."

"Oh, 'cause me, I get these Captain 'Save-a-Ho' types all the time, want me to talk about my childhood right while I suck they dick and shit. Oops. Can I say 'dick'?"

"We'll bleep it," I said.

"Sure?"

"Absolutely. *Bleep*. Just like that."

"That's cool. Funny thing is, everybody always want to know why you a ho'. It not all complicated, you know? It's the damn money, honey!"

"I see. Nobody forced you?"

"You mean like my Uncle Ray or somethin' like that?"

"Exactly."

She dug into her purse for a tissue and blew her nose. I read her at once. She was covering up. "Am I making you uncomfortable?"

She shook her head. "You think talking about that slime-ball, lame-dick, pencil-necked, circus-geek, cheesy mother-fucker of a stepdaddy make me uncomfortable? Oh, *hell* no. Whatever make you think that?"

"Okay. Just checking."

"Let's just say this. Mommy, she had her some bad taste in men."

This was not a wise time or place to do therapy. I shifted gears. "Do you work for yourself, or do you have a pimp?"

"White boy," she said, "only a fool be out here alone without no man looking after her. I ain't no fool."

"I can see that. Does he treat you okay? The man you work for?"

"He okay," she said. She was already shutting down. I was losing her.

Before I could say anything else, Jerry piped up from behind the camera. "Can you talk a little more about the other
thing, like going down on the guy while he asks you questions?"

"Jerry, shut up."

"Okay."

I took one last shot. "What's his name? Your pimp. The
man looking out for you."

Her eyes narrowed with suspicion. "Why you want to
know?"

"No reason, I was just asking. A first name is fine."

"You ask questions like that 'round here, you could end
up dead," she said. "You want to be dead?"

"No, ma'am."

"Good thinking. We done now?"

"Well . . ."

"*Kaching!*" she said. It sounded like a sneeze. She smiled
broadly and closed her purse again.

"I beg your pardon?"

"I done rung up the sale, and you ain't got no change
coming, neither." She turned on her heel and walked away.
As she reached the corner, she looked back over her
shoulder and winked at Jerry. "Boy, you get some money
together, you come and see me. I don't mind scars at all."
And then she was gone.

"Smooth as ice cream," Jerry said. "What a team. I think
we really had her going there."

I sighed. "Do me a favor, and keep your metaphorical
erection zippered next time."

"It wasn't metaphorical at all, a second ago."

"That's more information than I needed, Jerry."

"Mick," Jerry said. "Check it out."

The girl was a knockout. She wore a long blonde wig,

big sunglasses despite the darkness, a tight red blouse, and some sprayed-on jeans with sparklers glued on the thighs. She walked in spiked heels that made her hips sway dangerously and cast long shadows along the sidewalk. The girl was chewing gum and swinging a large, pink purse with an autographed photo of a well-known boy band on the side. At first glance, I took her for a teenager with a heroin habit, out to make a buck.

"Jesus," Jerry said. He whistled.

"Shut up and use the camera." I glanced over at the alley across from the Carlton Arms and saw a man standing there in the darkness. He stepped forward. Average height, muscular arms, dark-skinned. I didn't recognize him. We continued to pace the sidewalk as if shooting film.

"Damn it, this is business," I barked. Jerry jumped. "Keep your mind on your work."

Jerry caught on to the charade. "Yes, sir. Sorry."

The new girl appeared to see us for the first time. She stopped and looked me over. She turned her head and stared at Jerry and his camera. Finally she walked by without stopping.

"Excuse me."

The girl ignored me. Under her breath she said: "Pretty wimpy, Mick. Be a little more forceful."

"Miss," I said again. No response. "Hey, over here, bitch."

Darlene whispered again. "That's better." Louder, she said, "What's your fucking problem, buddy?"

Jerry nearly dropped the camera in surprise. I'd recognized her from the outset, but just barely. I spoke with teeth clenched. "Not bad, babe. All those years walking the streets paid off."

"Screw you, Callahan," she muttered. And then louder:

"What do you want? I'm busy, here."

"I can see that. Can I ask you a few questions?"

"About what?"

I caught movement from the corner of my eye. There were two men standing in the alley, now. One was carrying a baseball bat. A tingle jogged rapidly up my spine.

"We're shooting some footage for a documentary, lady. We will take your face and any objectionable words out of it later, but we would like to talk to you about your work."

"My work," she said, projecting her voice for effect. "I'm an actress."

"I see. What kind of acting do you do?"

Darlene blew a gum bubble. It popped. "First I act like you turn me on," she said. "Then I act like I give a shit about who you are and what you have to say. Then I act like I came. Oh, and I'm expensive."

A long, dark red Lincoln Town Car slid around the corner, four plump tires sizzling on the hot pavement. A distinguished businessman with perfectly coifed hair sat behind the wheel. He wore an open-necked silk shirt and was smoking a thick cigar. Jerry saw him, lowered the camera, and slipped it behind his back. He needn't have bothered. The man only had eyes for Darlene. She smiled. "Check this out."

"Baby?"

Darlene walked over, swinging her hips. "Good evening, sugar. Are you looking for a good time?"

"Absolutely," the man said. He blew two smoke rings, stuck out his tongue, and licked the air. "How much for a blow job?"

For a long moment I half-expected Darlene to whip out a pair of handcuffs and arrest the guy out of habit, but she stayed in character. "I was just telling this red-necked country boy over here that I don't come cheap, baby."

The man stared at me. "Like I said, how much?"

Darlene held up three fingers. "Three hundred."

The man roared with laughter. "You've got to be fucking kidding me, a three-yard piece of ass in a neighborhood like this? This isn't Vegas, girl."

"Take it or leave it," Darlene said.

"Hey." I walked over and tapped Darlene on the shoulder. "I'll take it."

The driver blinked. "You're not serious."

"Serious as a heart attack," I said, loudly enough to be heard by the men in the alley. "And it's three hundred just to have a conversation."

The driver blew another three smoke rings, deliberately aimed at me this time. He gunned his engine. "Fuck the both of you, then."

I reached in through the window and used two fingers to flick the tip off the long cigar. Hot sparks fell down onto the driver's silk pants and those expensive leather seats. He took his foot off the brake and the car jerked forward. Swearing feverishly, he tried to pick up the hot coals. That meant taking his hands off the steering wheel. The Lincoln rolled up onto the curb, and the left rear door scraped itself raw on a metal post. The driver shrieked and jerked the wheel too far right, so the vehicle dropped back down into the street with a crunch that bent the left front fender.

"Prick!"

Red faced, the driver sped away, still slapping at the seat between his legs. Darlene's mouth was twitching when I risked a sidelong glance.

There were now three young men standing in the alley, just watching.

Darlene held out her hand. I peeled off three hundred dollars in twenties from a substantial roll and she tucked them between her breasts. Under her breath, she said: "You're not getting this back, you know."

I ignored her. "Jerry?"

Jerry brought the camera up, adjusted the lens a bit. A red light winked on near the monitor, and he nodded. "Rolling."

"How did you get into this line of work?" I asked.

"I do what I want to do," Darlene answered.

"Do you have anybody who represents you? Some of the girls say it's too dangerous to work the street without a pimp."

Darlene snorted derisively. "I don't need no fucking man taking my money. I can take care of myself."

"Have you worked this area long?" The men in the alley were conferring among themselves. I tried to pay attention to Darlene as she answered the questions, but I was taking measure of the situation and barely aware of her voice. I only caught a part of her response. My gut tightened and several moments passed.

". . . so, I thought I would come down here for a while and check it out," she said. "This is my first night."

"What is your name?"

"Rose," Darlene said. She blew another bubble.

The charade had gone on long enough. I nodded. "Well, Rose, good luck to you."

"Thanks sweetie," she said. She walked away. The men in the alley continued to watch. It was impossible to act as if they weren't there. Jerry raised his eyebrows, asking if we were done with the game. I wasn't sure. I watched Darlene walk back up the block. She neared a smaller alley on the other side of the avenue. I glanced back at the three men, who were following her with their eyes. They were still there.

I looked back up the street. Darlene was gone.

I took off running, tracing her steps, arms pumping. When I got to the smaller alley I turned cautiously. The alley was well lit; a porch lamp from a nearby bar spread a wide, yellowing pool of light and shadow. Darlene was on her knees in a pile of flattened garbage. A tall, skinny Caucasian male with carrot red hair held a long, straight razor to her throat. He was whispering in her ear. I edged closer, mouth dry, pulse racing. *Well, he's Fancy's boy and he's definitely white, so that's one, anyway.*

"Come on somebody else's turf with a big mouth, bitch, and you don't live very long."

"Easy," Darlene said, breathing rapidly. "Let's talk about this for a minute."

The man looked up. His face was pitted with acne scars and he had the yellowing teeth of a heroin addict. He spotted me and growled low, like a junkyard dog. "Back off."

Darlene moved the second his attention wavered. She slipped her open palms between his forearm and her chest, gripped, and pulled. As the man fell forward, slightly off-balance, she simultaneously rose slightly and squatted, lifting him with her strong legs. She turned her shoulder and rolled him over her and down onto the pavement with an audible thump. Somehow she ended up with the razor, too. Darlene eyed it with distaste and threw it in the garbage.

The man was up in a flash. He tried to get by me to escape. I tripped him, grabbed his shirt, and slammed him into the brick wall. Then I did it a second time, just for scaring the crap out of me.

"What's his name?"

"Huh?"

I slammed him again, and this time I thought I heard a rib pop. The thin man cried out. "Who sent you?"

"Let go, dude."

I grabbed one of the man's hands and bent the little finger back. He squealed like a pig, bared those bad teeth.

"Okay, you're gonna know soon enough anyway. The top dude around here is a black guy, name of Fancy."

"Fancy sent you?"

"No. His people, though."

"What did his people tell you to do?"

"They said nobody wasn't in his stable should be working these streets. I was supposed to scare her off, man. Okay, maybe cut her a little, but not kill her or anything."

"That's it?"

"That's it."

I let go. His legs gave out and he fell forward, striking his chin on the pavement. He whimpered, checked his mouth for blood, and then sat up on his knees.

"You tell Fancy something for me, okay?"

"Yeah, yeah."

I grabbed his hair and pulled. The man looked up. His lip was bleeding and his rheumy eyes went wide. "You tell him what used to be his isn't his anymore," I whispered.

"Shit, man. Are you fucking crazy?"

"You tell him we don't answer to him, or to anybody else. There's a new game in town. Any part of that you don't understand?"

"No."

I let him go. The man ran to the end of the alley. He turned back, shook his head in amazement, and then disappeared into the night.

"Well," I said happily, "that ought to stir things up."

Jerry had taped the whole exchange. He looked at me as he lowered the camera, then let out a long rush of frightened air. He moved his baseball cap around again, pointing backwards, and stroked his scar. "Oh, man. I hate it when you say that."

SIXTEEN

The Carlton Arms Hotel was a funky, claptrap building with nondescript, bland rooms that reeked of alcohol, marijuana, and sex. It had ancient, iron fire escapes gone orange with rust and brick-rimmed windows with splintered frames and broken panes of glass. In any other neighborhood, it would have been condemned, but here it served a purpose.

The bored clerk at the counter was studying the racing form. He didn't look up when we walked in. He held a room key in one hand and an open palm in the other. I gave him cash. Our trio stood frozen for a few moments, repeatedly pushing the elevator button. Jerry was sweating and his eyes were bugged with anxiety.

"Elevator ain't working," the clerk said, still looking down. He turned a page and wrote down some ideas. "Your room is on the second floor."

The stairs creaked like coffin lids. The burgundy carpet in the hallway stank of urine. I memorized the layout and noted the bulbs above all the doors were behind wire mesh to keep someone from breaking or unscrewing them. This hotel had seen its share of violence.

I glanced both ways. I opened the room, went in first, checked the closet and the bath, then motioned to the others. Darlene immediately tore off the wig she had been wearing. She shifted her clothing around, pulled padding out of her bra, and took out a .38 special and two speed loaders. She checked the gun and tucked it into the waistband of her jeans.

"Man, I don't get it," Jerry said. "I hope you know what you're doing, Mick. A guy could get killed this way. Incidentally, what *are* you doing?"

"I'm making him mad."

"Oh, no shit? Well, we'll be lucky if he doesn't firebomb the whole fucking hotel after what you just said."

"Relax, Jerry," Darlene said.

"Oh, sure. Just relax." Jerry looked around the room. Gang graffiti festooned the peeling wallpaper, and the lampshade and curtains were yellowed from smoke. The aging pieces of furniture—a well-worn double bed, end table, and one armchair—were pocked with cigarette burns.

"Another high-class establishment," Jerry said. "I lived better than this in Dry Wells." He sat down on the edge of the bed and bounced. The springs squeaked. "What do we do now?"

I moved the chair over by the window and the fire escape, sat in the chair, leaned back, and closed my eyes. The gallows humor had worn off, and now I just felt sad, bitter, and overtired. "We wait."

"For what?"

"For Fancy to process what he hears and come to a decision. Then he'll make his move."

"And?"

"And then we'll make ours."

"Let me guess," Jerry said. "He kills us, and then we die?"

I shrugged. "Given time, I think he'll be more puzzled than angry."

"You *think?* Oh, great."

"I don't know if he will remember my face from the night I took Mary," I said. "But if he does, that will make him even more curious."

"So he'll want to talk to us instead of just take us out?"

"Exactly."

"Why?" Jerry asked.

"First I took one of his girls for what I told him were personal reasons, and now I show up again a few weeks later, as if I am doing a documentary on hookers."

"Yeah, so?"

"So, then I finally act like the truth is that I actually have a stable of my own girls. One of those three things has to be a lie, right?"

"So my life is riding on his curiosity."

"In a way."

"You're giving him an awful lot of credit, Mick," Darlene said. "Jerry has a valid point. Some of these pimps wouldn't be interested. They would just blow us the fuck away without missing dinner."

"He won't."

Jerry flopped back on the bed and put his hands behind his head. "What makes you so sure?"

"Darlene, you take first watch, okay?"

She glanced at the time. "Four hours?"

"Good enough. Wake me at two and I'll take the second."

Jerry closed his eyes. "Wake me when it's over." He covered his face with a pillow, then threw it across the room. "This thing stinks," he complained. "It smells like blow jobs and cheap perfume."

"So, enjoy."

"Up yours."

Time crawled. I tried to meditate, breathed slowly and

evenly, but did not sleep. I heard Darlene check the locks on the windows and the door. She went into the bathroom and washed her face.

"Mick?"

"What, Jerry?"

"I have to ask you something."

"Shoot."

"Did anything . . . happen between you and Mary when she stayed at your place?"

"No."

"That's not why she didn't want to see me?"

"I told you the truth, Jerry," I said. The lie burned, but came easier the second time. Don't they always? "Nothing happened. I think you're letting your imagination get to you."

"I'm acting bonkers, man. I'm sorry."

"That's okay."

"I don't know what's wrong with me. I'm drinking too much. I don't usually get high all the time. I'm not a . . . you know."

"I know. Forget it."

"Yeah. Okay."

"Get some sleep, Jerry."

A lie of omission or misdirection is a lie just the same, I thought. *Was that love?* A few moments passed. Darlene flushed the toilet. She turned out the lights before leaving the bathroom, returned to sit quietly on the floor with the gun in her lap. I could see her face in the gloom. After a while she closed her eyes, but my instincts told me she was awake.

Eventually, Jerry started snoring. Voices passed in the hallway, two men arguing. I opened one eye. Darlene was already at the door with the gun pointed down at the floor.

The men passed by and she returned to her sitting position. I couldn't rest.

"You okay?"

Darlene nodded. "Fine, go back to sleep."

"Can I ask you a question?"

"What?"

"It's the shrink in me," I said softly. "I just can't help but wonder why you're so down on men."

Darlene leaned closer and patted my hand. "Not very tactfully done, Mr. Therapist. I'm sure you already figured it out."

"I have my suspicions. Your sexuality is intense, but it blows hot and cold. You seem to have what we call an approach-avoidance conflict going on. From the vibe I get, I'd say someone was inappropriate with you when you were little."

She chuckled, bitterly. "If you call molesting a girl who is only eight acting inappropriately, I guess that's true."

"Okay, thanks for telling me."

"What do you care?"

"I just wanted to understand you better."

"Go back to sleep."

Time crawled. Some people entered the room directly above, took a noisy shower together, and had aggressive, loud sex. The springs creaked, the headboard pounded the wall, and a man grunted repeatedly. Finally he groaned and the couple fell silent. Against all odds, I tried to empty my mind.

At two o'clock, Darlene started across the room to wake me. I waved her back and nodded. She made a pillow out of a bath towel and stretched out flat on the floor, the gun at her side.

She closed her eyes. I yawned and closed mine, too.

Scratching sounds startled me. Something like a rat, moving somewhere in the wall? I opened my eyes again. The room was velvet black and the cheap alarm clock was not showing the time, so the power had been cut. I eased forward out of the chair and down onto my knees. The scratching came again.

The window slid open, almost silently.

A figure rolled over the sill and down onto the carpet, slick as a long cobra. I kept my eyes fixed on the window, looking for more shapes, but nothing else moved.

The man began to crawl across the carpet, moving towards Darlene and her weapon. I saw the tip of the long blade of a hunting knife glinting in the moonlight, probably held between clenched jaws. I gauged the distance, jumped out of the darkness and onto his back, rammed a knee down into his spine.

The man arched in pain and tried to roll away. I grabbed for the handle of the knife. I guessed wrong and cut my fingers, grabbed hair and twisted, then tried again. My fist closed over a forearm. I realized I'd surrendered too much leverage and started to change positions.

A flashlight blinded us. "Freeze, motherfucker," Darlene said. "Let go of the knife and put your hands flat on the floor, or I'll blow your brains all over this carpet."

"Don't shoot."

Jerry turned on the lights. "The fuck?"

Another white guy working for Fancy. He was in his early twenties and had long, greasy blond hair. He had dropped the knife. Darlene held the 9mm pressed against his forehead. She reached out and took the hunting knife, then slid it away, under the bed. The mattress squeaked as Jerry moved again.

"The fuck is going on?"

The phone rang, then rang again. I released the man and went back to the chair, closed and locked the window as the phone rang a third time. I used my shirt to stop my two fingers from bleeding, reached over and picked up the telephone. I didn't say anything.

"You're awake, I see. Is my man still alive?"

I cleared my throat. "We haven't killed him yet."

"How courteous of you." A rich voice with a clear English accent. It was Fancy. "I would prefer that you didn't, even though he has proven to be something of a disappointment to me."

"Okay. We won't, then."

"I assume you wish to meet?"

"Yes. Do you know why?"

Fancy laughed. "My dear Mr. Callahan, you must think me an uncultured fool."

"You know me?"

"But of course. Incidentally, I quite enjoyed that special you did on the crystal methamphetamine laboratories in northern Nevada. It was quite informative without being unduly sensational. Top-notch work."

"Thank you," I said, a bit dazed. "Perhaps you'd like me to autograph an eight-by-ten photo?"

"We shall see. Now, do not panic, Mr. Callahan. And please tell your lady friend not to shoot."

Darlene was still pressing the 9mm down into quivering flesh. She raised an eyebrow.

I shrugged. "He said, don't panic and don't shoot."

The door burst open. Darlene tried to bring the gun up. Two large kids, clearly gang-bangers, entered the room. Each had an AK-47. One covered me and one aimed his directly at Darlene's face. Darlene considered and rejected several options, all in a heartbeat. She sighed, lowered the pistol, and sat back against the ripped wallpaper.

"Well," she said to me, sarcastically, "looks like your idea is working out just great so far."

The gang members stepped farther into the room. One moved past the bed, his gun trained on a trembling Jerry, and backed away into a far corner.

Fancy entered the room. His chiseled features seemed darkly amused. He wore a mink coat despite the sweltering heat. Even though I towered over him, he was more impressive in the small, crowded room than he had seemed weeks before. His jewelry glinted. He clicked off his cell phone with his good hand. Feeling foolish, I put the hotel phone back in the cradle.

"You recognized me the first time?" I asked, with a dopey smile on my face. "Man, do I feel dumb."

Fancy smiled and I noticed that one front tooth was made of solid gold. "Of course I did, Mr. Callahan. And it was simply fascinating to watch you in action, I might add. One hears the stories, but . . ."

"Do you know why I came back here tonight?"

Fancy shrugged. "I suspect you'll tell me soon enough." He gestured to his followers. They cocked their weapons and aimed. "Now, at the risk of stating the obvious, please do what I tell you to do or these men will kill you. Is there any part of that instruction you need me to repeat?"

"We got it."

Fancy faced Darlene, then Jerry. "Miss Hernandez? Mr. Jover?"

I blinked. "All our names, too? I'm impressed."

"I get information because I pay well. This way, please." He turned his back, strode out the door, and down the hallway.

I got to my feet. The white kid with the greasy hair gave

me a dirty look and stepped back. I helped Darlene stand. Jerry was pale as he rolled over on the bed and swung his feet down to the floor. I went to the doorway and motioned for him to follow.

When I stepped out into the hall, Fancy was standing several yards away, near what appeared to be a utility door. It had DANGER ELECTRICITY, written in large block letters. I turned around. Jerry came out first, followed by Darlene and then the two gunmen. When I looked back, Fancy had unlocked and opened the door. It led out into a bricked-up fire escape. We followed the small man down the metal frame, our footsteps ringing like wind chimes.

The secret passageway led down into the alley, but Fancy kept walking. The rest of the steps led into an expanded sewer area below the street. Someone had cleaned and painted the walkway. I noticed that drainpipes had been placed below the grates so that the area would be undetectable from above. In fact, the workmanship was impressive. Electric lights made the passageway feel less claustrophobic.

Several yards later, I gauged we had crossed beneath the busy street packed with hookers and johns and gone under what had appeared to be a deserted warehouse. Fancy went up some cement steps. He was whistling to himself. I looked back. The armed guards were trailing us, weapons still at the ready. I followed Fancy up concrete steps.

We entered an immense workspace. Extraordinarily bright lights were flaring in one far corner and professional-grade video equipment was running. Four naked people were having loud and noisy sex before cameras, while a man circled around them with a hand-held unit for close-ups. Jerry stopped in his tracks. He watched until the guard poked him from behind with the barrel of an AK-47.

Fancy was already opening another door. He walked into a plushy furnished business office. Security cameras banked one wall, a huge entertainment system another. The longer walls were covered, from floor to ceiling, with books. I recognized what appeared to be first edition copies of American classics such as Salinger's *Catcher in the Rye* and Hemingway's *For Whom the Bell Tolls*.

"Would you care for a drink, Mr. Callahan? Oh, excuse me. Of course, it is well known that you no longer imbibe. What about your friends?"

"No thanks," Darlene said.

"Well, I could use a beer," Jerry said. "In fact, I could use a few."

Fancy chuckled. He nodded to one of the gang members, who went to an oak bookcase, pulled, and opened a hidden refrigerator. He extracted a German beer and opened it for Jerry, who chugged half in one gulp. Fancy took off his fur coat and dropped it over one end of a plush leather couch. He wore a tight white-knit shirt, made of some expensive fabric. He had the sleeves rolled down, as if to cover his withered left arm.

The small man motioned for his three prisoners to be seated. I sat down directly opposite the desk, in a straight-backed wooden chair. Jerry and Darlene sat on the couch. The gang members kept us covered.

"Well, well." Fancy drummed his good fingers on the desk. "What are we to do with you three?"

"I'm here for Mary." I watched carefully. Either Fancy was a gifted actor, or he really was startled.

"If memory serves me," Fancy said, "you're the one who took her out of my care a few weeks ago."

"She's gone."

"I see." Fancy sat forward and the chair squeaked. "And

so you decided to come here to beard the lion in his den?"

"Something like that. I tried to call, but you weren't listed in the phone book under P."

Fancy frowned. "That kind of cheap shot is beneath you, Mr. Callahan, and may I say that it would not be wise to annoy me any further."

"Okay. I'm listening."

Fancy pursed his lips. "I am no angel. I think I've already made that perfectly clear. I have committed my share of felonious actions. But I have also never made a bird stay with me that wanted to fly away."

"You tried to stop the two of us."

"Not at all!" Fancy laughed. "Or you would be dead. I let her go with you, Mr. Callahan, because I recognized you. Since I knew you no longer did drugs, you were probably telling the truth."

"I was."

"I also knew that you had some money of your own. I thought you had come merely to help the girl."

"I did. So why didn't you let us go without a fight?"

"When you stood up to my boys, and acquitted yourself so very well, I felt vindicated."

"Because?"

"It was obvious that you were capable of protecting her from her enemies. And so you both lived, and you were allowed to drive away."

I was puzzled. "Her enemies, or yours?"

Fancy stroked his chin with his right hand. His left lay on the table as if tortured to death. "As I said before, *her* enemies."

"Who are you talking about?"

"That I do not know, Mr. Callahan," Fancy said. "The girl came to me seeking protection and gainful employment as a prostitute. She claimed she had some people after her. I hear these things all the time."

"And you try to help?"

"I do my best."

"I'll just bet you do," Darlene said. Her voice dripped venom.

Fancy started to address me again, but then broke off to confront her. "Young lady." His cultured voice was heavy with irony. "Please spare me the cynicism. You may choose to believe it or not, but I am merely a good businessman. I protect my girls, and if anyone hurts them I see to it at once. This girl Mary had heard of my reputation. She sought me out; I did not pursue her."

"You exploit women," Darlene said.

Fancy gestured towards the warehouse and the filming going on beyond his office wall. "Those people are actors, albeit bad ones. They have contracts. They receive thousands of dollars a week each, just for performing sexually for the camera. They have pension plans and IRAs and insurance. They come here for one reason and one reason only, because I give them a better deal than my competition."

"The Italians?" Darlene asked.

Fancy did not answer.

"And do you give them better protection, too?" I felt my heart sinking. Mary was not here, and if she wasn't, she was probably dead.

Fancy nodded. "I give far better protection."

I sighed. "And you're telling me that she came to you because she felt she was in danger?"

"Yes."

"Why should I believe you?"

Fancy leaned back and shrugged. "You will have to, be-

cause there is nothing else for it. Can you imagine my reputation if I didn't play fair with my girls?"

"Good heavens, no," Darlene said. "I can't imagine."

"I know who you are and I know where you work, Sergeant Hernandez." Fancy's tone was sharp flint; it threw
sparks. "If you were not a policewoman, you would already
be dead. You will stop insulting me."

One of his lackeys covered her mouth, but not too
harshly. Darlene sighed and nodded that she'd gotten the
message. He released her, so I relaxed.

"Thank you," Fancy said. He turned back to me. "I'm a
rich man, Mr. Callahan, rich, but not particularly greedy. I
believe that keeping the people around me content serves as
something of a life insurance policy. Can you comprehend
that? My competition cannot."

Slowly, I nodded. "Yes. I can imagine that otherwise the
life expectancy in your line of work would be minimal."

"What I may lack in brawn, I more than make up for in
brains."

Here goes nothing. I leaned forward casually and rested
my palms on the desk. I locked eyes with Fancy and smiled.
"What kind of a deal did you cut for those children?"

"What children?"

"You know what I'm talking about."

"No, Mr. Callahan, I do not."

"The kids in the dirty movies."

Fancy glared back with the eyes of a hungry shark. A
long moment passed. "If I snap my fingers, you die."

I nodded. "I realize that."

"You have a big mouth."

"I know that, too. So why haven't you killed me yet?"

"I'll be honest with you. I'm not sure," Fancy said. "Five
seconds ago, you were inches from being buried alive in ce-

ment and dropped in Big Bear Lake."

"You haven't answered my question." The rage oozing from Fancy felt as solid as the furniture. We stared and no one blinked.

"Mick?" Jerry said softly. His voice cracked thin and adolescent from the tension. "Can I just interject something here?"

"No."

Come on, I thought, *why is this taking so long?*

Finally, Fancy looked away. "I do not exploit small children, Mr. Callahan. I suspect you, as a therapist, can intuit why."

Perhaps because you can relate to them so well, I thought. "Maybe I can, but I still need to ask you one last thing, and that's if you have ever heard of a little boy named Manuel Garcia. His nickname is Loco."

"Loco Garcia? No. I have not heard of him."

He is lying about something, but what?

"I do *not* traffic in children."

"Okay."

"This is a spurious rumor spread by my competition."

"Why?"

"It is obviously intended to attract the attention of the FBI, because they want to shut me down, and it would be so delicious to them if the law were to work to their advantage." He stood up suddenly, and his men reacted. Weapons were cocked.

I felt the tension rise again and swallowed. "Easy, gentlemen, we're just having a conversation here."

"Mr. Callahan? May I call you Mick? Let me repeat this one more time. I do not know of your Loco Garcia. I do not exploit children." Fancy leaned forward over the desk, bad arm tight against his chest. His voice grew cold. "And I am not fond of those who do."

"Okay."

"Can you guess what happens to people I am not fond of, Mick?"

"I think so."

"Then kindly do not raise that point again."

I had run out of options. "I believe you." Darlene was still glowering. I felt like crossing my fingers. "I'm sorry if that question gave insult."

Fancy sat down. "If I decide to let you go, what will you do next?"

I told him.

SEVENTEEN

"It is my considered opinion that you have less than twenty-four hours to go," Hal Solomon said. The image on the monitor was so crisp he might as well have been sitting in the hotel room. He pinched the bridge of his nose, adjusted his reading glasses, and patted down his silver hair. Hal seemed weak, exhausted. When he moved in the chair, he grunted with pain.

"Still feeling poorly, Hal?"

"Merely suffering from jet lag, young stallion. I am now in Japan."

He's bullshitting me again. "What in the world for?"

"This poor girl and the child pornography issue truly depressed me. I felt a sad longing to walk the gardens of Kyoto. Such things come over me from time to time. In any event, do you wish to see the rest of the film? As I said, I think you have only one day to go."

"Until what?" Jerry looked confused. He glanced over at Darlene, but she was cleaning her pistol.

"In less than twenty-four hours, the giant Burning Man will be set afire and the festival will end," Hal said.

I sighed. "Mary will probably disappear and, along with her, any chance of finding out whether or not any of this leads to the boy."

"What makes you say all that?" Darlene asked.

"Think about it. Everything keeps pointing that way.

221

Someone has been playing games with me from the start. Burned patches in my yard, strange phone calls, the guy with the tattoo. I'm starting to wonder if Mary showing up was as much a part of the whole picture as her disappearance."

Hal looked quizzical. "What do you mean by that, Mick?"

"She told me she was trouble, more trouble than she thought I could handle."

"So?"

"At the time I was convinced she was talking about bringing Fancy down on my neck. Maybe she was trying to warn me about all the rest of it, but couldn't go through with telling me the truth. She was too afraid of whoever put her up to contacting me."

Jerry frowned. He looked worn and sullen. "Why would anyone send her after *you?*"

"I don't know. But I think she felt caught between a rock and a hard place. She couldn't tell me the truth, but she didn't want to set me up either. She couldn't go through with it, so she ran."

"And someone caught her," Jerry said. It was not a question.

"Yes. And unless we keep following the trail, we're never going to find out who that was. Hal, is anything particularly special about this year's Burning Man Festival?"

Hal looked down at his notes. "Not really, another large host of rebellious anarchists, recreational users of LSD and mushrooms, artists, bikers, the odd and the curious are gathering in the empty flats to celebrate a few days of chaos."

Jerry started hopping up and down, as if bored. "There was one thing. The local law supposedly doesn't want the actual burning of that giant figure to happen this year, even in Nevada."

I motioned for him to sit down. "Kind of renders the event meaningless, doesn't it?"

"Exactly," Jerry said, and scratched his chin. "So, what I heard is that a lot of people are threatening to just go ahead and torch something anyway. Any excuse to party. Hey, sounds okay to me."

"So there could be a major incident of some kind."

"Assuming the police choose to intervene," Hal said. "From what I gather, they don't take this all that seriously."

"Still, it is classic stuff," I said, "polarizing between the conservative and the liberal. The letter of the law versus the will of the people. Maybe that part of it is more meaningful than we think."

"I don't know much about this thing," Darlene said, "but aren't the vast majority of the folks there pretty harmless?"

"Absolutely," Hal said. He coughed and grimaced. "In fact, one might argue that such an event serves a valid sociological purpose. A blowing off of steam, shall we say."

I sipped soda. "At least one person there is far from harmless, but talk about finding a needle in a haystack . . ."

Hal changed gears abruptly. "Folks, did you believe what Fancy told you yesterday?"

"Me, I think he's a lying sack of shit," Darlene spat.

"I don't know. I believed part of what he told us."

Darlene sneered. "Which part?"

"I think he is actually proud of his operation, the way he treats his people and tries to protect them. He's arrogant, and he sees himself as a kind of ghetto Robin Hood."

"While he exploits young women and little children?"

"Easy, Darlene, I have no intention of defending the

man or his lifestyle. I was just making an observation."

"What else do you believe?" Jerry asked urgently. "Do you think he knows where Mary is? Was he lying about that?"

"I'm sure he was lying about *something*, but I'm still not sure what."

"While you were bearding your lion, I made three reservations from Ontario airport to Reno," Hal said. "Since everyone in the world seems to know who you are anyway, I made them under your real names."

"Reno?"

"There is no service, nonstop or otherwise, to the middle of the desert. To Black Rock or whatever it is. One must improvise."

"It does make the most sense to fly there, rent a car, and drive out to the site," I said. "Flying will save us a lot of time."

Darlene was already moving. "Then let's go."

"Black Rock. When Mary called the last time, she said that, then a word that sounded like 'tent.' "

"And that means?"

"I guess we'll find out in a few hours. Hal, I want to talk to you alone for a second. Stay on."

Darlene shrugged and gathered up her things. She and Jerry left to load the vehicle. I sat down at the computer. "Stop lying to me, Hal. It's gotten worse. Tell me what's going on."

Hal started to speak, stopped. He closed his eyes, and when he opened them again he looked ancient. "I'm actually in New York, son. Emergency surgery is scheduled for tomorrow morning."

"For the bile duct thing? What's the rush?"

"They don't know for sure," Hal said. "But as of now it

appears to be an infection of the bilary tract. I believe it is called ascending cholangitis, and it is something especially serious in a person my age. At the risk of seeming dramatic, with this condition added to my acute pancreatitis, the situation has now become rather grave. I had hoped to deceive, rather than worry you. I apologize."

"What is your prognosis?"

"Let us just say that the surgery has been described as messy, risky, and in no way guaranteed to work."

"And if it *doesn't* work?"

"Callahan," Hal said mildly. "Have I told you lately that you are valued?"

"Jesus." I rubbed my palms together. The room felt cold. "Come on Hal, knock it off. You're going to live forever."

"Most definitely not, but with luck just a bit longer."

"You seem pretty calm."

"Well it is my own damned fault, is it not? It seems that all those years of alcoholism and debauchery have finally caught up with me."

"I may be right behind you."

"You may indeed. Be certain to warn the revelers at the festival, to wit: There is a reckoning."

"They wouldn't listen. We didn't."

Hal shrugged. "And so now we cut me open and rearrange my innards. Disgusting."

"Are you frightened?"

"Oh, yes." The old man smiled. "Very frightened indeed."

I choked back tears. "You are valued, too."

"This I know. And now, please go find those missing people."

We kept to ourselves as we traveled. Virtually no conversation took place; each of us was lost in thought, the tension continually growing.

Jerry was jealous, frightened, and confused. He drank too much on the airplane and nodded off; meanwhile, Darlene, doubting my judgment, flipped through some magazines like an enraged housewife ignoring a husband in the doghouse. I think she felt naked without the gun she'd had to surrender until landing. For my part, I stared out the window and wondered at a strange quality of my life, an odd quirk that led me, again and again, to violence.

Reno airport is large and gaudy. Hundreds of slot machines, all multi-colored and highly seductive, grin and chirp their greetings. The two-way mirrors make the walk to the baggage area seem endless. The bars are generally packed, the seats before the rows of one-armed bandits filled with desperate people clutching paper buckets and spilling their lives out one lonely quarter at a time.

At the counter of the car rental agency, we printed out a map.

I selected a white Volvo station wagon and ordered it delivered with a full tank of gas. We rode a small company van to the pick-up area, still virtually silent. There was no debate about driving. Jerry packed the suitcases and camera gear into the back of the wagon.

"Why do we still need this shit?"

I shrugged. "It's really just a way of protecting Darlene. This way she's moonlighting on a legitimate project. And if anyone happens to recognize me, it makes sense why I'm here."

"You say so." Jerry sighed. He got in and stretched out.

Reno is flat and, in the smothering summer, the roads out of town are straight shots into emptiness, like furrows in a pool table that's surrounded by pastures and grazing cattle.

Time passed, civilization fell away.

I drove on through the blistering heat of the desert, drinking in the scent of the sage and the eerie, vast emptiness that is central Nevada. Darlene slept in the passenger seat. An inflated headrest kept her neck erect. Jerry sprawled out on the back seat, his dusty boots resting on the expensive video camera's black padded case. From the CD player, a woman with an Appalachian twang sang: *"I only miss you when I'm breathing . . ."*

Finally, I noticed the markers: Charcoal, smoke and flame. Some were gaudy, homemade stick-figures with arrows pointing due west. Some were painted cardboard, with large red letters that screamed "Burning Man This Way."

As a cloud of dust cleared, I saw a nearly naked man in some kind of a thong waving cars into a crowded parking area. I pulled over and rolled down the window. The guy was clearly stoned and almost lavender from sunburn. He had a pistol hanging from his waist like a second phallus. He grinned and leaned in the window, pupils dilated and mouth reeking of pot.

"Howdy folks," he said. "Welcome to Black Rock."

"This is it, huh?"

"First time?"

"Sure is."

Jerry awoke and rubbed his sandy eyes. "What?"

Darlene let the air out of the neck brace. She looked out the window at the huge rows of cars. A few hundred yards away sat a massive expanse of flat, white sand, littered with hundreds of tents of all shapes, colors, and sizes. Green portable toilets seemed randomly placed throughout the camp. Towering over it all was a grotesque, massive stick-man, built of wood and neon piping.

"What the hell is that?" Darlene asked.

The man laughed. "Why, that there is Black Rock City. It's a tent city, ma'am." He eyed the camera on the seat. "Now, hold on here," he said. He put his hand on the gun. "Ain't no press allowed."

Darlene almost reached for her own weapon, but I motioned for her to be still. "No press? Exactly, my man."

"Huh?"

I beckoned him closer. "Shit, dude, that's our whole act. There's no film in that camera. My friend here, he doesn't even know how to run the fucking thing. Our act is that we pretend to be from the press, and get people confused and pissed off, but all the while it's all just a put-on. Get it?"

The man grinned. "That's pretty cool. I won't tell."

"Great," I said. "Where do we park?"

"Anywhere along in here. There's only one rule, folks. Live and let live. People are here to break out and be free, so don't judge anybody and they won't be judging you."

"Sounds great to me," Jerry said. He meant it. "Total freedom."

"It's about love," the man said solemnly. "Real love between the brothers and the sisters."

"Cool," I said, at a loss for anything else to say. "Thanks a lot."

"Sure thing."

We drove away, spewing dust. Darlene shook her head. "Did I just see what I think I saw?"

"What was that?"

"Some sunburned dumb-ass running around in a thong with his butt cheeks hanging out, carrying a loaded weapon?"

"Well, we don't actually know that it was loaded."

The sound of gunfire peppered the ridgeline. Faint rebel

yells floated across the empty sand. A line of cars was driving by some scarecrows and paper targets, calmly blowing them to pieces. A cardboard sign introduced the event as DRIVE BY SHOOTING. More distant gunfire, more voices screaming.

Darlene looked at me, eyebrows raised. "You were saying?"

"Nothing."

"I was under the impression firearms had been banned from this event years ago."

"Maybe they're shooting blanks."

She considered. "Maybe. You want to be the one to find out?"

"You first."

Jerry yawned. "We'd better find a place to camp. It will be dark in just a few hours. I need a drink."

"They kind of frown on alcohol," Darlene said.

"So, I'll have a hit on a joint."

I frowned. "Take it easy, Jerry. I need you to have your head on straight, okay?"

"No problem, boss."

A little too much edge to his voice, like he hasn't forgiven me yet.

We walked along, our senses gradually overwhelmed by organized chaos. People painted various colors went dancing by, many clearly on psychedelics. A few were openly smoking marijuana, others just carrying sticks of incense. Small fires were lit everywhere, and attendees were cooking everything from hot dogs and veggie burgers to fish steaks. Coolers overflowed with cans of non-alcoholic beer, diet soda, even some contraband wine coolers and pre-mixed cocktails. Loud music flowed from every conceivable direction; we heard drumming, rap songs, country music, and amateurs randomly picking at amplified electric instruments.

The largest tent had "Black Rock City" spray painted on the side of it in large black letters. Darlene and I exchanged looks and shrugged. We walked in, carrying our small suitcases and sleeping bags. I looked backwards and noticed Jerry was not following us. I tapped Darlene on the shoulder.

"Watch these," I said, not too concerned. I marched back outside and looked around. Jerry was standing near a pile of old mattresses that lay off to one side, away from the main path. He was shooting something with the videocamera. I jogged over. A moaning couple was having sex in the shadows; her legs were wrapped around his waist and they were both oblivious to the world around them.

"Turn that off," I whispered.

Jerry sighed and spewed a plume of smoke. His eyes were already red. He'd bummed a hit, and was faded. "Can't blame a guy for trying."

"Yes, I can, and for getting stoned, too. Do you want to get yourself killed? You'd best stay sober and remember what we're here for, Jerry. Keep your mind on the job."

"Sorry," Jerry said. "I just can't quite believe this place."

I surveyed the area. "Me neither."

The afternoon sun was cooler, allowing more movement. Three nude girls rode by on bicycles with neon tubes threaded through the spokes. A mime performed in the middle of the walkway, wearing only a makeshift codpiece and facial makeup.

We passed an open tent and peered in. A group of men wearing feathered Native American headdresses were solemnly passing around a giant bong instead of a wooden pipe.

We walked into the largest tent, scanning the interior for Darlene. She waved us over to a small space she had cleared. She had unrolled the three sleeping bags and then surrounded and marked off an area with our extra clothing and gear. She spread her hands.

"Welcome to our hotel suite."

Jerry wriggled his eyebrows. "No mini-bar?"

"I'll call room service," Darlene said dryly. She sat down on her sleeping bag and stretched. "Maybe they'll send one up."

"You do that," I said.

"Mick, I do have a small piece of news."

"What's that?" We sat down next to her. Stretching suddenly seemed like a very good idea. I straightened my legs, bent forward, and reached for my toes. It hurt. My bad knee popped.

"See that strange-looking creep over there?"

I looked around the tent. "Can you narrow that down some?"

"I mean that white-haired old guy, the one in the top hat and tails and green swimming trunks."

I found him, taking cash from some new arrivals. "Got it."

"He takes the camping fees and coordinates the cleanup tomorrow morning. He said he thinks he might remember having seen Mary in here yesterday."

I blinked. "Go on."

"I gave him the description, and he said he thinks he saw her with three other people. He remembers because she looked like she didn't want to be there. One guy kept slapping her and pushing her around. He was talking in English, or sometimes in pretty bad Spanish."

"Why does he think it was Mary?"

"He used her name. More than once."

I pondered. "This guy who hit her, what did he look like?"

"Big bastard, all buffed out. That's why nobody had the guts to stand up to him. Guy had his head shaved clean, and he wore some kind of a nose ring. Sound like anybody you know?"

Oh great, just great, some mountain of a skinhead. "Not really."

"There was a woman along, too," Darlene said. "Brunette, glasses. He doesn't remember anything else about her."

"You said three."

"That is the weirdest part. There was a child with them, too. A little boy."

I felt it in my bones. "How old?"

"He didn't know, Mick. He guessed nine or ten, maybe. The kid only spoke Spanish, from the sound of it, so it could be our kid."

"Could be." I thought for a moment. "One thing worries me; they're not exactly hiding from us, are they?"

"Lot of guns around here."

"That crossed my mind, too."

I suddenly realized Jerry hadn't spoken. He was sprawled out on a sleeping bag with his head on the camera case, one hand wrapped around the handle for protection. Once again, he appeared to be sleeping . . . or passed out.

"Jerry?"

Groggy. "Huh?"

"You stay here and watch our stuff, okay? Darlene and I are going to go see what's going on."

"Yes, master," Jerry said, "whatever you say." He yawned and closed his eyes again. "Wake me if you need something."

"One hour, okay?"

"Got it."

Darlene asked: "Or what?"

"Or he blows the whistle and calls the local police to come looking for us. What did you think?"

"Oh."

As we walked away, Darlene looked back. She seemed puzzled. "He's not really going to sleep again?"

"I sure hope not. Jerry is a lot smarter than he looks. He can take care of himself."

"Except when there are naked women and drugs around."

The afternoon sun was a reddish, watercolor smear on the skyline. An oval mirage shimmered on the northern desert, and vultures circled carrion to the west. The sweating, teeming mass of inebriated humanity had compacted upon itself and become one giant canvas-covered bacchanal. Something stirring and primitive was taking place, and the incessant drumming, low and rhythmic, felt wildly erotic.

After a moment, I stripped off my shirt and grabbed her hand. "Let's look natural."

I was only partly serious. Darlene leaned into me, and I felt an electric charge. We walked briskly, surreptitiously scanning the surroundings. The nude oddities increased and were by turns amusing, overwhelming, and then finally just deadening. We passed bottomless mock-priests and nuns in white collars and body paint, a wagon that served lemonade directly from the tap spigot or in a paper cup, three beautiful, young, topless girls who sat reading magazines.

There was an intelligent symmetry to the camp's layout, although at first glance it seemed to have evolved by accident. The improvised "tent city" patterned out from the center in an interlocking series of squares. The toilets were well placed; each served one long row of "art" exhibits. Despite the apparent chaos and confusion, the vast majority of celebrants seemed playful and harmless. We saw two young men begin to argue, but the people around them intervened and broke up the fight before it got started.

"Okay, I give up," Darlene said. She had moved up on her toes to whisper in my ear, and her breath gave me chills, despite the blistering heat. "What are we looking for?"

"Damned if I know, just anything that could be linked to Mary, Loco, or Fancy, child pornography, or even some big, ugly bastard with a shaved head and a nose ring."

I realized we were nearing the outer rim of the tents and approaching rows of parked vehicles. I turned and scanned the horizon. A small trail led off into some low dunes. I tugged Darlene's hand.

"That way."

"Any particular reason?"

"Mostly because it doesn't look so crowded. Look, I'm betting the clues were meant to bring us to Burning Man tonight. And whoever took Mary didn't even try to hide, right?"

"They wanted us to know they were here."

"But if you plan on harming somebody, do you want to do it in public, or in private?"

"Point taken," Darlene said. She tilted her head and looked up at me with an impish grin. "Jesus, Callahan, for a minute there I thought you actually wanted to be alone with me, for some reason."

"Oh. Well, maybe that too."

"God, that's so sexy," Darlene said. "The word 'maybe' is such a turn-on for a woman."

"Oh, cut me some slack."

We moved away from the crowds and into the last row of parked cars, still holding hands. Two handsome, young gay men strolled twenty yards ahead of us. They were clearly lovers.

"I get the feeling there's no privacy anywhere," I said, a bit more regretfully than I'd intended.

"Mick?" Darlene whispered. She tugged on my arm. I bent down and turned my head. She grabbed my face, adjusted it, and kissed me. The moment lasted.

I finally pulled away. "Yes."

Darlene grinned. "Yes, what?"

"To whatever you were thinking."

I will never understand how I noticed it. After all, the late afternoon was filled with the smoke of cooking fires and the sound of firearms discharging. Somehow, an atavistic dread clutched at my stomach when I saw a small plume of smoke rising from an indentation in the cracked, white ground at the far outskirts of the parking area.

"What is it?" Darlene asked.

The two men who had been walking ahead of us came racing back, shouting something.

I jogged ahead of Darlene, who had already slipped the handgun into her fist. One of the young men was crying and waving his arms. People responded from various angles and began to flood into the area. Meanwhile the other boy cried, *"Jesus!"* over and over again.

When we got to the top of the small rise, I looked down into the gully at the source of the smoke and my gorge rose. A blackened human figure lay in the middle of the indentation, curled in the fetal position. The clothing was burned off, the flesh roasted dark in places, cracked and meaty red in others.

It was a woman. She was still breathing. Her dark hair was nearly singed away, and the pretty face had gone rigid with agony. Her teeth were bared in a macabre grimace. A videocassette lay near her outstretched fingers, a large piece of tin near her bare feet. The tin had two words spray painted in black: FILM THIS!

"Oh, God, no," Darlene said. She clutched at my elbow. "Tell me that isn't her, Mick."

I was too stunned to respond. I heard the sound of someone vomiting nearby. I fixed my gaze on the darkening horizon as tendrils of smoke stung my eyes. More and more people arrived, wept, and wailed. A woman called that she was a nurse and began tending to the burned woman. I tried to gather strength. I swallowed and forced myself to look again.

A few yards away, also in the gully, lay another figure: This one was a man, someone unknown to me. He wore blue jeans, a western shirt with a string tie, and was clutching a small gun and what seemed a suicide note. The man had apparently placed the gun under his chin and fired. Most of his face was gone, and part of his forehead had shattered and sprayed itself up onto the baked dune.

"Mick, tell me," Darlene said urgently. "Is that Mary?"

We heard the wail of an approaching ambulance. I forced myself to look more closely at the burn victim. The attending nurse was now sobbing. I ran my eyes over the face and body again, studied the heaving bosom and the grimace of agony frozen on those once-pretty features.

. . . Loco slowly came to his senses. He was surprised that he could see. There was no blindfold, but it was pitch black within the van anyway. It was no longer moving. He vaguely remembered that they had photographed him again, this time alone

and in his underwear. His mouth tasted terrible. They must have changed drugs, because he felt worse than before. His head was pounding. It took him several moments to remember the metal panel and the loosened screws.

His hands were bound again, but he fingered the panel and pulled up. A slight crack of fading daylight entered the van. He grinned in the darkness and pulled again. The metal screeched and he froze. It would move no farther. After several attempts, he realized he needed to loosen more screws. He groped at the back of his belt, and then began to cry.

The screwdriver was gone. They had taken it while he slept.

EIGHTEEN

"What's the story?"

We were back in the tent, sitting on sleeping bags. I had my arm around Jerry, who was crying and trembling. He had already gotten high again. All around us, the revelers continued the final night's party, most unaware that something horrific had just taken place. The police had cordoned off the crime scene, but it lay too far outside of the main camp to have affected the festivities.

"I used the cell phone," Darlene said. "I called the hospital and I asked if anybody was taking up a collection for the poor girl, what happened, things like that. Nobody would tell me anything. It took a few calls, but I finally got a nurse with a big mouth."

"And?"

"They don't know her name, but she is not expected to live. The nurse said that is probably a blessing in disguise."

"Yeah, it is. What do the local cops think?"

"The official line is murder-suicide."

"Fuck that!" Jerry tried to stand up, but failed. He had been sobbing for several minutes. His face was red with rage. "Are they fucking crazy?"

"You can't blame them, Jerry," Darlene said. "On the surface, it looks pretty open and shut. They found a note in the guy's fist. It said he loved her and couldn't take her behavior any more."

"Oh, right."

"Jerry, it claimed Mary was shooting porn films involving little children. It said he couldn't get her to stop. Remember the videotape that was near her feet, Mick?"

I knew what was coming. "The nurse said a cop told her what was on it. And it was Mary, doing pornography."

"Of course."

"What about the man?" Jerry asked blearily. He took another deep hit on a joint someone had given him. "Who was he?"

Darlene sat down and hugged her knees. "DOA, no identification of any kind on the body. Naturally, that means it will probably take a couple of weeks to identify him from dental records, so their cover story will hold up at least that long."

"That's long enough." I patted Jerry on the shoulder, fumbled around for a canteen, and drank some water.

Darlene waited and, when I didn't continue, she asked, "Long enough for what, Mick?"

"Long enough to kill me and get out."

"Well, maybe it's time *we* got out."

"Not yet."

"I know that if I get too mixed up in this, it could ruin my career and cost me my pension, but I'm angry as hell too, Mick. I'm thinking whoever did this also shot Donato that night, thinking he was you."

"Bet on it."

Jerry was several moments behind the conversation. "What did they do, just pick some poor, stoned kid at random and blow his brains out to set up an alibi for killing Mary?"

"That's exactly what they did."

239

"We're not leaving," Jerry barked. His eyebrows pranced. He was slurring his words. "We can't. Whoever did this has to pay. We owe it to her, Mick." He reached over and grabbed my sleeve. "We owe it to Mary, man."

"I know that."

"I need a drink," Jerry said. "In fact, I need a six-pack."

"No, don't get any more fucked-up than you already are," I said sternly. "It won't help anything." I got to my feet. "I'm going to the john. I'll be back in a couple of minutes. We'll put our heads together and figure out what the hell to do next."

When I walked outside, the wind was picking up, moaning soft and low. Sand stung my eyes and I covered them with my palm. Several people were struggling to hold some cheaper cloth tents upright, but the sudden storm knocked them down like dominoes.

I walked to the portable toilet, looked around, but saw no one in line. I knocked and, after a moment, opened the plastic door and went inside. The light bulb was dying. The toilet was full, the odor atrocious, but I used it and stepped back outside. The harsh wind stopped as abruptly as it had started, and the desert air smelled like ozone. A light rain began to fall. The scattered drops felt warm and oily; there was an electric crackle in the air that suggested a bigger storm was approaching.

"Good evening, Mr. Callahan."

I whirled, put my hands up to defend myself, and saw someone standing in the shadows, smoking a cigarette. The orange ember dropped to the ground in a shower of sparks. A foot ground it out. The man stepped out into a pool of moonlight. He wore a ridiculous pair of Hawaiian shorts, a plain blue short-sleeved shirt, and a pair of expensive running shoes with no socks. A platinum Rolex adorned his wrist.

"Agent Fields, I love your outfit."

"The things my job requires of me," Fields said. He spoke with an obvious disdain for his surroundings.

"Where are Laurel and Hardy?"

"Who?" Then Fields registered the reference. He smiled. "I have dispatched my somewhat dim-witted subordinates to other locations. They should catch up to us by tomorrow."

I moved to the wall of the portable toilet and leaned against it with one knee up. I wanted my back covered. "To what do I owe this privilege?"

Fields squinted at me and spat on the ground. "I don't like you, Callahan."

"That's disconcerting."

"You know why?"

"Nope."

"Because you lied. I thought we had agreed we would share information." Fields strolled closer. "But I haven't heard a word from you. And then I check my surveillance camera from Pomona again, and what do I find? Mr. Radio Jock himself, a hooker, and some redneck punk are poking around a fucking Federal investigation without even bothering to check with me."

I studied the man and thought about Mary. The edge of my vision darkened and my temper flared. "Agent Fields, I am having a very bad day. Just what the fuck do you want from me?"

Fields stepped in close with one hand in his pocket, as if on a weapon. His demeanor was threatening enough to raise the hair on my neck. "I want Fancy delivered to me with enough evidence to put his tiny black ass away for good. And you are supposed to help me nail him."

"Yeah, I did talk to him. He was straight-up about some

of the shit he does, but he denied having anything to do with kiddy porn."

"And you believed that? If Fancy cops to hurting kids, then he is as good as dead, assuming he ever has to do time again. Cons hate child abusers, and a little bastard like that would never be safe with the general population."

"He was pretty persuasive."

"What the hell did you expect he would do, confess?"

"I don't know what I expected. Look, Agent Fields, I would like to help you out, but my interests here may be different from yours."

"I thought your interest just ended up barbecued on a spit," Fields said. He sneered. He was now close enough for me to smell the mint on his breath. "Or am I wrong about that?"

I glared. "Who the *fuck* do you think you are?" My voice was low and raspy and the blood was roaring in my ears.

"I'm the man," Fields said calmly. "So I can lock your sorry ass up any time I want."

"Is that so? Well, right now all you are is halfway to dead. I could rip you apart like greasy fried chicken."

"Then go for it."

I stopped myself from responding. *Why is he baiting me like this? What does he hope to gain?*

"Time's running out," Fields said. "Hear that?"

Gunfire was exploding all over the camp. People were wandering away from us, towards the giant effigy at the center of the city. The climax of the festival was only a couple of hours away.

"Guess it will all be over soon, one way or another."

"Goddamn you, I could shoot you where you stand," Fields said. "And no one would know it was me."

"You would know."

"Shit." Fields bared his teeth. "Mark my words, Callahan. If I thought you were taking Fancy's side in all of this, I would do that and not give it a second thought."

I forced myself to relax. "One thing I can guarantee you, I am not on Fancy's side."

Fields read my eyes for a long moment. Finally he stepped back until he was at a safe distance. The hand holding the gun left his pocket. "If that's true, then help me nail that pervert. Stop screwing around and work with me, here. We both know he did this to your girl."

"*How* do we know?"

"Come on. Mary was a slut in some of his movies, and on his string of street whores, and she ran away. How much do you need?"

"Some hard evidence would help," I said. "Now, there's a concept for you."

"Don't be a smart ass. What do you know so far?"

"We think the boy with her was some nobody, just a poor schmuck who happened to wander by. They killed him as part of the cover story."

"Why such a dramatic statement?"

"The message was intended for me."

"Why?"

"Somebody wants me dead."

"Then why not just kill you?"

"Because they want me to suffer first."

"I figured that part out a long time ago, Callahan," Fields said. "That's why my boys and I have been sticking to you like flies on shit. And the 'somebody' is that little prick Fancy. He's a proud man. Nobody walks off with one of his string and gets away with it. Nobody."

"Then why did he let me go both times I saw him?"

243

"You said it yourself. He knew we were watching. Besides, he wants you to suffer first, so he led you here. And you are suffering, aren't you? You almost saved her, Callahan. How does it feel to have been maybe just five minutes late?"

Seeing the spark in my eyes, Fields quickly dropped his hand back into the pocket of his shorts and backed away. A drunk staggered between us and tried to open the door to the portable toilet, but couldn't grasp the handle. Fields and I stood there, in tense silence. After a long moment, the man pissed on the ground and went back to camp.

"You were on a roll, Fields. Don't push your luck like that again."

"Jesus, wise up," Fields said. "Your girl was most likely working for Fancy all along."

"How do you figure that?"

"She was probably jacking you the whole way. Maybe she was supposed to rob you or set you up for something, who knows? But Fancy wanted it done. Then, the way I see it, she probably felt guilty once she sobered up and couldn't go through with it. When she tried to run, Fancy sent his boys to track her down."

I nodded. "Some of that feels right. She once said she was more trouble than I could handle."

"It's Fancy."

"It looks that way."

"I fucking want him," Fields said. He began to move away, back into the shadows. "We'll be watching you, staying as close as we can. I know you're going to lead me right to him."

"Can I ask you a question?"

Fields didn't answer, but he stopped walking. I surprised him by closing the distance myself. The man looked uncomfortable. "You know where he lives and where he works. Why haven't you just gotten a warrant, gone in there, and closed him down?"

"It's not that simple."

"The hell it isn't."

Fields grew sullen. I laughed softly. "It's because you don't really *want* to arrest him anymore, right?"

"Fuck you."

"You want to kill him. It's gotten that personal for you, after all these years. You want to shoot him right between the eyes."

The agent shook his head. "Now you're pushing *your* luck."

"No, I'm not, because you still need me. Don't sweat it, Fields. If I can lead you to somebody who's been kidnapping and raping kids, I probably will. And if you should kill that miserable son of a bitch, I'll maybe look the other way, too. It's no skin off my nose."

"Good. Then we have a deal?"

"Not necessarily; I said probably and maybe."

"Talk straight, damn it."

"Okay. You'd better think about this, and think about it long and hard. I know I'm stating the obvious, but you're an officer of the law. You're about to cross a line that will completely change your life, and definitely not for the better."

"What do you care?"

I shrugged. "I'm a shrink, remember? It's my curse. And I have crossed a few of those lines myself, in my time. I remember a great line from some movie or another: 'When you dance with the devil, the devil don't change.' "

"Thanks for the warning, but I can take care of myself." Fields melted back into the darkness. "You better watch your ass, Callahan," he said as he disappeared, "these boys play hardball."

"I already noticed."

But Fields was gone.

I walked back towards the camp, mind racing. *Is Fancy smart enough to throw me this far off his trail? And if so, why did he bother?*

I made my way back to the tent. The party was growing wilder, and I had to move several drunken revelers out of the way. One woman, high enough to be delusional, kept shoving her bare breasts in my face. With a chill, I realized how easy it would be to kill someone in such a madhouse. I paused for a moment, made a major decision in a heartbeat. I opened the cell phone, dialed, and spoke urgently, then folded it and put it back in my pocket with a small, fervent prayer that I was right.

A few moments later, Darlene said, "I tend to agree with Agent Fields." She sat near the campfire, hugging her knees. I sat cross-legged beside her. We were trying not to shout, but still be heard above the perpetual drumming. That brought our faces close together. Improbably, considering the circumstances, I found it difficult to resist kissing her.

"How so?"

"I think Fancy is a brilliant and dangerous man," Darlene said, "who built his own little kingdom right there underground. He even has his own standing army. Mick, he may be worth hundreds of millions of dollars already. He's got an awful lot to lose."

"And Mary may have known some of his secrets?"

"Exactly. My God, that poor girl."

I picked up a large stick and threw it into the fire. Orange and white sparks soared high into the night sky like a colony of butterflies. "That poor girl," I repeated, dully.

Darlene let a few seconds pass. "Mick, what are we going to do now?"

I sat up, startled. "Damn. Where is Jerry?"

"Off shooting pictures again or maybe getting even more stoned. He told me he would stay close to the lit areas. I doubt that Fancy would be interested in him anyway."

"Meaning it's me he wants?"

"Meaning it's *probably* you. Think about it, Mick. Mary didn't say much, but she could have told you everything she knew. You'd be a direct witness, too. Jerry and I have nothing but hearsay. You could really help Fields blow Fancy's operation wide open. He can't have you running around with information like that in your head."

"So why not just shoot me?" An awkward silence followed. "Sorry, I wasn't thinking. But he let me go both times. Why?"

"I don't know. Like you said, the FBI has a fucking camera there, right? Fancy knew all about that, obviously. He couldn't kill us then, without the FBI knowing all about it."

"But out here?"

"Out here he can."

"Have you checked on Donato?"

"Good idea, it's been a while. Give me the cell phone. I want to call the hospital and see what's up."

I handed her the small phone clipped to my belt. Darlene went back into the tent in search of something akin to privacy. *Why not just shoot me? Nice one, idiot,* I thought, miserably. *You're just batting a thousand.*

"Mick?"

I looked up. A drunken Jerry was on the other side of the fire, waving his baseball cap. He was staggering through the crowd with a brunette who looked vaguely familiar. I had also noticed her in the tent, earlier in the day, when we had all first arrived. She was now wearing torn cut-off jeans, a tight blue halter, and a pair of large, dark glasses. She carried a jug of cheap wine. Jerry waved, while the girl fondled his crotch.

"Jerry!" I called. "Come back here, damn it!"

Jerry held up ten fingers, as if to say "back in ten minutes." He put his hat on, took a swig from her wine bottle, and followed the pretty girl out into the parking area. I wanted to stop him, but estimated the distance and realized I'd never be able to catch up. *Better to stay in one place and let him find his way back.*

I checked my watch and noticed the time. *I don't like this, something isn't right.* My gut knotted. Okay, maybe Jerry needed to get laid after all he'd been through. Was that a kind of love, too, the simple celebration of sexuality with a complete stranger? One could argue that it was, but it was only an experience. Isolated people, many of them drunk or stoned, celebrating and coupling with abandon, but for no particular reason: *existential hedonism.*

Oddly enough, I felt no trace of my disease. I had no wish to break my sobriety and join in. In fact, the hungry mindlessness I saw around me unaccountably filled me with a deep and profound sadness. It occurred to me that Mary, like most humans and perhaps like me, had lived, and died, knowing very little of real love.

A tattooed man began filling his mouth with lighter fluid and spitting fireballs into the air. A drunken crowd cheered him on. The yellow flame looked magnificent in the gathering darkness, almost spiritual. The inky night sky was littered with sparkling stars. I remembered something a famous theologian, perhaps Paul Tillich, had once said about alcohol. He had called it "cheap grace."

Someone tripped and fell against me. I reacted without thinking, grabbed the man by the shirt, rose to my knees, and pulled. The figure fell forward, partly into the fire. He began to scream and slap at himself. Several people reached down and pulled him away from the blaze; they rolled him in the dust to help kill the fire.

Everyone started laughing, and the stoned man got to his feet, embarrassed. He was clearly not hurt, but also in no way dangerous. He did not even seem to be aware of what had just transpired, and I'd almost killed him.

Easy, damn it.

I rubbed my face and tried to relax. Suddenly Darlene plopped down beside me. She handed over the cell phone. "I left it on," she said. Her face was expressionless and pale in the firelight. Moisture glimmered in her eyes.

"Darlene?"

She didn't answer me. One solitary tear rolled down her cheek. I put an arm around her shoulder.

"Honey? Are you okay?"

"Poor Mary is dead," she said. It took a moment for the words to fully register. I felt my own tears burning. I pinched the bridge of my nose to stop them, held her close. Darlene was trembling.

"I called about Mary first," she said. "The nurse said she died a little while ago. She had a bad reaction to the heavy pain medication. She said again that it was probably a good thing. She called it a mercy."

I felt a wave of rage roll over me and fought back an absurd urge to laugh. I bit my lip to stay silent. "And what did they say about Donato?"

"I called the hospital, and your friend Suzanne was there," Darlene said. "I asked her how Larry was doing.

They ran into a lot of complications. Peanut told me that he got some fluid in his lungs, and the damned machines were breathing for him. At first he was just too weak to function on his own, but he pulled out of it a few hours ago. The doctors are just amazed. They say it's because he is in such good shape. Peanut says they think he has a better than even chance at a full recovery."

"A different kind of mercy," I said bitterly.

"Mick, what are we doing out here?"

"I don't know anymore."

"Let's just go home."

I hugged her. "I was thinking the same thing. I want to get you and Jerry back to L.A. on the first flight out of Reno in the morning."

Darlene tensed her shoulders. She looked up. "And you?"

"I have a score to settle," I said.

"Then we both do it."

"I'd rather leave you out of this. I want you to keep your badge."

"You're going after Fancy?"

I didn't answer her, but the lines on my face felt carved. Darlene shook her head. "I'm in this to the finish," she said. "But maybe we ought to put Jerry on a plane. Where is he?"

"He went off with that girl, the one we saw earlier. He said he'd be back, but he's smashed, for Christ's sake."

I realized with a start that more than half an hour had passed. I looked through the crowd, but saw no sign of Jerry. Suddenly I noticed a pair of grinning teenaged girls wearing matching bikinis. They were playing with a large, digital videocamera.

It was Jerry's camera, and the black case lay open on the littered ground. A shiver down my spine.

Just then, the cell phone rang.

NINETEEN

"Hello, Mick. How are you?"

It was a woman's voice, artificially intimate, warm and syrupy. Familiar, but I couldn't place her. *The girl Jerry had wandered away with, the one who had playfully grabbed at his crotch?* I covered one ear and tried to listen. I was hoping sounds would give me a clue to her location.

"Who is this?"

She laughed, covered the phone for a moment, and then came back on again. "You really don't know, do you?"

"I can barely hear you," I said truthfully. "Why are you calling me? What do you want?"

"It's what *you* want that counts. Do you want to see your geek friend alive?"

Darlene was tugging at my sleeve. I gently waved her away. She caught the expression on my face.

"Yes," I said, alerting her. "Yes, I want to see Jerry alive."

Darlene jumped to her feet. She palmed her gun and looked around the crowd, as if she suspected we were being watched. The night was turning totally surreal, a sweating dementia in the desert. Seeing no one staring directly at us, she grimaced and shrugged. I thought furiously and decided to stall, got to my feet.

"Are you alone?"

"Did you just say something? I can't hear you." I walked

251

in a circle and moved the phone around, then fiddled with the volume to buy time. "Hold on a second. That's better."

"Stop fucking around and listen to me."

"Okay, okay."

"I want to know if you're alone," the woman said.

"I'm alone." *She can't see me.*

"What happened to the woman who came with you?"

"She's in the tent right now, changing clothes or something. I'm alone, believe me." I tried to speak with my eyes. Catching on, Darlene raced back into the tent. I saw her unbuttoning her blouse as she ran.

"Listen up, Callahan," the woman said. "I'm only gonna to say this once. Any mistakes, your friend is dead. You listening?"

I stopped moving. "Sure, I'm listening."

"I'm going to tell you where to go and what to do. You're gonna follow my directions, okay? Hey, and you will come *alone*."

"Alone."

"If you disobey us, your geek friend is gonna be burned alive tonight. You understand me?"

"I understand."

"Stay on the cell phone and talk to me all the way. Got that?"

"What was that? I lost you."

"I said stay on the phone, goddamn it."

"Okay."

Out of the corner of my eye I saw Darlene emerge from the side of the tent, struggling with clothing. She was disguising herself, donning a "hooker" costume: blonde wig, padded bra, and tight pants. She had already applied red lipstick. She looked like a completely different woman. I knew she would try to follow me.

"You there?"

"I'm here."

Darlene walked away from the tent. Her costume blended in with the eccentric crowd. She kept one hand inside her purse, clearly clutching her gun. She nodded and waited for me to move.

"Walk towards the parking area," the voice said.

I started moving and trusted that Darlene would follow from a safe distance. I did not look back. "I'm walking."

"Don't talk to anybody, just move."

"Right."

In fact, I barely noticed the people I passed. They were just colors and shapes in costumes. The air was coated with the sickly-sweet stench of marijuana. I pushed on, clearing a path with one arm while the other clutched the cell phone, moving against the flow of traffic. People were beginning to cluster around the effigy, eager to participate in the climactic moment. I stopped once, to allow an intimidating group of bikers to go by. Not a good time to get in a brawl.

I pushed some more people out of the way and passed the spot where I'd spoken to Agent Fields. I was at the edge of the camp. My mouth went dry at the thought of walking out into the darkness, unarmed and alone. I scanned the horizon as I moved, saw nothing but the indifferent stars and miles of parched, cracked earth.

"Hold it," the voice said.

On a hunch, I kept walking.

"I said, hold it!"

"Sorry. I didn't hear you." I stopped. *Well, they sure as hell can see me now.*

I looked around again. There were several small orange fires bobbing and weaving at the outer rim of the camp.

People were dancing naked and shooting water pistols at one another. Something warm and wet struck my face, then my right arm.

I heard a sound like dozens, and then hundreds, of tap shoes moving closer. A hard rain began to strike the parched earth, canvas tents, and the Plexiglas roofs of the portable toilets. The air rippled with static electricity as a low grumble of thunder rolled over the foothills and down onto the empty, white plain. Another warm wind whipped the tents and tugged gently at my sweaty clothing.

"Callahan?"

"Yes."

A huge trident of lightning rippled the bluish skyline. Another bolt, shaped like a spider web, hit only seconds later. I felt primitive and totally alone, a man lost in the immensity of nature. The moment brought back a vivid memory of my childhood on the ranch; one evening I'd stood alone in an immense field of whooshing alfalfa, watching the approach of a violent storm. I wondered, as I had then, if I was about to die.

"What the hell is going on, lady?" Thunder rolled like sheets of tin. "Can you tell me what I'm waiting for?"

The phone was silent. Then I spotted a Highway Patrol car moving slowly among the parked vehicles to the north. Perhaps long accustomed to all the commotion, the officers inside watched the revelry with amusement. I saw a flash of white teeth within the car, and an extended arm pointing things out, as if to a less-experienced partner. The two men seemed to enjoy the nudity.

"You still there?"

No answer. She must be right over there, near the police car, I thought. *She is afraid to talk.* I searched the vehicles and tried to fix her probable location in my mind. The last two lines of vehicles, perhaps? I stretched my hands in the air and casually pointed in that direction as I brought them down again. Unfortunately, I had no way of knowing if Darlene had seen or understood that gesture.

Anyone hiding between those two rows of parked cars would have been able to see me as I crossed the camp and neared the toilets, except for one brief moment when a large van blocked the view. And that was when she'd told me to stop walking. I had continued on, and left her line of sight for a moment. That's what made her nervous.

Great. Now I know where you are, but so what?

The Highway Patrol car eased its way down the line, honking occasionally. People good-naturedly scrambled out of the way. It slowly vanished into the gloom, red taillights winking out as it turned the corner.

Her voice came again. "Start walking."

"Where to?"

I thought I saw Darlene Hernandez, but wasn't positive. She might have been at the edge of a campfire, dancing around and acting bombed out of her mind. She did not appear to be watching me, but I prayed she was staying alert.

"I said, where do you want me to go?"

"Go about fifty feet to your right. There's another campfire. See it?"

A group of people had ensconced themselves on a slight rise, where they had a full view of the giant Burning Man. When it went up in flames, they would be occupying some prime real estate. The group seemed oddly subdued; I moved closer. They were high on something very sedating, perhaps heroin, or even a downer like Oxycontin.

"Sit by the fire," the woman said. The phone hissed and cracked.

I sat down just at the edge of the camp, behind a teenage boy with waist-length hair, who was strumming a battered acoustic guitar. I crossed my legs and kept the cell phone tucked under my chin. My neck had begun to ache. A pretty redhead in a one-piece swimming suit offered me a beer. I shook my head, although I found myself absurdly tempted. *I'm probably as good as dead anyway. What difference would it make?*

"What now?"

"Just stay put."

The air was humid from rain, and it was still quite hot. A woman came dancing along. She was spraying cold water into people's faces, using a plastic spray-starch bottle. She looked a bit like the woman I had seen with Jerry, but she wasn't wearing sunglasses and was dressed a bit differently, and she passed so rapidly I couldn't tell. She sprayed the mist, hit me square in the face, and moved on to the next person. I rubbed my eyes and let her go by.

People started drumming again and all around me folks began to pound on things. The guitar player flipped his instrument over and slapped the back of it in perfect syncopation. I felt my whole body vibrating with the undulating, almost sexual rhythm. I drifted for a moment, lost in the sound as my mind counted the beats. *Jesus, what's the matter with you? Pay attention!*

"Hello?"

There was no answer. I tried to remain calm, but it was hard not to think about Mary, about whether or not Darlene had picked up my trail, about what might have happened to Jerry. So I listened to the music again. It was haunting and rich in texture and seemed to empty the mind in ghostly waves that receded and returned. I literally felt myself dissolving into that rhythm.

Something is wrong with me. Something is wrong with me . . .

I watched the fire, feeling like I had a target stapled to the back of my shirt. A terrible dread seized me. I imagined myself in the scope of a sniper's rifle, and only seconds away from certain death. *Stop it!* Against my will, I pictured how my head would explode outward, pieces of skull landing in the campfire as my blood sprayed the festival participants. *Stop it! Something is wrong with me.* My eyes filled with tears. I imagined how ugly I would look on the cold, hard autopsy table. I heard the ghastly growl of the bone saw as it approached my scalp. How sad.

What the hell? Have I been drugged?

I stood up and shook like a wet dog, grabbed some bottled water from a nearby cooler, splashed it over my face and into my eyes. It burned and my eyes flowed with tears. So I splashed them again. I swallowed the rest of the bottle without pausing for a breath.

Hold on, hold on. Where the hell is Darlene?

A bearded old man sprinkled some powdered chemicals into the blaze. I instantly forgot who I was, what I'd been doing. I dropped the plastic bottle and watched all the beautiful, bright colors dancing in those blossoming flames. The wondrous sight overpowered the sounds around me, and suddenly the whole world went abruptly, entirely silent. I sank to my knees again and started to cry. *So beautiful.*

Someone was moving near the outer edge of the group. I looked, but couldn't see the person clearly. I thought it might be a man, tall with sinewy muscles and bottomless eyes. This man had leathery skin, flesh gone dark from years of hard labor in the burning heat of the desert sun. Was that a cowboy hat? Yes. And he wore a weather-beaten old brown cowboy hat.

It was my stepfather, Danny Bell.

I jumped to my feet and screamed in terror, but the towering figure moved closer, like a buzzard circling road kill. The rain stopped abruptly, and then resumed again, as if orchestrated to coordinate with the drumming. I looked around for help, but no one seemed to know what I was seeing, or to care. Somehow a man who had been dead for nearly twenty years had decided to attend the party, and they hadn't even noticed.

But how can this be happening? It's not happening. I've been drugged.

. . . I wasn't standing, wasn't screaming. I was still sitting down. I had only thought about standing and screaming. But weren't thought and action essentially the same thing, merely a host of electromagnetic impulses, shaping themselves to move in a particular direction? Perhaps I had only thought of seeing Danny Bell, then, and my mind had done the rest . . .

Drugged. I've been drugged . . . LSD?

. . . But if I didn't look, I would also never have to know. Did an event actually exist, if it was not personally *acknowledged?* Couldn't the mind just reshape electronic impulses, so that a terrible event could be reversed? If I wanted Mary to be alive, then why couldn't that be so? An exciting concept . . .

. . . Yes. I was sure of it. Mary could be sleeping in my guest bedroom again, or on the couch talking to Peanut, and none of this would have ever happened. All I had to do was be certain that these things were not true, and they would immediately not *be* true. Somehow I knew that this concept was valid, even the eternal wisdom behind all things. *He's not really there!* I swallowed my fear and looked up . . .

Danny Bell was standing directly over me.

And I was little Mick Callahan again, small and shrieking in terror. I had no control over my thoughts, voice, or limbs. I kicked and thrashed about on the ground, all alone. Virtually no one noticed, and those few that did laughed at me, amused by how high I was. *Can't last forever, a few hours tops. Got to hang on.* I shut my eyes and willed Danny Bell to be gone. I opened them again, and Bell was still there. I groaned.

"You're not real, Daddy Danny." My voice sounded foreign.

He reached down, grabbed my shirt, and dragged me to my feet. He slapped me across the face. "Hello? You home, motherfucker?"

Danny Bell, sneering. He spat on me, or was that another raindrop? Yes. Rain. The storm had started up again. So had the wind; it was sighing like a soprano in my ears, it was starting to carry me away. I was soaking wet, bone tired, and very cold.

Hallucinogenic, sprayed in my eyes. It will pass soon. Hang on.

"Say something," Danny Bell said. He was smiling. His teeth were long and had been filed to sharp points. He licked his lips like a cannibal approaching the stew pot. "Aren't you glad to see me, Mick?"

I tried to speak, but my tongue had never weighed this much before. I felt myself sliding away, sliding away, going way down into a foul-smelling blackness . . .

Some time passed, seconds or hours, I wasn't sure. Then a painfully bright light bulb hung in space just above me, and I magically flew through the air. I landed on my side, on something hard. I smelled dust.

The light winked out again.

For just a moment, I thought I saw myself as a little boy, standing right there as solid as could be, in a pair of torn and dirty blue jeans, except this little boy wasn't me and he was saying something in Spanish, over and over . . .

Something that sounded like Meester, *por favor, por favor!*

TWENTY

"Are you thirsty?" Hal asked gently. He was naked, except for a white hospital gown sprinkled with dark blood. He turned away, bare buttocks hanging out, and turned back. One lone light bulb swung in black space above him, making his whole head shine. Glitter flew up and away from that mane of silver hair, glowing like sparklers on the Fourth of July. Hal was kneeling at my side. He held up a canteen and unscrewed the top. He offered me a drink of water.

"Yeah, I'm parched," I said. "What the hell are you doing here?" I took the canteen and drank greedily.

Hal chuckled and took off part of his head. I squirmed backwards and bumped into someone's knees, turned, and saw a pretty little Hispanic boy, maybe nine or ten years old, with black hair and eyes. I did not recognize him at first. The little boy was visibly terrified. I shook my head, desperate to clear the cobwebs.

"Hello," I said. "You look at lot like Loco."

The boy nodded vigorously, as if desperate to communicate something. *"Hola, hola."*

Where am I? I turned around again. What I'd thought was Hal was a brunette in her twenties. She was holding a wig she had been wearing and had just removed. I rubbed my eyes. They still burned. I brought myself back into focus.

261

"Did you spray my eyes with LSD?"

"Good guess. I just watered down the nine, though. Nice shit, huh?" The girl poured the rest of the canteen over my head and stepped back. "Wake up, Callahan. It's payback time."

I looked around. Suddenly it registered who the boy was. "Hey, you are Manuel! Loco?"

"Si," Loco replied. *"Si."* He seemed relieved to be recognized. I patted his hand and looked around.

We were in the back of an empty motor home or a large van of some kind. A metal side door opened and Jerry flew in. He bounced off the back wall with a clang and landed near Loco, then fell limp and rolled to a stop. Jerry was talking to himself, but the words were inaudible.

"Oh boy, oh boy," someone said. I looked up. A man that looked exactly like Donny Boy stepped through the door and stood above us. In fact, I marveled at the vividness of the hallucination. Donny Boy's frame seemed even beefier than it had months before, as if he had deliberately gained weight. Oh, and his head was shaved. He had taken to wearing a nose ring. He also had a new tattoo on his forearm that looked oddly familiar. The hallucination kicked me. Hard.

"Hey, asshole, don't you remember me?"

My mouth dropped open. "You're real?"

"Oh, that's right, you're still high," Donny Boy said. "How did you like your little trip? We thought it was the least we could do."

I gaped stupidly. After the mess up in Dry Wells, the cops went looking for Donny Boy where I'd left him tied up, but he'd never been found. He was alive—and now he'd come after me. Donny Boy kicked Jerry. He glared at the girl. "Goddamn it, Frisco, ain't he up and around yet?

What did you put in that shit?"

Frisco. His girlfriend from Dry Wells. They never caught her, either.

The woman picked up a pump shotgun and covered us. Suddenly it hit me where I'd seen her before. Frisco had followed us and been spotted several times, first back at my gym, then in an alley the night I'd first faced Fancy. Hell, I'd even sat near her at an AA meeting and nearly recognized her again at the festival. She had changed her hair color with wigs, worn glasses and different clothes each time, but it had always been Frisco.

So, we were right. Mary must have been a part of it from the beginning.

Donny Boy squatted down on his powerful haunches. He grabbed me by the hair and yanked. "You got things figured out, yet?"

I licked dry lips. "I think so, not sure."

"Shit, I gave you too much credit. I thought you'd start wondering when your maid's boy got snatched."

"I only got that part just now."

"You're a dumb shit."

"Yeah." I felt like I was about to pass out again. "I guess you're right." Donny Boy slapped my face. It hurt.

"Stay with me," Donny said. "Mary was one of us. She never really left. Shit, she called me soon as she ran out of money. She sorely needed her drugs, that girl."

I shook my head, stalling for time. "I don't understand . . ."

"Like Frisco said, it's payback time, dude. We've been tracking you for months, closing in one step at a time."

"But why drag me all the way out here?"

"Why? Shit, can you think of a better place for a junkie to die? I hate you, Callahan. You blew our drug operation wide open. You kicked my ass and left me for dead. You killed my friend Bobby Sewell. You took away my first chance to be a fucking millionaire."

"I didn't kill anybody."

Donny ignored me. "I swore I'd pay you back if it took me the rest of my natural life. Taking your maid's kid here was my first move. I expected you to come after him. But shit, all you did was offer a couple grand as a reward and talk it up on your show. What a pussy."

"Sorry to disappoint you."

Donny grinned and flexed his muscles. "Poor Mary, she never did like the kiddy porn thing, so I just kept her high. She seemed okay with hooking for Fancy and calling to set you up. She didn't really get cold feet until you got her clean. Then she stopped cooperating, so we had to go in and get her back. I really had to hurt her to get her to call you that last time, to get you to follow her here. She actually thought she was in love with you, man. Can you imagine that?"

"You're a sick bastard."

"So, we had to teach her a lesson. Hell, I taught her real good, too, didn't I, Callahan?"

I kicked at his crotch, but I was still weak, off-balance, and confused. Donny Boy punched me and I went down tasting blood. I wiped my mouth as Donny whispered, *"Oh boy, oh boy"* again.

"It took a while, but we're back on top," Donny said. "You just can't keep a good team down. That prick Lowell Palmer had himself a real first-rate kiddy porn collection. Frisco had an old boyfriend who was a genius about all the Internet shit, so we let him set things up for us."

Frisco yawned. "And then he went and got all pissed off and shot the poor geek. Another smart move, Donny."

Donny Boy ignored her. "Anyway, we started selling that collection off for downloading. Jesus, what a cash cow that was! Didn't take us but a month or two to realize how much we could make if we started shooting more of our own stuff."

"By kidnapping kids like Loco and then killing them once you're done?"

Donny didn't answer. His smug look said it all.

"So you're the new competition," I muttered. I was still dizzy.

Frisco frowned. She lowered the shotgun. "What did he just say?"

"Who cares?"

"Donny," she said, "use your brain just once. What did he just say about us being the new competition? What does he know?"

"Never mind. Callahan ain't going to be saying much of anything pretty soon. Except maybe 'Please don't shoot!' " Donny Boy howled with laughter. "Or should we just cut his throat?"

Frisco sighed. "Oh, don't start with that crap again, just get it over with and let's get the hell out of here."

"Where am I?" Jerry said. He sat up. His hands were tied behind his back. Frisco shifted the shotgun to one arm, grabbed another canteen, and threw some water in his face.

"Sit up," she said. "You're back among the living. It was just a bad trip, that's all."

Jerry stared at Donny Boy and Frisco and blinked a couple of times before it all registered. He gave me a sad half-smile. "I really messed up this time, didn't I, Mick? I'm sorry."

"Jerry, this wasn't your fault."

"Can it," Frisco said. She kicked Jerry, tied a gag in his mouth.

"Por favor?"

Blanca's nephew Loco was tugging at my sleeve. I saw Donny glower with rage and reach for the boy. I rolled and put my body between us.

"You. *Estúpido!*" Donny Boy said. "Shut the fuck up."

"We done with him yet?" Frisco asked.

Donny thought about it for a moment. He shrugged. "All we got on him is those regular pictures by his own self," he said. "Why not get one down-and-dirty video before we waste him?"

She rolled her eyes. "You mean you want to do him?"

"Just to get a movie," Donny Boy protested. "You know I ain't no faggot, Frisco. You know that. Hell, this is just business."

"We've been dragging his little ass around for months," she said. "I say kill them all at the same time. Let's just start with a clean slate."

Donny Boy scowled. "I guess maybe you're right about that." He seemed disappointed. *"Oh, boy.* Damn." He looked over at us and his face lit up again. He kicked me in the side and got a genuine groan. "But I want to have some fun with this dude."

Frisco sighed. "Oh, Donny."

"Let's get out in the flats a half mile or so," Donny Boy said. "So no one will hear him screaming."

"What do you figure happened to the girl who was with them?" This woman Frisco wasn't stupid. "There was no sign of her."

Donny Boy shrugged. "Who cares? It's just some twat like Skanky. She can't hurt us. Get up there and drive."

Frisco paused to light a joint. She took a long hit,

stubbed it out, found her keys, and left the van through the sliding side-panel door. I struggled to sit up. Donny Boy produced a snub-nosed .38 special. He kicked me halfheartedly. I went down again. I began to babble under my breath, nonsense designed to add to an appearance of helplessness. Inside, my mind was in high gear. *Time is running out, better do something soon.*

The van started with a sputtering roar. The engine sounded powerful and finely tuned, belying the vehicle's battered and dusty interior. We lurched forward as Frisco changed gears. I could picture us easing out into the throng, moving only a few feet at a time. The horn blew and then blew again, as Frisco ordered people out of the way. Excited party animals were screaming and shouting all around us. Cries for help would be useless in such an environment.

"What? Huh?" I said, as if still heavily drugged. "You say something, Jerry?"

"*Oh boy,*" Donny said. "Enjoy that high, Callahan. It won't be lasting much longer."

I peeked at the child. Loco was curled up in a ball in the corner of the van, knees up against his chest. His eyes were surprisingly alert. I could tell he was evaluating how to make a run for it. I winked. The boy's pupils dilated slightly, but he was a tough kid, his expression didn't change. He wriggled his fingers as if to say he'd understood the sign.

I sat up, acted dizzy, and then pretended to pass out. I allowed my head to strike the metal floor with an audible clang. Donny Boy laughed. I lay still. From where I was sprawled, I could see that Jerry was moving too.

The crowd noises around us grew fainter. Time ran out. The gears grunted, groaned, and hoisted us over a low dune. We had passed the outer rim of the camp and begun heading out into the empty flats. The party behind us would go on until dawn—and by then we would have all been tortured to death.

The van began to limp and bounce to the front and the right. A flat tire? Donny Boy glowered and stood up. He braced himself against the wall of the van and bellowed at Frisco. "The fuck is going on?"

"Don't know," Frisco said. Her voice was faint over the thumping and banging.

"Damn!"

Another tire blew, this time the rear right. The vehicle started to growl and stumble around in a useless circle. I fought down a smile. Darlene must have shot out both tires on the right side. Donny Boy hissed like a snake, and whispered to himself.

The hissing sound. It had been Donny Boy, wearing a black Halloween mask, who had attacked me near the radio station. He had the Burning Man tattoo on his forearm.

The van ground to a halt. Donny Boy screamed: "Watch them while I get that bitch."

He slid the door open. A bullet missed him by inches, a ricochet that went screaming off towards camp. Donny Boy jumped out and rolled across the sand. He fired twice into the darkness, forcing Darlene to change positions. I started to get up and found myself eyeballing the twin barrels of the pump shotgun.

"Get down," Frisco said. I obeyed, dropped down on my knees. She got into the van and slid the door closed behind her. I stared up into her stoned, brown eyes and watched her dazed thinking process. I saw her come to a decision as clearly as if she had said it aloud: *What am I waiting for?*

Donny is gone! Why not just shoot them all now?

I was moving before I was fully conscious of the decision. I gathered my strength and came up under the gun, sweeping it high with one shoulder, only vaguely aware of the explosion that ripped a hole in the ceiling of the van. I temporarily lost hearing in my right ear.

I brought my head up under her chin and heard a satisfying crack. Frisco bit down on her tongue and sprayed a light trail of blood. She stepped backwards and tried to bring the gun around. I hit her with an uppercut, turning fast and putting my whole body into the blow. Frisco dropped the shotgun and flew back into the far wall with a clang. Her head snapped against the metal, her neck bent sideways, and her eyes rolled back in her head. She dropped suddenly, loose-limbed and dead.

"Let's get out of here."

Jerry was standing, trying to loosen his bonds. Loco ran to Frisco and efficiently searched her pockets. He returned with a knife and cut Jerry free. He looked at me with hope in his eyes.

"We will take you back to your aunt," I said, knowing the boy did not understand English. "Blanca. Blanca."

Loco grinned from ear to ear.

"Down," I motioned rapidly. "Stay down."

I used the shotgun to smash out the interior light, slid the door open as quietly as possible, and dropped to my knees in the hard-packed sand. The little boy followed, then Jerry. The noise from the festival was constant, yet after a few seconds I heard a gunshot nearby and what was unmistakably Donny Boy's voice: *"Oh, boy!"*

"I don't know how many shells are in this thing," I said quietly. "So it seems to me discretion is the better part of valor."

"I'm down with that," Jerry said. "What do you want me to do?"

"Darlene is probably going to try to lead him back towards the camp," I said. "She'll be trying to buy us some time. Once Donny figures that out, he'll turn back this way to be sure we're dead. You go north and then back around to camp. I'll go south, after Darlene. Let's move."

Jerry grabbed the boy by the hand. Loco snatched his arm away and then relaxed. He nodded. Jerry started to crawl north and the kid followed him. I listened and heard another shot. I took off, running fast and low, trying to find Darlene in the darkness. I still felt a bit dizzy, but now the adrenaline was pumping and clearing my system of the drugs.

Someone is coming, full tilt boogie. I located a tiny crevice in the desert floor, rolled, and then fell face-down in the dirt. Donny Boy came charging through the darkness. Now that my eyes had adjusted a bit, I could make out the bright white of snarling, perfect teeth. Donny was chuffing along like a sprinter, elbows crisp and knees pumping high. He had a look of single-minded determination. He ran right past me and over towards the van. When he saw the door standing open, he increased his speed. He jumped into the van, boots crashing down harshly, and found Frisco dead. After a second of silence, there came a long, keening wail.

"You motherfucker!" Donny Boy screamed. "I'm going to pick your flesh off with pliers, Callahan. I'm gonna make you beg."

I lay still, came to a decision, slipped the cell phone out of my pocket, and spoke into it, articulating as clearly as possible under the circumstances. Then I broke the connection. I placed Darlene in my mind. I gauged the distance to camp, the visibility by starlight, and my speed against

Donny Boy's. Suddenly I jumped to my feet.

"Come and get some, Donny. I'm right here!"

Donny screamed and jumped down out of the van. He started running and he was fast. I took off, broken-field style, the shotgun held with the barrel down towards the ground. I willed myself to hold back a little, to let Donny Boy gain. I wanted to lead the man away from Jerry and Loco, farther out into the desert.

I tripped, fell, and rolled. Now there would be no time for games. I got to my feet again, felt my ankle twinge, and ran harder. This time I sprinted back towards the van. A bullet whistled by my ear, close enough to sound like an angry insect. I ran under the night sky, legs weakening. The drugs had sapped my energy.

I felt a stitch in my side and changed directions again, then reversed field and started back towards camp. I wanted Darlene to have a decent shot. The noises in camp included gunfire. No one had heard us yet. I figured maybe she could take Donny out of it, and we could simply melt away into the mob. I felt sick, now. I needed water.

"I'll kill you!" Donny screamed. He wasn't firing, probably afraid of wasting shells. We ran on. I was heading for the lights, people, and safety.

Suddenly I saw Darlene standing up near the edge of the parking area. She was waving her hands and screaming. It hit me that she was trying to signal that she was out of ammunition. I considered whirling and firing at Donny, but reminded myself that I might have only one shell left, or even be holding an empty weapon, so this was no time to risk a hasty shot against a moving target with nothing but starlight to see by.

I increased my speed. Darlene looked to her right and waved again. She had Jerry and the young boy approaching.

Now I was in pain. I had a queasy, slow motion feeling, now, like a man in a marathon who suspects he may not have the strength to finish. I risked a look over my shoulder and saw that Donny Boy was stumbling, weakening, and running out of breath too. He fell to his knees, then got up and came on again.

Jerry and Loco raced along the rim of the parking area and caught up with Darlene. The party went on behind them, participants dancing like naked savages by firelight. Jerry and the boy bent over and tried to catch their breath.

"Come on!" Darlene screamed. I found the last of my reserves and increased speed one final time. I heard another bullet screech by my ear, and somehow above the din of the party heard it smack into the trunk of a parked car not three feet from Darlene. I whirled, knelt down in the sand, and pumped the shotgun. Donny saw me and tried to come to a stop, arms pinwheeling comically. He threw his hands up, palms out.

"Mercy," he cried.

I fired. The shotgun slammed painfully into my shoulder and something cracked in my neck. The explosion was deafening. Donny Boy spun around soundlessly and dropped out of sight. I pumped the shotgun, but my touch told me no fresh shell entered the chamber. I threw the empty weapon down and stumbled back to the firelight.

I ran into Darlene's arms. I was soaking wet from rainwater and sweat and gasping painfully for breath. "Is he dead?"

Darlene kissed me. "I don't know, but I've got two speed loaders in the tent, so let's move."

The four of us limped into the human chaos, and I realized that the climax of the evening was nearly upon us. The gigantic stick-figure was now lit with neon tubing. It stood towering over the mob, and people were gathering into tight little groups, chattering in anticipation of the burning. Darlene led the way, tapping people on the shoulder, elbowing them aside, punching one drunk in the stomach to clear a pathway. I stumbled behind her, then Jerry, and finally Loco.

As we approached the tiny city, a fat man wearing large plastic breasts with a huge, fake penis blocked our way. The noise from the celebration was deafening. When Darlene tried to move the man aside, he giggled and hugged her. I'd regained some wind, so I worked my way closer. Suddenly the man frowned, a puzzled expression, as a piece of his skull disappeared. He fell to his knees and dropped face-down on the foam rubber breasts, his shattered head pumping bright blood in a thin, precise stream. Someone screamed.

I turned and saw Donny Boy fighting through the crowd. He was favoring one arm, which was smeared with crimson, and still holding the smoking pistol in the other. His eyes were wild with rage and pain. He was perhaps twenty yards away and closing. I groped for my cell phone, but it was broken. Just then, Donny Boy tried to fire again and realized his own weapon was empty. He threw the gun down and charged.

"Go! Move it!" I called.

Jerry and Loco simultaneously grabbed Darlene's arms and forced her to go faster. She complained and started to fight her way free, but then decided to try for the spare ammunition. The three of them vanished into the crowd.

I turned to face Donny Boy. I grabbed a large piece of lit firewood and waved it in front of me. Donny Boy smiled and began to circle. Meanwhile, three people glanced at us with clear disapproval. Assuming the dead man to be passed out, they stepped over the corpse and moved on. The climax of the festival was obviously of more interest than a common street brawl.

No one was facing backwards, so no one noticed the dark pool of blood flowing out from the prone body.

"*Oh, boy,* I been waiting for this," Donny said. He kicked some sand up and charged. I blinked the dirt from my eyes. Donny Boy crashed into me and knocked both of us into the fire. I screamed with pain. We rolled back out onto the parched ground, clubbing one another with closed fists, going for the nose or the chin.

I slipped one hand free just as I suffered a terrible shot to the jaw. I shook it off and grabbed Donny Boy by the ear, squeezed, and twisted. Donny Boy bleated like a goat and elbowed me in the teeth. I tasted blood. I let go and clawed at his eyes. I was losing the fight.

Weak, I'm too damned weak from the drugs.

Donny Boy rolled on top and hit me on the jaw. Fireworks went off in the heavens above, neon colors blazing through the evening sky. The crowd went "ooh" and "ah" and for a very blurry second I thought of Memorial Day back in Dry Wells, and then it occurred to me that this time I was really about to die. I saw my stepfather Danny Bell standing in the shadows, watching us. Danny seemed very disappointed in me.

"So long!" Donny Boy said. He had a rock in his fist. He raised it up high, started to bring it down. I felt an empty sense of hopelessness that my life had come down to this. Danny Bell said: *Don't you fucking quit on me, boy, don't you do it!* I grabbed the thick wrist with both hands and held it in place. That one action took everything I had. Then I bucked like a horse and yanked to my left. Donny sat back in an effort to keep his balance, and I threw him off. I drove a fist into his throat. Donny Boy gagged, but made it back up to his knees and bent over me. I hit him again, and it hurt, but he held on. Meanwhile, I was now completely exhausted.

"Ouch."

Donny Boy looked startled. He clutched at the back of his head and fell heavily forward, right onto me. I pawed my way free and looked down at Donny, who was just stunned. He sat up, fingering his scalp; his hand came away red and wet. Someone had fired at him. I scrambled backward in the sand, eyes searching the crowd for Darlene.

Agent Fields stood at the edge of the shadows, holding a 9mm automatic in one hand and his ID in the other. His badge glinted in the firelight. He was smiling sweetly, warmly.

"FBI," he said.

Fields put the badge away. He slid closer to Donny Boy like a vampire, almost magically, as if his feet weren't even moving or touching the ground. I flinched and then realized that I was still hallucinating.

"Thank God," I said, or tried to say. My mouth wasn't working very well. Fields pulled Donny Boy's bloody hair back and stared deep into his eyes. He laughed and looked at me.

"This piece of shit is the new guy in town? This is *him?*"

I nodded. "That's him."

"By himself?"

"His partner was a girl. She's dead. There was some computer geek in on it too, but they took him out yesterday. He probably got greedy."

Fields shook his head, amused. "Jesus, he isn't much to look at, is he?"

Donny Boy tried to stand up. He froze when Fields

275

cocked the gun. "Say your prayers, dickhead," Fields said softly.

Donny Boy had seen the badge. He smiled at Fields. "Aren't you going to read me my rights?"

Fields shrugged. "Nope." He put one palm up to shield himself from the splatter. Donny Boy screamed. Fields shot him execution style, right in the head. Blood and brains blew up and away in a fountain. Donny turned into a large bag of sticks and crumbled to the ground.

"Wait." I got up on my knees. "Are you out of your mind?"

Fields walked closer. "You had me pegged correctly, Callahan. I had no intention of arresting the bastard."

"Goddamn it, Fields."

"And I also have to hand it to you. It looks like you were right about Fancy after all. He's only a pimp."

"I can't believe you just did that."

"Believe it." Fields searched, found the ejected shell casing, and put it in the pocket of his slacks. He armed the weapon again and pointed it my way. "Can't have you telling on me, can I?"

I shrugged. "About what? I didn't see anything."

Fields laughed, lowered the weapon. "Come on now, Callahan. Under that country boy act, I know you're smarter than most people. You've probably figured out what's really going on. Tell me the truth."

"Maybe." A large star of white burst overhead, and the crowd screamed its approval. "And could be I have already passed the information on to somebody else."

"I doubt that," Fields said. "Not out here, anyway." He aimed the gun.

"Cell phone."

"What?"

"I said cell phone. I broke it somewhere along the way, but it was working fine a few minutes ago. Want me to show it to you?"

Fields frowned. "No. Keep your hands where I can see them." He lowered the gun, considered his options. "All right, I'll indulge you for a moment. What did you say, and to whom?"

"Q and A, Fields." I took a deep breath. "My turn first. An associate told me you lived pretty well for a cop, and that cover story about having a rich relative worked okay for her, but I couldn't stop thinking about how expensive your clothes looked. That watch is worth ten grand. I thought about how unorthodox and over the top your methods were, right from the start, and how the mysterious kiddy porn bad guys always stayed one step ahead of the law. So, it crossed my mind, what if that's because he *is* the law?"

"Not much to go on."

"True enough, so it wasn't until you showed up here without backup of any kind that you gave yourself away. That's what tipped me for real."

"Oh, nonsense," Fields said, a bit offended. "How would you know that was more than simple dedication on my part?"

"I know."

"What, because you're such a good shrink?"

"No, because it violates FBI procedure. Also, nothing else made sense in context, taken with all the other little hints. One question."

"Hurry."

"Do you run the kiddy porn outfit, or do they just pay you for protection?"

Fields pursed his lips. He paused, shrugged. "Protection, of course. I'm no freak. I don't dirty my hands with

277

the day-to-day operation; I just get a decent piece of the action. Hell, if you can't beat them, join them."

"That's why you were so obsessed with finding these losers, to eliminate the competition."

Fields smiled. "And we have, thanks to you," he said. He raised the gun and aimed carefully. "Oh, one last thing, Callahan."

Don't do it, don't do it. "Okay."

Fields asked: "Who did you call?"

"Who?" I wanted more time. I did not want to die. "Maybe I'm not going to tell you that."

"Suit yourself." Fields smirked, but his eyes were empty. He started to pull the trigger.

"Wait! I'll tell you, damn it. It was . . ."

Movement all around us. Just as I felt overcome by a wave of dizziness from the drugs, somehow the very night itself sprang to life; the shadows wrinkled and changed shape in an eerie way, then moved in a confusing blur of fists and feet. Fields grunted with alarm, made a strange, gurgling sound . . .

. . . And simply vanished.

I rubbed my eyes and peered into the dark. I had seen some black fabric, Ninja style, and a bit of motion, but that was all. I got to my feet and stumbled away.

I met Darlene, Jerry, and Loco at the edge of the parking area. She was carrying her revolver and they had our backpacks. Darlene looked stunned to see me alive.

"Let's get the hell out of here," I said. The noise had intensified. The climax of the festival was only a few moments away.

"What happened, Mick? Where the hell did he go?"

"I'll tell you later." I was totally exhausted. "Jerry, go get the wagon, okay? We'll wait right here."

Darlene spoke to Loco in rapid Spanish. *"Te vamos a llevar a la casa. Estás salvo ahora,"* she said. *"Tenga paciencia."*

The brave little boy sat down and hugged his knees again. The fireworks were ending. The entire crowd had moved into the center of the camp to congregate around the Burning Man and watch the climactic event. No one paid us any attention. Jerry had a straight run to the wagon and an easy drive back. He pulled the wagon into the area with a spray of dust. I motioned for the others to get in, searched the area with my eyes, but saw nothing. Finally, I simply waved my arm in the air and got into the car.

"Drive."

Darlene spoke to Loco in Spanish again. *"No te preocupas. Vamos a llegar pronto."* He smiled and began to cry with happiness. She turned back to me. "I told him we're going to get him out of here, and that he should just be patient. Now what the hell is going on?"

"Listen up," I said. "We will be in a world of trouble here, if we don't get our stories straight. Can we trust Loco to help us out?"

Darlene translated the question. Loco nodded with enthusiasm. "Tell him our lives may depend on his honor."

"It's okay," she said. "He's with us."

"Tell him this," I said, thinking aloud. "We just came here to make a documentary. He broke free of them on his own. He was wandering around and then recognized us because his aunt works for me. Loco told you in Spanish that the man who had abducted him and photographed him for sexual reasons was somewhere in the crowd. You told Jerry and me about it, and we all decided just to get him the hell out of Dodge."

Darlene translated. "Okay," she said. "What else?"

"That's it. He can tell the truth about everything else. He remembered having met me before and came over. He just got lucky."

"Will this work?" Jerry asked.

"It has to work, but it is going to look like one hell of a coincidence to the authorities."

"So we all stick to the story. Got it. What else do I tell him to say?"

"Tell him he ran away when they were not looking. When the cops check things out tomorrow, they will find two dead suspects. Eventually they will also figure out that their man Fields was here, too. Then they can put the story together any way they want."

"You mean any way that makes the bureau look good?"

"Bingo, and without us having been involved in that part of it."

Jerry headed for the highway. He hit the bright beams. He spoke over one shoulder. "Fields was crooked?"

"He was with the other outfit," I said. "He protected the kiddy porn group that Donny was competing with."

Behind us the feet of the Burning Man finally burst into flames. The crowd shrieked approval and the booming, macabre echo carried across the foothills. I rolled my window up to shut out the screams, both real and imagined. Darlene was still puzzled.

"But what actually happened to Agent Fields?"

"I called Fancy a couple of days ago," I said. "I asked him to have us tailed from a distance. He put his best people on it. Then I called him again from the desert just a while ago. I told him that Donny Boy had murdered Mary, and what I had started to suspect about Jack Fields. I promised him we would look the other way."

We drove on through the blackest of nights, only half

aware of the spectacle still going on behind us, shrinking into the distance as red fire roared up to heaven. Loco began saying a rosary under his breath.

Darlene suddenly caught on. She shuddered. "Oh, my God."

I glanced in the mirror. The red and orange flames had finally reached the eye of the Burning Man.

Jerry drove on in silence, finally shook his head. "I still don't get it. So where the hell *is* Agent Fields?"

I looked back at the giant, burning effigy. The fire had consumed it and the crowd was shrieking in ecstasy.

"Fancy's boys got him. My best guess is that he is somewhere up in that thing with a gag in his mouth, and that they're going to need dental records to identify him."

EPILOGUE

"They think they got it all." I put the telephone down and crossed my arms. I felt dazed, but happy. "Hal is going to pull through."

She took my hand, tugged, and led me back to where we'd been lying. I stretched out flat and sighed. This was pretty close to heaven on earth. I counted my blessings—a littered dinner table with melting candles, an empty bottle of non-alcoholic champagne, plus an old gray cat purring nearby, a fireplace with a nice, fat log sizzling in it, and some cool jazz playing on the radio.

"Damn, that feels good," I sighed.

"It's supposed to."

Darlene poured some more warm oil onto her hands and continued to massage my aching muscles. She chuckled. "Did you see that little girl who finally broke Loco's birthday *piñata?*"

"She was really excited."

"When she took off the blindfold and saw all that candy, I thought she'd jump right out of her party dress."

"She was damned cute. Do you think Loco had fun?"

"He seemed pretty happy. I know Blanca was." Darlene fell silent. "Mick?"

"Yeah?"

"How do you think that boy will turn out, after what he's been through?"

I thought for a long moment. "Loco is a brave boy, Darlene. Still, it's hard to say. From what I hear, the family has managed to keep things pretty quiet around the neighborhood. They also agreed to let him see that therapist that I recommended, the one who specializes in child sexual abuse. She's the best, and Hal said he'd pay for it indefinitely."

"He's a sweetheart."

"Yes, he is."

"Still, the poor kid . . ."

I rolled over, pulled her head down, and kissed her nose. "Jerry came from foster care. I grew up with alcoholism and physical abuse. You were sexually molested."

"And your point would be . . . ?"

"You turned out okay," I said, trying to lighten things up. "One out of three ain't bad."

"I'm serious."

"Okay, I know you are, but the truth is only time will tell. I think he's got a good shot, let's put it that way."

The jazz song faded and a commercial spot began. One candle on the dinner table hissed and then sputtered into smoke. Darlene smiled as I stroked her bare skin.

"You're beautiful."

The phone shrieked, startling us both. I groaned and rolled over, scratching my sore elbows on the shag carpet. I answered it on the third ring.

"Hello?"

"Mick? It's Leyna. Leyna Barton. Have I caught you at a bad time?"

"Yes."

"Oh. Can I try again tomorrow?"

"Don't bother." I broke the connection, left the phone off the hook, and rolled over again.

"Who was that?" Darlene asked.

"Wrong number."

The commercial spot came to an end, a station ID played and then the tape of an earlier show resumed. When my voice came over the radio, I was still talking animatedly about wanting to find a good, workable definition of love.

"Listen to that bullshit," I said wearily. "Somebody could almost believe I know what the hell I'm talking about."

Darlene kissed my broken nose. "Sometimes you do," she said. "Sometimes you do."

About the Author

Harry Shannon has been an actor, a singer, an Emmy-nominated songwriter, a recording artist in Europe, a music publisher, a film studio executive, an acclaimed author of horror fiction, and a free-lance Music Supervisor on films such as *Basic Instinct* and *Universal Soldier.* He is currently a counselor in private practice. Shannon's short fiction has appeared in a number of genre magazines, including *Cemetery Dance, Horror Garage, City Slab, Futures, Crime Spree, Lenox Avenue,* and *Gothic.net.* Shannon's script *Dead and Gone* was recently filmed by director Yossi Sasson, for Dark Haze Productions. His first Mick Callahan novel, *Memorial Day,* is also available from Five Star Publishing. He can be contacted via his website, www.harryshannon.com.